What did he think she was?

Some kind of easy target? A cheap thrill? Or a woman on her own who was desperate for any kind of attention?

He was a man who, by his own admission, had been called eccentric and was prone to going against the norm. Isobel couldn't think of any other reason why the earl of Invercaldy would find her attractive....

ANNE MATHER began her career by writing the kind of book she likes to read—romance. Married, with two children, this author from the north of England has become a favorite with readers of romance fiction around the world. In addition to writing, Anne enjoys reading, driving and traveling to new places to find settings for her novels.

Books by Anne Mather

STORMSPELL
WILD CONCERTO
HIDDEN IN THE FLAME
THE LONGEST PLEASURE

HARLEQUIN PRESENTS PLUS
1567—RICH AS SIN
1591—TIDEWATER SEDUCTION
1663—A SECRET REBELLION

HARLEQUIN PRESENTS
1492—BETRAYED
1514—DIAMOND FIRE
1542—GUILTY
1553—DANGEROUS SANCTUARY
1617—SNOWFIRE
1649—TENDER ASSAULT

Don't miss any of our special offers. Write to us at the following address for information on our newest releases.

Harlequin Reader Service
U.S.: 3010 Walden Ave., P.O. Box 1325, Buffalo, NY 14269
Canadian: P.O. Box 609, Fort Erie, Ont. L2A 5X3

ANNE MATHER

Strange Intimacy

Harlequin Books

TORONTO • NEW YORK • LONDON
AMSTERDAM • PARIS • SYDNEY • HAMBURG
STOCKHOLM • ATHENS • TOKYO • MILAN
MADRID • WARSAW • BUDAPEST • AUCKLAND

ISBN 0-373-11697-7

STRANGE INTIMACY

Copyright © 1994 by Anne Mather.

This edition published by arrangement with Harlequin Enterprises B.V.

® and ™ are trademarks of the publisher. Trademarks indicated with ® are registered in the United States Patent and Trademark Office, the Canadian Trade Marks Office and in other countries.

Printed in U.S.A.

CHAPTER ONE

Isobel wasn't precisely sure when she decided she had made a mistake.

She had had doubts in the beginning, of course. But she had managed to dismiss them as cold feet. It was quite a step, moving from the familiar surroundings of the flat in Earl's Court to the Highlands of Scotland. Even if she was going at the invitation of a friend. Even if there was a job waiting for her, and a comfortable house, into the bargain.

Cory thought she was mad. And perhaps, without her daughter's constant carping, Isobel might have thought so, too. But, contrary to popular opinion, Cory's attitude had only served to convince her she was doing the right thing. Anything that would remove her thirteen-year-old daughter from the unhealthy influences of the crowd she was running around with at school couldn't be all bad.

Nevertheless, Isobel had faced the prospect of the move with some trepidation. In fact, since Edward passed away, she had faced most problems that way. For so long, he had insisted on making any decisions for her, and uprooting herself and Cory from the only home her daughter had ever known was quite an undertaking.

But then, no one had expected Edward to die. At forty-five, he had many years ahead of him, she had assumed. He hadn't been a drinker; he hadn't smoked; he had been a pillar of the community. And his mother had pronounced—without hesitation, when Isobel had first broached the possibility of their moving to Scotland—that it was a pity *she*, Isobel, hadn't been driving, when the jack-knifing wagon had smashed through the barrier on the M25, killing Edward, but leaving Isobel with only minor cuts and bruises. After all, Edward had still had so much to do with his life, whereas she hadn't even tried to share his faith.

Which was true, Isobel had admitted—though silently, to herself. And it was something she had berated herself for many times since Edward had died. Her unwillingness to accept the Jewish faith had been the source of so many arguments between them. But, although she supported any and every charitable cause they espoused, and she had many Jewish friends, her own feelings were too ambivalent to make such a momentous decision.

Besides, she had never believed that religion, of any persuasion, was more important than human compassion. Her childhood had been spent travelling with her father, from one impoverished part of the world to the other, and he had always maintained that faith in oneself was more important than faith in some mythical god. Isobel didn't know if she believed him either, but she was sufficiently persuaded to give both beliefs a chance.

Edward, however, had had different views, although at the time of their marriage he had assured her he would never force her to do anything. But fourteen years, and numerous arguments, later, Isobel had been obliged to accept that his promises had been ambivalent, too.

And it was the main reason why she and his mother had never got on. Or was that carrying understanding a little too far? Mrs Jacobson had never wanted her son to marry anyone. She had been quite happy caring for him, and making his life comfortable. An orphaned teenager, without a penny to her name, who had been trying to come to terms with her father's death at the time, had never figured in her scheme of things.

Looking back, as she had done many times in the months since Edward died, Isobel had had to admit that maybe Mrs Jacobson had had a point. Perhaps he had been too old for her. Perhaps she had been looking for a replacement for her father. Whatever, the years they had spent together had been mostly happy. At least as happy as most of their friends within their cloistered community.

Edward's sudden demise had been a blow to all of them—even Cory, who had spent the last two years of her father's life doing everything she could to frustrate him. Ever since she'd left the private school, which Mrs Jacobson had insisted on her attending, and started at the local comprehensive, she'd become a problem. Of course, Edward's mother had maintained it was because Isobel had deprived her of her identity, by putting her into the state-school system. Isobel—and Edward, when he wasn't being brainwashed by his mother—had called it something else.

Sheer bloody-mindedness, Isobel had opined, when for the umpteenth time Cory's headmaster had reported on her daughter's delinquency. Playing truant, using bad language, indulging in petty shop-lifting—Cory had been found guilty of them all. Far from trying to get good grades, and maybe even get to university, as Isobel had once hoped to do, Cory had done everything she could to upset her parents. And, what was more, she wasn't ashamed of it. She actually enjoyed the notoriety it gave her.

Occasionally, Edward had worried that perhaps they should have allowed his mother to go on supporting Cory in private education. But Isobel had persuaded him otherwise. Mrs Jacobson's influence on their daughter's life had already been untenable, with Cory quoting her grandmother's words whenever she didn't get her own way.

Edward's death, ten months ago, had given Isobel a brief breathing space. In the vacuum of their shared grief, she and Cory had been closer than they'd been for years. Isobel had even begun to hope that some good might come from Edward's accident. That Cory had begun to realise how short life could be. And it might have happened, if Mrs Jacobson hadn't chosen to interfere again.

Until Edward's death, Isobel had had a part-time job, in a local solicitor's office. Because she had married so young, and become pregnant almost at once, she had been forced to wait until Cory started school to learn the most basic secretarial skills. Edward had never wanted her to work anyway, and only the fact that Cory's clothes and shoes were so expensive had enabled Isobel to persuade him that she should get a job.

And Isobel had enjoyed it. She didn't enjoy spending her days attending her mother-in-law's coffee mornings, or listening to her mother-in-law's friends gossiping about anyone who didn't conform to their strict code of conduct. Isobel had no doubt that she herself had suffered the same fate, once she started working for Gordon Isaacs. But her hours were flexible, and she was always there when Cory came home from school.

Edward's death had changed things, however. In the new, tougher financial circumstances in which she had found herself, Isobel knew a part-time job would not be enough. The insurance Edward had left would barely cover the mortgage on their apartment. And what with food and light and heating, all subject to inflation, she knew she needed full-time employment to cover all their expenses.

That was when Mrs Jacobson had suggested they move in with her. Her house, a rambling Victorian mansion, in St John's Wood, was far too big for one person, she said. There was no earthly need for Isobel to work, when everything she owned would come to Cory on her death anyway. She'd be glad of the company—and the help about the house—and she was sure it was what Edward would have wanted.

Isobel had panicked then. There was no other word for it. The idea of moving in with her mother-in-law, and becoming an unpaid servant in her house, was something she couldn't even countenance. Perhaps she was unkind; perhaps she was ungrateful; perhaps she was foolish! But Isobel knew there was no way she could accept such an arrangement. Cory was hard enough to control as it was. With her grandmother's support, she would become downright impossible.

And that was only part of it. Isobel knew she would never be allowed to live her own life in that house. Without a job, without friends, without *independence*, she would have no life at all. It just couldn't happen. She was sure she'd go mad.

And just when she was at the end of her tether—when Mrs Jacobson had started bribing Cory with expensive CDs and other presents, with promises of holidays in the United States, and the chance to decorate her own

room when she came to live with her grandmother—
Isobel had run into Clare Webster in Oxford Street.

She and Clare had been at school together. By the
time she was fourteen, her father had decided that the
peripatetic type of education he could give her, as an
antiquities professor, was not enough. In consequence,
he had enrolled her at a good boarding-school for girls
in Sussex, and although Isobel had protested her father's
word was law.

Besides, after a few weeks, she had started to like it,
and her father's promise that if she worked hard and
got the necessary qualifications he would allow her to
work with him had been a very potent incentive. And
she had found a good friend in Clare, the daughter of
a London surgeon, at whose home she had always been
made welcome.

But time, and circumstance, had not decreed that their
friendship should last beyond their schooldays. Clare's
father was a Scot, and when his own father, a country
practitioner, had been taken ill Dr Webster had
transferred to a hospital in Glasgow, so that he could
be nearer his parents.

That had happened just weeks after the two girls had
left school, and less than a month after Isobel's eight-
eenth birthday. But Isobel had been preparing to go to
South America at the time, to join her father for a year's
sabbatical, before continuing her studies at Oxford, and
she had been too excited about her own future to worry
about missing Clare. It was only when news came that
her father had been killed in a rock-fall that she realised
how isolated she was. She had no close friends, no relations, and precious little money. In the depths of her
grief, she had been forced to get a job in Sainsbury's to
support herself, and all her hopes for the future had been
buried in Yucatan.

That was why, when she met Clare in Oxford Street,
it had seemed so prophetic. It had been almost fourteen
years since they'd seen one another, and although, in
the beginning, they had kept in touch by letter, the
passage of time had eroded even that connection.

But Clare had recognised Isobel at once, even if Isobel
had not been quite so sure. But the expensively clad

woman in fine tweeds and pearls bore little resemblance
to the plump teenager Isobel remembered, and it was
soon obvious from Clare's attitude that she had married
rather well.

Her insistence that they go somewhere and have lunch,
so that they could catch up on one another's news, had
initially aroused a polite but fairly uncompromising refusal. She was due back at the office in less than half
an hour, Isobel had explained, not altogether regret-
fully, in no mood to listen to Clare going on about the
difficulties of getting a taxi in London these days. Isobel
couldn't remember the last time she had ridden in a taxi,
and with the prospect of another round with Mrs
Jacobson that evening looming on the horizon she was
desperate to think of some way to head off another
confrontation.

But Clare wouldn't take no for an answer, and her
sudden reversion to the girl Isobel remembered had her
agreeing to ring Gordon and beg an extra hour. It was
a rather special occasion, she'd consoled herself, and
perhaps Clare might have an idea as to how she could
extricate herself from Mrs Jacobson's clutches.

And she had. Amazingly, Clare had had the perfect
answer to her problems. Her father, who had given up
his hospital duties when his father died, and taken the
senior Dr Webster's place in Invercaldy, required a com-
petent secretary. Until recently, he had made do with the
rather elderly retainer, who had worked with his father
for the past forty years. But now Miss McLeay had
retired and gone to live with her sister in Dundee, and
her job, and the comfortable cottage she had occupied,
were both vacant. And Clare had insisted that her father
would offer the job to Isobel in an instant if he thought
she'd take it.

Isobel had not been so convinced; not then. The very
idea of changing not only her job, but her whole way
of life, was decidedly daunting. And, despite Clare's
reassurances, she'd doubted it was that easy. In Isobel's
experience, jobs, and houses, were not freely available.
Certainly not in London, anyway. People wanted qualifications, and references; and what about other appli-

cants? Not to mention the landlord of the property, who might have other plans for its disposal.

But Clare had cut through her protests. The village—Invercaldy—practically belonged to her husband's family, she'd declared. Her husband, Colin Lindsay, was brother to the present Earl of Invercaldy, and in consequence she had no hesitation offering the job—and the cottage—to Isobel.

Even so, Isobel had demurred. The idea was attractive, there was no doubt about that. Moving from the grimy streets of London to the clean mountain air of the Highlands of Scotland sounded like heaven. But she was practical enough to know that living in unfamiliar surroundings, far from everything she had known these past fourteen years, was something of a pipedream. Besides, there was Edward's mother to consider. She might not like her much but she was Cory's grandmother.

Promising Clare she would think it over, she had gone back to work with a real feeling of regret. It would have done Cory good to get right away from all the unfavourable influences of London. She was already afraid of what the future might hold.

And then, when she'd arrived home that evening, everything had exploded. She'd come into the flat to find Cory hunched sulkily in a chair, and Mrs Jacobson on the phone, talking agitatedly to whoever it was on the other end of the line.

But, although she'd attempted to get her daughter to tell her what was going on, Cory wouldn't answer her. And pretty soon Isobel had got the picture. It became obvious from Mrs Jacobson's speech that she was speaking to the headmaster of the school which Cory attended, and before she could ask what was happening she heard Edward's mother telling the man that she was withdrawing her granddaughter from the school.

She had tried to take the phone then, but the other woman wouldn't let her, and short of causing the kind of scene she knew would be reported in the staffroom Isobel could only seethe in silence. But when Mrs Jacobson had eventually put down the receiver and announced that Cory would be attending a private girls' school in St John's Wood from now on; that, as they would be moving to Mornington Close, it would be more convenient anyway, Isobel had blown her top.

She hadn't intended mentioning the job in Scotland. During the afternoon, and on the way home, she had decided she would have to rough it out as best she could. But when Mrs Jacobson had informed her that, as Isobel had no control over Cory, she was taking charge of her granddaughter, Isobel had known she had no choice.

The row that followed had been messy, and Isobel would have preferred not to have had it in front of her daughter. The news that Mrs Jacobson's decision had been precipitated by learning that Cory had been caught sniffing glue behind the bike sheds was worrying enough, without having her own character questioned into the bargain. And then, when Isobel had tried to take the heat out of the situation by mentioning the offer of the job in Invercaldy, Edward's mother had made that damning statement about Edward's death. That Isobel had always known Mrs Jacobson blamed her for the accident was bad enough; to be told she'd be better dead was something else.

And so, in spite of Cory's tears, and Mrs Jacobson's recriminations, Isobel had phoned Clare at Claridge's and accepted her offer. Hearing that Mr Webster was more than happy at the prospect of meeting her again was some consolation, and when they boarded the Glasgow train at King's Cross some three weeks later Isobel had felt confident she had made the right decision. Besides, it wasn't an irretrievable one, she'd told herself. If things didn't work out, they could still come back to London. The apartment might be in the hands of an estate agent, but once it was sold their money would be invested, and they could always start again.

And, initially, as the train sped north through rural England, basking in the sunshine of an unseasonably warm September day, Isobel was able to ignore Cory's sullen face, and enjoy the journey. After all, until her father died, she had spent her life living in different places. Just because she seemed to have put down roots these past fourteen years didn't mean she couldn't pull them up again.

And it would be good for Cory, once she stopped feeling sorry for herself. Apart from a couple of holidays in France, she had hardly travelled at all. She knew virtually nothing about England, let alone Scotland, and it was time she stopped thinking that London was the centre of the universe.

It was about the time the train started to run through the Glasgow suburbs that Isobel conceived the fact that, in spite of everything, she wasn't sure she had done the right thing, and by the time they pulled into Glasgow Central she was convinced she had made a mistake. Cory had scarcely spoken the whole journey, and then only when Isobel had spoken to her first. The tears and tantrums she had indulged in, in an effort to make her mother change her mind, had given way to an aggrieved silence, and with every succeeding minute she had made it plain that she would never accept the moral limitations of living in a small village. She would be a misfit, a rebel, far more conspicuous here than she had ever been in London.

The train was slowing as it pulled into the station, running alongside another high-speed train that was presently moving in the opposite direction. Isobel had a crazy urge to open the offside door, and transfer herself, Cory and their luggage on to the southbound train. Oh, to be back in London, she thought. Why had she ever imagined she could go through with this?

The train stopped, coming to a halt with a grinding screech of brakes. All around them, passengers were gathering their belongings together, ready to depart, and, realising she couldn't sit there indefinitely—even if Cory seemed indifferent to their arrival—Isobel got to her feet.

'Are these your cases?'

A middle-aged man, who had been sitting across the aisle from them since the train stopped in Edinburgh, spoke in a soft Lowland accent. Observing Isobel's efforts to herd herself, two holdalls, a duffel bag and her recalcitrant daughter off the train, he was offering his assistance with the suitcases she had still to deal with.

'Just these two,' she agreed, nodding gratefully, as she tried to haul an unwilling Cory out of her seat, without being too obvious about it. 'Thanks very much. They are rather heavy.'

'No problem,' said the man, allowing them to precede him out of the compartment. Isobel did so, pulling Cory along after her, and stepped down on to the platform with a feeling approaching despair.

It was much colder here, she noticed at once. In London, her thin cords and Edward's old flannel shirt, worn with a thigh-length cardigan, had been enough. Here, the cool breeze invaded the open neckline of her shirt, and whipped strands of streaky brown-blonde hair about her face. She was glad she had confined her hair in one chunky plait for the journey. She had the feeling that anything else would have come adrift.

'Is someone meeting you?' the man enquired, as he set her suitcases down beside her, and Isobel turned towards him with a nervous smile.

'I—no,' she said, glancing a little bewilderedly about her, alarmed to find that Glasgow was so much busier than she'd imagined. 'No, I have to change trains,' she explained, relating Clare's instructions. 'We're going to Fort William, you see. Would you happen to know what platform the train goes from?'

'Well, I know the train you want, lassie, but I think you'll find it leaves from Queen Street,' the man replied with a rueful grimace. 'That's about a fifteen-minute walk from here. I think you'll have to take a cab.'

'Oh, great!'

Cory uttered the first unsolicited sounds she had made since leaving King's Cross, and Isobel gave her a warning glare before turning back to their informant. She wasn't exactly thrilled with the news herself, but she had no intention of showing it.

'A cab,' she echoed, nodding, and the man pointed helpfully towards the exit she should take.

'I'd offer to show you the way myself, but my wife's waiting for me,' he added, and it was while Isobel was assuring him that she could manage quite well on her own that she saw, out of the corner of her eye, another man watching them, with a faintly speculative expression on his face.

The platform had virtually cleared now, most of the other passengers having hurried away for buses or cabs, or been greeted by waiting relatives and friends. The few people who were left were, like themselves, stragglers, who were unfamiliar with their surroundings, and were taking a little time to get their bearings.

But the man watching them now was none of these. Indeed, she didn't think he had disembarked from the train at all. Propped against the wall of the waiting-room, his hair long, and slightly rumpled by the breeze, he looked as if he had been there some time. But his suede jacket, which hung open on broad shoulders, was obviously expensive, and the black shirt and narrow black woollen trousers it exposed did not look like chain-store chic. Low-heeled black boots completed his attire, and Isobel, who was not in the habit of noticing men, or what they wore, felt an uneasy prickling down her spine. Who was he? she wondered. And why was he watching them? She didn't know anybody in Scotland. Particularly not a man whose lean dark features bore all the harsh beauty of his Celtic forebears.

'I'm not carrying a load of cases,' Cory declared rudely, as the man who had helped them off the train walked away, and Isobel turned on her daughter with thinly veiled frustration.

'We don't have a load of cases, Cory,' she retorted through her teeth, and then drew herself up to her full height as the other man—the man who had been watching them—pushed himself away from the wall, and came strolling loosely, but purposefully, towards them.

'May I be of some assistance?' he enquired, and Isobel was briefly shocked by the fact that there was not a trace of a Scottish brogue in his voice. She had been so sure he was a Scot, and his lazy drawl disconcerted her.

'Um—no,' she replied, refusing to meet his eyes. She had read somewhere that so long as eye-contact wasn't established a woman had a chance of avoiding an unpleasant encounter. She looked beyond him to where a porter was wheeling a trolley on to the platform, and, grasping Cory's arm, she said, 'Go and grab him, will you? He'll help us with these, and show us where we can get a taxi.'

'Must I?'

Cory was obviously more interested in what was going on between her mother and the stranger than in summoning the porter. And, judging by the way she was looking up at the man through her lashes, Isobel guessed that in a year or so she would be facing yet another problem with her daughter.

'Yes, you must——' she was beginning, when the man spoke again.

'You are Isobel Jacobson, aren't you? I heard you call your daughter Cory, so I was pretty sure I was right.'

Isobel swallowed, and this time there was no avoiding those eyes, which she saw, with some amazement, were almost as black as his hair. 'Who are you?' she exclaimed, as Cory propped one hand on her hip and adopted what Isobel privately called her provocative pose.

'Rafe Lindsay,' he said, his thin lips parting to reveal slightly uneven white teeth. 'Clare's brother-in-law. I had to come down to Glasgow on business, so I offered to meet you and drive you back to Invercaldy.'

Clare's brother-in-law!

Isobel gazed at him, as if she still couldn't believe it, and his smile broadened into a grin. 'Do you want to see my driving licence?' he offered, putting a hand inside his jacket, but Isobel quickly came to her senses. No one else but an associate of Clare's would have known who she was, and who Cory was. But Clare had said her husband was brother to the Earl of Invercaldy, and this was definitely not the Earl. He was too young, for one thing—probably only a couple of years older than herself—and no member of the aristocracy that she had seen would ever wear his hair so long—it overhung his collar by a good two inches at the back. Well, not in this century anyway, she amended, recalling Bonnie Prince Charlie's followers' luxuriant locks. And, come to think of it, Rafe Lindsay did have a look of one of those swarthy Highlanders—if he really was a Scot. A younger brother, perhaps?

But, 'That won't be necessary,' she informed him, rather primly now. And then, causing Cory to give her a disgusted look, 'You don't have an accent.'

It was a foolish remark, and he would have been quite at liberty to ignore it, but instead he chose to answer her. 'Noo? Och, if I'd ha' known you'd prefer the vernacular, I'd no ha' tried to hide ma brogue,' he mocked, with all the broad Scottish vowels she could have wished. Then, summoning the hovering porter with an ease Isobel could only envy, he indicated the luggage. 'My car's outside. Shall we go?'

For the first time since they had left London that morning, Cory looked positively cheerful. After exchanging a challenging look with her mother, she slung her canvas holdall over her shoulder, and started after Rafe Lindsay and the porter. Evidently this new development met with her approval, anyway, and Isobel knew she ought to feel grateful for that at least. But, as she followed them, she was aware that her own feelings were decidedly mixed.

CHAPTER TWO

'WHATEVER possessed you to do such a thing?' The Dowager Countess of Invercaldy gazed at her eldest son with undisguised displeasure. Then, twisting the pearls at her throat with a restless finger, she went on, 'What kind of an impression is she going to get of the family, if you choose to behave like one of your own workers? Good heavens, Rafe, I don't know what your father would say if he were still alive!'

'I doubt he'd regard it as a hanging offence,' remarked her son drily, lifting the cut-glass decanter and pouring a generous measure of whisky into his glass. 'I only gave the woman a lift, Mama. I didn't abduct her for God's sake!'

'No. But you didn't *know* her!' retorted his mother. 'Approaching her at the station, like a common adventurer! What must she have thought? And what will you do if she tells everyone that the Earl of Invercaldy—picked her up?'

'I did.' Her son swallowed half the liquid in his glass.

'Rafe, you know perfectly well what I mean. She's quite at liberty to say whatever she chooses. She might even accuse you of being so—eager—to meet her, you drove down to Glasgow for just that purpose.'

'That's rubbish, Mama, and you know it.' Her son regarded her with rather less tolerant eyes now. He finished his whisky, and looked at her coolly over the rim. 'I had an appointment with Phillips. You should know—you made it.'

'I know that, and you know that, but no one else. I don't expect you're going to go about the village broadcasting your affairs to all and sundry.' She watched him pick up the decanter again, and her lips grew pinched as he poured another measure. 'I suppose I should be grateful you were sober at the time. You were sober, I

18

take it? You didn't go to Phillips' office stinking of alcohol, I hope?'

Rafe chose not to answer that remark, and, as if realising she was treading on dangerous ground, the Countess retrenched. 'What was she like, anyway? Clare says she has a young daughter. I doubt if she'll find Invercaldy very entertaining after London. Are they awfully southern? You know—the kind of people who think everything grinds to a halt north of Watford!'

Rafe turned, his refilled glass in his hand. 'I have no idea what they think of us, Mama,' he replied tautly. 'But they're not savages, if that's what you're implying. The woman seems fairly well educated, and according to Clare her father was some kind of historian. The daughter's another matter. Thirteen going on thirty, if you get my meaning.'

'A pocket Lolita!' exclaimed his mother disparagingly. 'I might have known there'd be something wrong with appointing an *Englishwoman*! Why ever did you let Clare persuade you that she knew best? They'll be settling into Miss McLeay's cottage now, and we'll never get them out!'

Rafe sighed. 'May I remind you that Dr Webster was in favour of appointing Mrs Jacobson? And she is going to work for him, after all. The Websters have known her for almost twenty years, apparently. But she and Clare lost touch after the Websters moved away.'

'*Mrs* Jacobson!' The Dowager Countess clicked her tongue. 'What's happened to her husband? Will you tell me that? She's how old? Mid-thirties? Forty?'

Rafe looked down into his glass. 'Younger,' he said flatly, not at all sure why he felt the need to correct her. It didn't matter to him how old his mother thought the woman was. She'd hardly spoken a word to him during the more than two hours' drive from Glasgow. While he'd been organising the stowing of their luggage, she had scrambled into the back of the Range Rover, and he had been left with the predatory Cory. Who had shown no qualms at all about ignoring her mother's orders, and climbed into the seat beside him.

'Very young to be a widow, then, wouldn't you say?'

His mother's voice intruded on his thoughts, and Rafe raised his glass to his lips. 'Clare said her husband had died in a road accident,' he declared at last, wishing she would give it a rest. In the Dowager Countess's opinion, anyone who had not been born north of the Clyde wasn't worth bothering about. 'Does it matter? You're not likely to have anything to do with her.'

'No,' his mother offered the grudging acknowledgment. 'No, I suppose you're right. In any case, they may not like living here. We can only hope.'

'Mmm.'

Rafe took the remainder of his drink across to the stone fireplace, propping one booted foot on the fender, and gazing down at the glowing logs. Although the building had a perfectly adequate central-heating system, there was enough wood on the estate to ensure a plentiful supply of fuel for the open fires his mother liked to keep about the place.

But now, as he stared into the curling blue flames, he discovered his own thoughts were not so easy to divert. Contrary to his wishes, he was curious about Isobel Jacobson. Her cool reserve had piqued his interest, and for the first time since Sarah had died he found himself thinking about a woman with something more than mild contempt. It wasn't that he was attracted to her, he assured himself, with characteristic candour. It was just that he felt sorry for her. It couldn't have been easy, finding herself a widow, with a daughter like hers to contend with. In his opinion, Cory—was that really her name?—required serious attention.

The view from the cottage windows was spectacular. Even in the fast fading light, Isobel had stood in her bedroom and stared and stared at the wonderful panorama of earth and sky spread out before her. She had seen fields, sloping down towards a vast expanse of water, with horned Highland cattle peacefully grazing in the reeds. And trees, bare in places, but in others showing the gorgeous colours of autumn. And mountains, fold after fold of dark-shrouded peaks, beneath a sky that had still been painted with the delicate shades of evening.

The sun had already slipped behind the mountains before Rafe Lindsay had parked his dust-smeared vehicle in front of the cottage, but the amber-shredded clouds had still borne the heat of the sun's passing. They had risen through pink and mauve to deepest purple, with here and there a prick of light that marked the appearance of a star. There was no moon, and the shadows had soon darkened into night, but Isobel had felt no sense of apprehension. It might be slightly premature, but she had already felt she could be happy here.

Which was surprising, considering her ambivalence during the journey, particularly the latter half. But she simply wasn't used to dealing with men on a personal basis. Not younger men, anyway. And definitely not men who looked like Rafe Lindsay. Living with Edward, who had been inclined to regard her as his property, she had got out of the habit of making friends with other men. Not that she had ever got into the habit, anyway, she admitted ruefully. After all, she had been married at eighteen. Apart from her father, Edward was the only man she had ever really known.

And it had been kind of Clare's brother-in-law to come and meet them, because from what she'd gleaned from his conversation with Cory her friend had been less than scrupulous with her instructions. It appeared that even if they had transferred themselves and their luggage to Queen Street Station they would have had to wait some time for their connection. And the train would have been slower, and less direct in its approach.

Nevertheless, she knew she had been less than sociable during the drive. She had left it to her daughter to make all the overtures, and she was quite aware that Cory had taken advantage of her position. But it would have been too embarrassing to chastise the girl in front of Rafe Lindsay, and instead she had spent the journey fending off the advances of a friendly retriever, who had shown his affection by licking her face.

Amazingly, the cottage had been unlocked, and their escort had made his departure, after depositing their luggage in the front room. Isobel had offered her thanks, albeit rather belatedly, and he had made some deprecating comment, but that was all. With a brief half-smile,

he had swung back into the powerful vehicle, raising his
hand politely before driving away.

Now Isobel turned from stowing the empty cases away
in the bottom of an enormous wardrobe, and found Cory
standing in the doorway. The girl had done little in the
way of unpacking, and her only real source of interest
had been in choosing the downstairs bedroom for herself.
Isobel hadn't minded. The dormer room, at the top of
the narrow staircase, might be smaller, but the view was
worth it. The cottage was so overfurnished that all the
rooms seemed tiny anyway. It was just as well they had
put their own furniture into storage. It was certain there
was no room for it here.

'When are we going to eat?' Cory demanded plain-
tively now, and, glancing at her watch, Isobel saw that
it was after eight. She had been so intent on unpacking
and putting their things away, so as not to waste what
little space there was, she had forgotten all about making
a meal.

'Oh—whenever,' she replied, glancing half contentedly about her. 'Clare said she'd leave some food in
the fridge. I suggest we go down and see what there is.'

'I know what there is,' declared Cory, not moving.
'There's some eggs, and cheese, and a pot of something
that looks like yoghurt. Honestly, you'd think we were
vegetarians! Why couldn't she have bought some
beefburgers or some steak?'

Isobel's contented air vanished. 'You should consider
yourself lucky that she's left us anything at all,' she
retorted crisply. 'And beefburgers aren't good for you.
They're full of fat!'

'So is butter, but she's left us some of that,' countered
Cory, not to be outdone. 'And there's only brown bread.
I ask you, brown bread!'

Isobel refused to let her daughter's attitude spoil their
first evening at the cottage. 'Brown bread won't hurt
you for once,' she remarked, gesturing for Cory to move
out of the doorway. 'I'll make omelettes. Cheese
omelettes. And we can have the yoghurt for dessert.'

Cory trundled down the steep narrow stairs ahead of
her, grumbling about the inconveniences of living in a
village. 'I bet there isn't even a McDonald's within thirty

miles,' she muttered, considering that a great distance.
But privately Isobel suspected the nearest fast-food establishment was a lot further than that.

'How old was this Miss McLeay anyway?' Cory asked
some time later, sprawled at the scarred pinewood kitchen
table, watching her mother prepare their meal. 'I bet she
was ninety if she was a day. All this old furniture! It
looks like it came out of the ark.'

'Well, I think it's rather charming,' declared Isobel,
looking appreciatively through the archway that divided
the kitchen from the living-room and viewing the lamplit
chintz-covered sofa and chairs with some affection. There
were too many occasional tables, of course, and even
Miss McLeay could not have wanted all these knick-
knacks. But the general impression was homely, and
Isobel thought it would look really cosy when the fire
was lit. For the present, they were making do with an
electric heater. There was an Aga in the kitchen, which
she thought might heat the rather antiquated radiators
she had seen, but that would have to wait until
tomorrow and daylight, when she might feel more
equipped to experiment.

'It's not very big, is it?' Cory persisted, as her mother
riffled through the drawers, looking for a cheese-grater.
'Grandma said it would probably be an old crofter's
cottage. Do you think that's what it was? Before the old
lady lived here?'

'Crofter's cottages didn't have central heating,'
retorted Isobel flatly, resisting the urge to take her
mother-in-law's name in vain. 'Have a look in that
cupboard, will you? Clare said the place was fully
equipped. There must be a grater somewhere. If not, I'll
just have to crumble the cheese myself.'

Cory got reluctantly to her feet and did as she was
asked. But apart from a couple of cans of soup, which
Isobel suspected must be well past their sell-by date, it
was empty.

However, she was not to be disappointed. An examination of the gas cooker solicited the fact that there was
a drawer at the bottom practically filled with baking tins
and utensils of all kinds. Among the clutter was a hand-

held grater, and Isobel carried it to the sink to wash as
Cory resumed her seat at the table.

'This Clare...' she remarked, after a few minutes, and
Isobel glanced up from the cheese.

'Mrs Lindsay, to you,' she corrected swiftly, and then
winced as her knuckles connected with the grater.

'All right.' Cory pulled a face. 'Mrs Lindsay, then. Is
she married to Rafe's brother?'

'She's married to *Mr* Lindsay's brother, yes.' Isobel
brushed the last of the cheese from her fingers, and
turned back to the pan. 'I expect you'll meet her
tomorrow. She said she'd pop by to see how we're settling in.'

Cory shrugged, evidently not impressed by this
prospect. 'I wonder if—if he's married?' she mused,
reverting to her previous topic. 'You know: Rafe. Oh,
all right.' She gave an exaggerated sigh at her mother's
expression. 'Mr Lindsay, then. He's really cool, isn't he?
Did you notice how long his eyelashes were?'

'I noticed you had a little too much to say for yourself,'
responded Isobel, choosing not to get into a discussion
about Rafe Lindsay's attributes, and Cory pulled a face.

'Well, at least I said something, instead of sitting there
like a dummy,' she retorted cheekily. 'You didn't even
cut a smile when he apologised about the dog.'

'I hardly know the man, Cory.' Isobel found herself
on the defensive once again. 'Just because he was kind
enough to offer us a lift doesn't mean I have to like him.
I thought he was rather arrogant, actually. I don't think
your father would have liked him.'

'Oh, well——' Cory's response to that was revealing
'—Dad wouldn't like any man who looked twice at you.
He's—he *was*—terribly old-fashioned.' She rubbed an
impatient hand across her eyes. 'I was always telling him
so.'

'Yes.'

Isobel surveyed her daughter with an unexpected rush
of emotion. Even though it was nearly a year since
Edward's accident, they could both be caught by an
unwary comment, and the remonstrance she had been
about to offer died unspoken in her suddenly tight throat.
But today had been a rather traumatic day, in more ways

than one, and she could only hope that in these new surroundings they might both find it easier to adapt.

'You're not going to cry, are you?' Cory's terse question hid a wealth of uncertainty, and with a determined effort Isobel shook her head.

'No.' She paused, before continuing deliberately, 'But I don't think you should talk about your father like that. He wasn't old-fashioned. Not really. He was just—not interested in current fads and fancies.'

'That's for sure.' Cory gathered confidence from her mother's calm response. 'But that doesn't mean you have to act like you're already middle-aged. I mean, you're not young. But you're not old either.'

'Oh, thanks.'

'And you must have noticed how attractive Rafe was.'

'Cory, how many more times do I have to tell you— I'm not interested in any other man, attractive or otherwise? Now, did you decide if you wanted cheese in your omelette or not?'

The impromptu meal was far better than even Isobel could have anticipated. The milk Clare had left for them was rich and creamy, and without the means to make filter coffee they had to make do with instant. But instant coffee made with fresh milk, and not the half-skimmed variety Isobel had usually bought at home, was almost an indulgence, and they were sitting enjoying their second cup when someone knocked at the door.

Not surprisingly, Isobel was loath to answer it. Beyond the faded floral curtains, the night was as black as pitch, and, although common sense told her they were far from the reach of thieves and muggers, old habits died hard.

'Aren't you going to see who it is?'

Cory was looking at her a little apprehensively now, and, realising she was in danger of alarming her daughter, probably unnecessarily, Isobel got to her feet. 'I suppose so,' she said, pretending an indolence she was far from feeling. But then Clare called,

'Isobel! It's only me!' and all her anxieties vanished.

Reaching the door in two strides, she turned the key and threw it open. And Clare came into the room on a cloud of French perfume. Her rich cream fur and long boots looked out of place in the shabby living-room, but, Isobel reflected, her own attire suited it to a T. The lady of the manor, calling on one of the peasants, she mused drily. But that wasn't fair. It wasn't Clare's fault that she had not bothered to change.

'Isobel, darling!' Clare exclaimed now, kissing the air beside her friend's ear with the smoothness of long experience. 'And this must be Cory! Hello, dear. Your mummy didn't tell me you were so grown-up!'

She went towards Cory, and Isobel saw her daughter draw back in some alarm. But happily, Clare didn't embarrass either of them by attempting to kiss her too. Instead, she contented herself with bestowing a charming smile on her, before turning back to her friend.

'Well, now,' she said. 'What do you think of this place? Isn't it cosy? Have you got everything you need?'

'I think so.' Isobel answered her last question first. 'I've unpacked, and we've had supper, and we were just dawdling over our coffee. Would you like a cup? I can easily——'

'Oh, no. No.' Clare lifted her hand in denial, as if the very idea was anathema to her. 'Colin and I have just got back from having supper with the Urquharts—Robert and Jessica Urquhart, that is—and I couldn't drink another drop.' She gave a rather girlish giggle. 'They're such a lovely couple. He's the local sheriff.'

'I see.'

Isobel nodded, and, as if realising she was being rather indiscreet, Clare glanced about her. 'I must admit, I'm amazed at the amount you've accomplished. And in such a short space of time, too. I quite expected to find you in the middle of things. The train must have been on time for once. Did Mr MacGregor collect you from the station? Well, of course, he must have done.' she smiled again. 'You're here, aren't you?'

'Mr MacGregor?'

Isobel felt slightly confused. Who was Mr MacGregor? She was sure the man had said his name was Lindsay. Well, of course he had. Cory had used that name earlier, when she had been berating her mother for not talking to him.

But, before she could say anything more, Cory chimed in. 'He picked us up in Glasgow,' she said, giving her mother a look of sly complicity. 'He said the trains aren't usually reliable. That's why he came to meet us.'

Clare turned to the girl now, a frown drawing her sandy brows together. 'Tom MacGregor drove all the way to Glasgow——' she began, a look of consternation marring her pale sculpted features, and Cory offered her mother a wicked grin.

'I think he said his name was Rafe,' she declared, with the careless skill of a seasoned campaigner. 'Yeah, it was definitely Rafe, wasn't it, Mum? And not MacGregor— Lindsay.' She tilted her head. 'Hey—that's your name isn't it?'

Isobel knew at once what her daughter was up to. It was obvious she resented Clare, and the vaguely condescending air she had adopted since her arrival. And, without her mother's inhibitions, she had jumped deliberately into the fray, enjoying the success of defeating the enemy.

Clare's jaw had dropped. 'Rafe,' she echoed faintly. 'Rafe met you in Glasgow! But——' her dismay was evident '—he doesn't know you, does he?' She caught her breath. 'You must be mistaken. Rafe would never——'

'I'm afraid that was what he said his name was,' put in Isobel unwillingly, quelling any further outburst from her daughter with a baleful look. She licked her lips. 'He did say he was your brother-in-law, Clare. I assumed you knew all about it.'

'Well, I didn't.' For a moment, Clare was too upset to guard her feelings. 'I can't believe it. Why would he do such a thing?' She looked angrily at Isobel. 'How did he know who you were?'

Isobel wrapped her arms about her midriff, feeling an unpleasant sense of distaste. Clare was over-reacting. There was no earthly need for her to behave as if she and Cory had solicited the ride for themselves. Good heavens, it was obvious what had happened. Rafe Lindsay had had to go to Glasgow for some reason, and he had decided to do his sister-in-law a favour and meet her friend. Only Clare wasn't behaving as if Isobel was her friend; she wasn't even behaving as if Isobel had a right to be here. Her whole attitude was one of outrage, as if Isobel had dared to impinge on her territory.

'I think he was just trying to be kind,' Isobel said now, aware that her voice was much cooler than it had been before. 'We were practically the last passengers to leave the platform. You hadn't explained that we had to change stations, as well as trains, and he came to our assistance. As I say, I assumed you knew.'

'No.' Clare took a deep breath, evidently trying to calm herself. 'No, I didn't. I wouldn't——' She broke off, and when she spoke again it was softly, almost to herself. 'I doubt if Colin or his mother knew anything about it either. But that's typical of Rafe. He's always been a law unto himself.'

'Yes, well——' Isobel wished Clare would just go now. Maybe in the morning she would be able to view what had just happened with an objective mind, but at this moment all her earlier doubts were rampant. 'I'm sorry if you think we've been presumptuous. It wasn't intentional. But now, if you don't mind, we are rather tired——'

'Of course.' With a rapid change of mood, Clare twisted her lips into a thin smile. 'Of course you must be tired. And I must be going. Colin will be wondering where I've got to. I promised I'd only stay a minute.'

Isobel forced herself to be polite. 'Thank you for calling.' She glanced towards the kitchen. 'And for the food. You'll have to tell me how much I owe you.'

'Heavens, no.' Clare was almost entirely in control of herself again, and, pulling a pair of thin leather gloves out of her pocket, she began to smooth one over her fingers. 'What's a few groceries between friends?' She allowed her gaze to pass over Cory, before settling on Isobel again. 'But I have to say, you know how to arrive in style, darling. It's not every employee who can boast that the Earl of Invercaldy was their chauffeur!'

CHAPTER THREE

WHEN Isobel awakened the next morning, she lay for several minutes just listening to the silence. For so long, she had been used to the sounds of people, and traffic, and even in the depths of night she had always been conscious of the city, living and breathing, just a few yards from her door.

But as she lay there, fending off the full awareness of what the morning might bring, the only sounds that reached her ears were the unfamiliar sounds of nature. There was a rook, making a nuisance of itself, high up in the trees that edged the cottage garden; a cow was lowing, its strident call more indignant than contented; and on the roof a pair of doves were cooing, their repetitive chorus probably what had woken her in the first place.

But that was all she could hear. There were no engines revving, no horns blowing, no jingle of the milk float, as it made its morning deliveries. There wasn't even the sound of the postman, whistling as he covered his round. Only the wind in the eaves, and an occasional creak as the old house stirred to meet the day.

There was no sound from downstairs either, which hopefully meant that Cory was still sound asleep. Well, it was only a little after seven, she noted, squinting at her watch which she had propped on the cabinet beside the bed. She generally had some difficulty getting her daughter up by eight o'clock at home. At home ...

Throwing back the covers—sheets, blankets, and an old candlewick bedspread; evidently Miss McLeay had not gone in for fancy things like duvets and Continental quilts—Isobel padded, barefoot, to the window. This was their home now, and she had to remember that.

It was cold, and she shivered in her short nightshirt, but she pulled the curtain aside, and looked out on that

strange but amazing view. And it was just the same, but
different. Now the sky was a diffused shade of palest
lavender, with a lemony tinge on the horizon, which
heralded the early rising of the sun. The mountains in
the distance were still wreathed in darkness, and the loch
was an opaque mirror, shrouded in mystery. Even the
cattle that stood at the edge of the water seemed
nebulous, and unreal, their shaggy coats steaming as they
waded in the shallows.

Isobel took an enchanted breath, and saw it film the
window with condensation. It reminded her of the fact
that she was risking getting pneumonia, standing here
without clothes. She might not mind there being no
traffic on her doorstep, but unless she could do something about the Aga she was going to have to dress more
warmly.

Grabbing her dressing-gown, which was, thankfully,
a warm towelling one, she tossed her plait over her
shoulder and went downstairs. At least she could im-
prove upon the bedding, once their personal belongings
arrived, she thought, as she walked into the kitchen. She
had filled two trunks with ornaments, books, and
bedding, as well as the clothes they had not been able
to carry. They should be delivered in a day or so. Until
then, they'd have to manage as they were.

When she drew the kitchen curtains, she got another
surprise. A huge black cat was seated on the windowsill
outside, evidently waiting for someone to let it in. After
filling the kettle and setting it on the hob, Isobel
unlocked the back door and opened it. And, immediately, the cat abandoned its perch, and strolled into the
room.

The air it brought with it was icy, and Isobel hastily
closed the door again, and went to turn on the electric
heater. 'I wonder who you belong to?' she murmured,
and then grimaced at the realisation that she was talking
to a dumb animal. 'Oh, well, I'm sure you'd like some
milk,' she added. 'I just hope I've got enough.'

The cat lapped eagerly at the milk she put down for
it, and then rubbed itself silkily against her bare legs.
'A friend for life, hmm?' observed Isobel drily, not
averse to having its company all the same. She had never

had a pet, even though she had occasionally suggested to Edward that they should get one. But Edward hadn't liked dogs, and Mrs Jacobson had declared she was allergic to cats, so despite her and Cory's appeals the subject had been closed.

The kettle boiled, and she made a pot of tea. Then she collected a cup and seated herself at the table, with the pot and milk jug close by. It had always been one of her favourite times of day, and here, with her elbows propped on the table, and a hot cup of tea between her hands, she felt almost optimistic.

And, after last night, she had not expected to feel so. Indeed, when she had gone to bed, she had felt decidedly depressed. But she was sure she must have exaggerated Clare's attitude, she thought firmly. The girl she had known could not have turned out as unpleasant as she'd thought.

Still—she caught her lower lip between her teeth—it had been a shock to her, too, to learn that Rafe Lindsay was the Earl of Invercaldy. She had no experience, of course, but to her knowledge it was unusual for a man with his background to put himself out for someone he didn't even know. And without Clare's knowledge, too. No wonder she had been aggrieved.

All the same, Isobel couldn't really understand why Clare had been so annoyed about it. It wasn't as if she had done anything wrong. In fact, she had refused his offer when he'd first made it, and it had been his explanation that had persuaded her to think that Clare had sent him.

She grimaced at that. Lord, what must he have thought when she'd told him she didn't want his help? And that awkward journey, when Cory had done all the talking. What had she talked about? Horror movies, mostly, Isobel seemed to remember. They were Cory's current obsession, and although she didn't recall Rafe Lindsay's making any particular comment about them he had listened patiently enough.

She pressed her lips together, and poured herself another cup of tea. He had been rather patient with both of them, she reflected, ruefully. And at no time had he given any hint that he was anything more than Clare's brother-in-law. Even when she had called him *Mr* Lindsay. She sighed.

And he had been attractive, she conceded grudgingly. Very attractive, actually. That was why she'd been so surprised when she'd found him staring at her. In the normal course of events, men like him did not stare at women like her. Her features were pleasant enough, she supposed, but no one could describe them as striking. Her face was round and ordinary, with wide-spaced hazel eyes, a fairly straight nose, and a generous mouth. She was not beautiful, by any stretch of the word, and although Edward used to tell her she was 'all woman' Isobel knew what he had really meant was that she was homely.

In addition to which she knew she could never aspire to Clare's style of elegance. She wasn't fat, but she certainly wasn't thin either, and only her height offset rounded hips and the full breasts that had always been a source of frustration to her.

Her hair was her only real asset, she thought. And, despite the fact that both Edward and his mother would have preferred her to have it cut, Isobel had clung to her own convictions. Besides, her father had liked it long, and it seemed a small thing to do to keep his memory alive. Loosened from the braid in which she invariably confined it, it fell in a beige silken curtain almost to her hips, and although it was sometimes a chore to wash and dry it was her one indulgence.

Pulling the braid over her shoulder now, she toyed with the elasticated band that secured it. Last night, she had felt too down-hearted to loosen the braid, and brush her hair as she normally did, and this morning it looked dull and untidier than usual. She needed a shower, she thought determinedly. Or a bath, as there didn't appear to be a shower in the bathroom. No doubt Miss McLeay considered showers a modern extravagance. But perhaps she could make some enquiries about having one installed—if she could just figure out a way to get the Aga working.

She had opened the firebox door, and was considering how to light it, when someone knocked at the back door. It was barely half-past seven. Far too early for callers, and she was examining her smutty fingers in some dismay when a man's head appeared outside the kitchen window.

It was Rafe Lindsay. *No*, the Earl of Invercaldy, she corrected herself hurriedly, staring at him as if he were some kind of mirage come to life. It was as if the thoughts she had been having about him had somehow conjured him up, and although she knew she couldn't be hallucinating the doubts were there.

'I found this in the car this morning,' he said, mouthing the words in an exaggerated way, so that even if she couldn't hear him she could read his lips. He held up a dayglo green and orange haversack, which Isobel recognised instantly as Cory's. 'Open the door.'

Isobel grabbed the nearest cloth, which happened to be a tea-towel, she saw with some impatience, and after a moment's frustrated hesitation scrubbed her fingers on it. Then, with a resigned glance at her towelling robe and worn mules, she did as he asked.

The cat, who had been washing his paws in front of the electric heater, came to arch its back against the newcomer's legs, and for a moment its appearance created a welcome diversion.

'Hey, Bothie, you've soon adopted your new mistress,' he remarked drily, bending to fondle the cat's ears. He straightened and looked at Isobel again. 'Do you like cats? He belonged to Miss McLeay, but she couldn't take him with her. Her sister lives in sheltered housing, you see, and they don't allow pets.'

'Oh—well, yes.' Isobel knew she sounded stiff, but she couldn't help it. It had been hard enough coping with his dark-eyed scrutiny the previous afternoon. It was infinitely harder when she was still in her nightclothes and she knew she hadn't had a wash, and her hair was a mess.

Rafe Lindsay, meanwhile, displayed all the self-confidence of his forebears. Even in soft denims and rubber boots—not green ones, she noticed wryly—with his hair tumbling about his shoulders, and a night's growth of beard darkening his jawline, he possessed the kind of understated elegance that only good breeding could achieve. Of course, his shirt was probably handmade, and his leather jerkin was definitely expensive. But it wasn't just his appearance that gave him that assurance. It was an innate thing, as natural as the lazy smile he now bestowed upon her.

'Good,' he said, and for a moment she couldn't remember what they had been talking about. 'For Bothie—Bothwell! Miss McLeay had a romantic heart,' he amended, propping his shoulder against the wall beside the door. His gaze slid over her, resting briefly on her hands, which were still scrubbing anxiously at the teacloth. 'Having problems?'

'I—why—no.' She thrust the cloth aside, and nodded at the canvas bag he was still holding. 'Thank you for bringing it back—um——' She couldn't bring herself to address him as 'my lord', even though he probably expected it. 'It's—er—it's Cory's.'

'I guessed as much.' But he still didn't hand it over, and Isobel shivered as the icy air probed beneath the hem of her nightshirt. 'You're cold. May I come in?'

'Come in?' echoed Isobel, as if she didn't understand the words, and then, realising that as this was probably his property she didn't have a lot of choice, she stepped back. 'Um—if you like.'

'Your hospitality overwhelms me,' he remarked mockingly, as he straightened and stepped across the threshold. He pressed the holdall into her nervous hands. 'I gather you've never used an Aga before.'

Isobel blinked, and closed the door, almost trapping the cat in her haste. Bothwell squeezed inside with an offended air, and went to repair his dignity on the living-room windowsill, while she pressed her hands together and faced her visitor. 'How do you know that?'

'The way you were looking at it, when I walked past the window,' responded Rafe drily. 'What's the word I want? Blankly? Yes, I think that covers it. Blankly!'

'You mean vacantly, don't you?' exclaimed Isobel shortly, forgetting for the moment that she had intended to apologise to him if she ever saw him again. 'I'm not an idiot. I'm just not used to open fires, that's all.'

'This isn't an open fire,' declared Rafe, without rancour. 'It's a wood-burning stove.' He took off his jacket and tossed it on to the nearest chair. 'Why don't you make a fresh pot of tea, and I'll take a look at it for you?'

Isobel caught her breath. 'You can't!' she said, aghast, feeling an unusual tide of heat invading her throat and neck. 'That is—I'm fairly sure I know what to do. I—just need some wood to light it.' She swallowed. 'Thank you, sir.'

Rafe turned and gave her a dark look. 'Sir?'

Isobel pressed her lips together. 'All right—my lord, then. You'll have to forgive me: I'm not used to dealing with—with the aristocracy.'

His mouth twisted. 'You've been talking to Clare.'

'It's true, then.' It wasn't until that moment that Isobel realised she had still hardly believed it.

'That depends what she's told you,' he retorted, turning back to the Aga, and rolling back the sleeves of his dark blue shirt over muscular forearms. Then, as if aware of her stillness, he glanced over his shoulder. 'Just make the tea, Mrs Jacobson. Milk but no sugar for me.' He paused. 'You do have milk, I take it?'

Isobel licked her lips. 'A little.'

Rafe expelled his breath on an impatient sigh. 'The cat,' he guessed flatly. 'Bothie, you old reprobate! You'll not have to be so greedy!' Then, with another rueful glance in Isobel's direction, he added, 'I'll have Archie Duncan leave you a quart every morning from now on.' He turned back to study the stove. 'He'll supply you with eggs and bacon as well, if you want it. Anything else, you can usually find in Strathmoor. Or, in an emergency, in the village itself.'

Isobel swallowed. 'Strathmoor?' she said doubtfully.

'That's our nearest town,' Rafe explained, examining the contents of a wood-box that was set beside the Aga. He looked round again. 'Didn't Clare tell you anything about the area?'

Isobel felt a need to do something, and went to fill the kettle at the sink. When he turned those penetrating dark eyes upon her, she felt as nervous as a schoolgirl, and although she told herself it was only because he had arrived before she was even dressed she didn't believe it.

'She—told me about the village,' she said, aware of the incongruity of her standing here in her nightclothes making tea for the Earl of Invercaldy. While he tried to light the stove for her, she added to herself incredulously. It was unbelievable.

'But not how to get here, or that you really need a vehicle of some sort to get around,' remarked Rafe drily, feeding kindling into the grate, and she had to struggle to remember what she had been saying. She was aware of him watching her as she put the kettle on to boil, and everything else seemed of secondary importance. She almost fumbled it, but all he said was, 'Pass me the matches, will you? I think this is going to work.'

Isobel handed him the box of matches, conscious of the cool strength in the long fingers that brushed hers. Crouched there, in front of the stove, he wasn't as intimidating as he was standing over her, but he still disturbed her in a deep, visceral kind of way. She told herself it was because of who he was, that she wasn't used to dealing with men like him. But it was more than that, and she knew it. His kindness disconcerted her: his familiarity broke down barriers she hadn't even known she'd erected; and his maleness was a threat to her prospectively safe and ordered future.

He lit the wood, made sure the damper was wide open, and closed the door. Presently, the reassuring crackle of the kindling could be heard, and Isobel expelled a relieved breath. 'As soon as it's going strongly enough, just add some of these small logs,' he said, stepping back to survey his handiwork. 'At least the flue seems to be clear. There's no down-draught.'

Isobel nodded. 'I'm very grateful.'

'Are you?' His responses were never what she expected, and she hurriedly tried to assure him that she meant what she said.

'Yes. It was kind of you to come and make sure we were all right,' she told him defensively. 'At least now we'll have some hot water. I—I would have had a bath last night, if—if, well . . .'

Her voice trailed to a halt, as the realisation that she was being far too familiar put a brake on her tongue. He wasn't interested in her personal needs, for heaven's sake. He was her landlord. She was just another tenant to him.

The kettle started to whistle, and with a feeling of relief Isobel went to make the tea. It necessitated emptying the teapot, and refilling it again, and she was glad of the time to reorganise her thoughts. For some reason, he seemed to have the power to reduce her to a stammering idiot, and she'd be glad when he went. After all, he had done his duty. They'd be unlikely to see him again.

'Do you think you're going to like it here?' he asked, as she was making a business out of warming the pot, and spooning in the tea.

She was forced to turn and face him. 'I hope so,' she said, avoiding any direct eye-contact, as she gathered another cup and saucer from the dresser. 'It's a lot different from what we're used to. London is so busy. You can't hear yourself think.'

'You won't miss the noise and bustle?'

'I don't think so.' She could feel his eyes upon her, and she gestured rather awkwardly towards a chair. 'Please,' she said. 'Won't you sit down?'

He hesitated for a moment, and she guessed he was used to waiting until his hostess was seated before sitting down himself. But, when she made no move to do so, he pulled out a chair from the table and straddled it. Then, resting his arms along the back, he reached for the cup and saucer she had set beside him.

Isobel took a breath. 'Can I get you anything else?'

He looked at her over the rim of the cup. 'What would you suggest?' he enquired, and although she was almost sure he was teasing her she didn't know how to answer him. All she could think was that Cory had been right about his eyelashes. They were long, and thick, yet decidedly masculine just the same. And his eyes weren't black, as she had thought, but a very dark and subtle shade of grey; deep, and intense—and dangerous to her peace of mind.

'Um—toast,' she muttered, in an effort to distract herself, but he only shook his head.

'The tea's fine,' he assured her smoothly. 'As soon as I've finished, I'll go, and let you get organised. I believe

John's expecting to see you later. It's not far, and there's a plate on the gate. You can't miss it.'

Isobel blinked. 'John?' Her confusion wasn't helped by his evident amusement. Then her brain began to function again. 'Oh—you mean—John—that is, Dr Webster.'

'Clare's father, yes.' Rafe's gaze was sympathetic. 'I guess she didn't tell you his name either, did she? Never mind. You can rest assured he doesn't stand on ceremony.'

'I do know Dr Webster,' retorted Isobel, not without some dignity. It was bad enough that he found her a figure of fun. She didn't want him to feel sorry for her as well.

'Good.' Rafe swallowed the remainder of the tea in his cup, and set it back on its saucer. 'Then that's three people you know in Invercaldy, isn't it?' he mocked. 'And I mustn't forget your daughter.'

'Oh—yes.' Isobel remembered why he had come. 'I—thank you for bringing her bag back. She's rather—forgetful, at times.'

'Is she?'

Rafe didn't sound as if he believed her, but he made no comment. Instead, he got to his feet and reached for his jacket. Then, slinging it over his shoulder, he raked back his hair with a careless hand, before taking a final look at the Aga. It sounded as if it was burning merrily, already heating the tiny kitchen, and creating an atmosphere of warm familiarity.

'I assume you know you can use this to cook with,' he remarked, tipping up a metal hood to expose four solid rings. Isobel hadn't known, and she suspected he knew that, but she managed to appear as if she had, and he dropped the hood again. 'You'll soon get used to it,' he added. 'And if you do have any problems, I hope you won't be too proud to ask for help.'

'No.' Isobel's fingers fastened on to the cord at her waist, and she twisted it tightly. 'I—thank you again, Mr—er——' She took a breath and lifted her eyes to his with some reluctance. 'I'm sorry. What do I call you?'

His eyes darkened. 'Rafe will do,' he replied after a moment, when she had been half afraid he was going to touch her. But his lips only curled into a tight smile, and without another word he stepped to the door and pulled it open. 'By the way,' he appended, pausing on the threshold to slide his arms into the sleeves of his jacket, 'don't let my sister-in-law grind you down, will you? Clare's got some decidedly middle-class notions, which we don't agree on.'

CHAPTER FOUR

HIS brother was waiting for him when Rafe got back
from Strathmoor.

Colin was seated at the desk in the library, making a
fairly inquisitive scrutiny of his brother's mail, and he
looked up rather guiltily when Rafe walked into the
room.

'Oh—you're back!' he exclaimed, pushing the letters
aside and getting hastily to his feet. 'I was just waiting
for coffee. I asked Cummins some time ago, and I
thought that's who it was.'

'Ah.' Rafe nodded, not embarrassing the other man
any more than he was already by saying he knew exactly
what Colin had been doing. 'Well, I'm sure it won't be
long now. I saw Mrs Fielding in the hall when I came
in, and she asked if I wanted the same.'

'Oh. Oh, good.' Colin's plump features mirrored his
relief. He rubbed his hands together, and edged round
the desk, well away from the incriminating letters.
'Damned cold day, isn't it?'

'Cold? Oh, yes.' Rafe regarded his younger brother
with some impatience. 'Did you want to see me?'

Colin shrugged. 'Not especially,' he said, running a
slightly nervous hand over his thinning hair. 'Just
thought I'd call in on my way to Dalbaig, that's all. I
want to have a word with Stuart.'

Rafe arched a dark brow. 'Kenneth?'

'No, Gordon,' amended Colin quickly. 'I want to make
sure those covers are well stocked for this weekend. With
Sir Malcolm coming, I don't want there to be any cock-
ups.' He grimaced. 'If you'll forgive the pun!'

'Mmm.'

Rafe was only listening to his brother with half an ear.
His mind was intent on other things—not least his
reasons for going into the Jacobsons' cottage that

morning. It didn't matter that he hadn't planned on
doing so, or that his intention had been to leave the haversack on the doorstep, where it was certain to be found.
As soon as he had passed the window and seen that Isobel
Jacobson was up, his reactions had been purely
instinctive.

And why? Why had he knocked at the door, and
drawn attention to himself like that? Oh, he had guessed
correctly that she was uncertain about how to light the
Aga. It had been obvious from the way she'd been
looking at it that she'd never used one before. But that
wasn't an excuse. Given her intelligence, she'd soon have
worked it out for herself. Anyone could light a fire. There
was no particular skill required. Just some wood, and a
match, and a moderate amount of patience.

But for some reason his reflexes hadn't responded to
logic. He liked to think it was because of what his mother
had said the night before, but he was honest enough to
admit that that wasn't altogether true. There was no
doubt that his mother's attitude had annoyed him, but
he hadn't been thinking of his mother when he'd knocked
at Isobel Jacobson's door.

'Er—hum!' Colin cleared his throat, and then patted
his chest, as if it hadn't been a quite deliberate attempt
to attract his brother's attention. 'Um—Clare tells me
you've met Webster's new receptionist.'

Rafe became aware that he had been staring out of
the long windows, without even seeing the reflective
waters of Loch Caldy, which lapped only yards from the
castle walls. But Colin's words had finally penetrated his
abstraction, and he focused rather grimly on his brother's
fair face. 'What?'

'I said, Clare told me you—you'd given her father's
new receptionist a lift yesterday,' Colin paraphrased
awkwardly. 'Bit of an odd thing to do, wasn't it? Mother
thinks you only did it to embarrass her.'

Rafe gave his brother an impatient look, and then
walked round the desk and flung himself into the worn
leather chair Colin had been occupying earlier. 'Our
mother is paranoid,' he said succinctly. 'And, as I
understand it, Clare used to go to school with Mrs
Jacobson. So she's not exactly a stranger to her, is she?

Or has Clare become so vain she's forgotten her own roots?'

'Of course not.'

Colin flushed now, and then turned with some relief when there was a sound at the door. After the most perfunctory of taps, Cummins, who had been in service at Invercaldy Castle for the past forty years, came into the room, carrying a tray set with a coffee-pot and fine china cups. 'On the desk, my lord?' he enquired, with barely a glance at Colin, and Rafe nodded.

'Thank you,' he said, as the old man lowered the tray in front of him. 'We can serve ourselves.'

'Yes, my lord.'

Cummins inclined his head deferentially, and then, with a half-hearted acknowledgment of the younger man, he walked rather stiffly out of the room.

As soon as the door closed behind him, Colin exploded. 'That fellow!' he exclaimed. 'If he weren't nearing retirement, I'd insist that you get rid of him, Rafe. He's barely civil at the best of times, and whenever I ask him to do anything he conveniently forgets.'

'He's old,' remarked Rafe quietly, making no move to pour the coffee. 'And he doesn't care for Clare's attitude either. Or had you forgotten?'

Colin expelled his breath on a noisy sigh. 'The man's a servant, Rafe!'

'He's an employee,' amended his brother evenly. 'And deserving of some consideration.' He paused. 'Particularly at half-past one in the morning.'

'All Clare wanted was some cocoa!'

'Which she could have made herself.'

'I doubt if Mrs Fielding would have approved of any of the family interfering in her kitchen.' Colin clicked his tongue. 'It wasn't as if she got him out of bed. If I remember correctly, he'd been spending the evening playing cards with Lucas.'

Rafe regarded him coolly. 'It was his evening off.'

'Oh, all right.' Colin came towards the desk, and splashed cream into one of the cups. 'The man's a paragon, and Clare's a snob!' He filled the cup from the coffee-pot, and then spooned in several measures of brown sugar. 'But she's just trying to uphold the family

honour. We are the local establishment, Rafe. We owe
it to ourselves to maintain a certain—decorum.'

Rafe's lips curled. 'Exclusivity, don't you mean?'

Colin looked up from tasting his coffee. 'What's wrong
with that?'

Rafe shrugged. 'If you don't know, I can't tell you.'

Colin sniffed. 'Don't think I don't know what you're
doing. You're just trying to divert attention from your
own shortcomings. OK, maybe Clare is a little brackish—
at times, but in this case I think she has a point.'

'Do you?' Rafe placed his hands on the edge of the
wood and, pressing down, brought himself to his feet.
His mouth twitched a trifle wryly, as Colin took a couple
of steps back from the desk, as if anticipating some sort
of physical retaliation, but all he did was cross the room
to where a tray of drinks resided on a bureau. He lifted
a bottle of single malt, and poured an inch into a glass.
'Fine. Your objections have been noted.'

'But they're not going to be acted upon, are they?'
exclaimed Colin, stung into a retort. 'And what's wrong
with coffee, at this time of the morning? Must you ruin
your constitution with that stuff before it's even
lunchtime? Honestly, Rafe, are you trying to kill
yourself?'

Rafe's expression was cold. 'Why should you care?'
he countered. 'If I weren't around, you and Clare would
have a legitimate reason for acting like the lord and lady
of the manor!'

'That's a foul thing to say!'

Colin's cup clattered noisily into its saucer, and,
looking at his brother's shocked face, Rafe felt a sudden
spurt of remorse. It wasn't fair to treat Colin as a
whipping-boy. He had never shown any resentment
towards his elder brother, and when Sarah died he had
done everything he could to ease Rafe's burden. Just
because Clare had turned into a right royal pain in the
butt was no reason to act as if Colin were personally to
blame.

'I'm sorry,' he said now. 'That was uncalled for.' He
grimaced. 'You caught me at a bad moment, Col. I'm
not in the best of tempers. You'll have to forgive me.'

Colin shook his head. 'Think nothing of it, old man,' he said gruffly, and Rafe thought how lucky he was that his brother was always willing to forgive and forget. 'I shouldn't go on at you as I do. Goodness knows, you've had enough to cope with as it is, without me sticking my big nose into your affairs.'

'Mmm.'

Rafe acknowledged his words silently, looking down at the liquid in his glass for a moment, before lifting it to his lips. But he only took a mouthful, allowing the undiluted spirit to numb his teeth and gums, before letting it slide smoothly down his throat. The truth was, he didn't really know how he felt. He'd thought he did. Until recently, he'd have sworn he felt the same now as he'd done when Sarah died, but he simply wasn't sure any more. For some reason, he had doubts, and they weren't exactly welcome.

Which was ridiculous, really. After all, when Sarah had died in childbirth, he had been convinced he'd never get over it. She had been so young, only twenty-eight, and having a baby had seemed such a simple, uncomplicated procedure. With all the advances in medical science, there should have been no danger of her dying in the delivery-room. But Rafe suspected the doctor hadn't even realised the baby was dead until its lifeless little body had been extracted from Sarah's womb. And Sarah had been so exhausted by the prolonged period of labour that she hadn't had the strength to withstand the massive haemorrhage that had followed.

It had happened so quickly. One week, he and Sarah had been picking out names for the baby, and the next he was standing beside her grave. And for weeks after that he had woken in the morning still expecting to find her lying beside him. He had had dreams where she was with him, laughing with him, talking with him, her diminutive frame still swollen with her blossoming pregnancy. Those dreams had been the worst, because when he had awakened he had had to face the ugly truth all over again. At least when his dreams had been cloaked in blood he'd known there was no hope.

So why was he now resenting the fact that he could think about what had happened without feeling that devastating surge of despair? he wondered. It couldn't be that after two years he had grown so used to the anguish, he had actually started to find pleasure in it. But no. He might never forgive himself for what had happened to Sarah, but anything else was unthinkable. He ought to be glad he was beginning to accept the inevitability of it all; glad that he was finally coming to terms with her death.

His mother would probably say that Phillips was responsible. It was she who had eventually persuaded him to let Phillips try and help him, and for the past six months he had spent a couple of hours each week listening to the old fraud tell him that trying to drown his sorrows in alcohol wasn't going to work. Of course, he'd known that for himself. Prolonged bouts of drinking had left him with nothing but a bad hangover, and in recent weeks he had started to restrict his intake accordingly. But his mother had begged and cajoled him to seek professional help, and it had been simpler to give in to her than suffer her tearful recriminations.

That was why he didn't believe Phillips had had anything to do with the way he felt now. Unwilling as he was to believe it, his change of mood seemed to stem from what had happened the previous afternoon. Which was the real reason he resented it, he supposed. It was infuriating to think that Isobel Jacobson—and her precocious daughter—should have had any positive effect on his mental condition. For God's sake, he had only gone to the station in the first place because he had known how it would irritate his mother. His mother might have succeeded in foisting her pet psychologist on to him, but he could still behave completely irrationally if he chose to do so.

Like this morning, he thought broodingly. Why had he felt that overwhelming urge to help the Jacobson woman again? It wasn't as if she was the kind of woman he had ever been attracted to. Apart from their obvious social differences, she didn't even look like his ideal woman. He preferred small women, like Sarah, not tall Amazons, whose shape was apparent even in a man's shirt and trousers. She had just been a means to ruffle his mother's feathers, and it annoyed him to think that she had caused him to act in a totally inappropriate way. Even the thought that she had, however briefly, attracted his interest disturbed him. He didn't want—he didn't *need*—that kind of complication in his life.

'Anyway,' Colin ventured now, evidently deciding that Rafe was still brooding over his wife's behaviour, 'I suggest we say no more about it, eh? I'm sure—Mrs Jacobson appreciated not having to wait for the local train. And at least she's had a decent introduction to the area. I'm sure old Webster will be pleased about that. It hasn't been easy finding a replacement for Miss McLeay, you know. There aren't that many people who'd want to move to a remote village in the Highlands, not when they've been used to—well, a much more—hectic environment.'

Rafe made no response. It would have been difficult to say anything without involving himself still further, and he had no wish to endure another argument with his mother. Her complaints were legion as it was, and he was tired of accounting for his actions to any of them.

So, instead, he took up his brother's earlier comments about the members of the hunting party who were visiting the estate that weekend. Sir Malcolm Calder had been an old friend of his father's, and Rafe suspected his main reason for coming to Invercaldy was to see his father's widow. Sir Malcolm's own wife had died some time ago, and Rafe didn't think it was his imagination that his visits had increased in frequency in recent years.

Not that his mother would appreciate having that fact pointed out to her, he reflected drily. The Dowager Countess considered it was now her role in life to ensure that her elder son fulfilled his duties as the Earl of Invercaldy should, and he was well aware that she considered two years a long enough period of mourning. Fairly soon, she was going to start introducing him to young women again, and, as with Sarah, he would be expected to make a suitable marriage.

He had met Sarah just after his own father's funeral. There had been many visitors to Invercaldy in those sad days following the old Earl's death, and one of them had been an old schoolfriend of his mother's, Celia Larson. A widow herself, she had brought her daughter with her, and, whether by accident or design, Rafe had found himself left to entertain Sarah Larson.

Inevitably, he had recognised that his mother must have had some hand in the affair, but by then he was sufficiently attracted to Sarah to forgive any heavy-handed manipulation on the Dowager Countess's part. And it had been time that he started thinking about settling down. Colin had already been married, even though he was two years younger, and with his new responsibilities Rafe was not averse to accepting his fate.

It hadn't been a marriage made in heaven, he knew that. Eight years his junior, Sarah had been younger than the women he was used to going out with, and incredibly naïve into the bargain. But she had been sweet and innocent and because it had taken so long for her to conceive they had had several years in which to get to know each other intimately. They had been friends as well as lovers, and although Sarah had never really enjoyed the sexual side of their lovemaking she had more than made up for it by being as loyal and affectionate as any woman could be. That was why he had been so devastated when she died. Were it not for the fact of his sexual needs, she would still be alive. Which was a terrible burden for any man to bear.

Colin left after assuring himself that Rafe was apprised of all the salient details concerning the weekend's house party. The guests would be staying at the castle, and although Colin and his mother had taken over the organisation of these events his brother didn't live in the main buildings. There were several lodges on the estate, and Colin and his family occupied the largest of these, a comfortable four-bedroomed manor house, about half a mile from the castle.

After he had gone, Rafe seated himself at his desk again, abandoning the glass of Scotch in favour of a cooling cup of coffee. He grimaced as the lukewarm liquid coated his tongue, but he decided against ordering a fresh pot. It was his fault he hadn't drunk the coffee while it was hot.

Even so, he was surprised that he should suddenly prefer cold caffeine to malt whisky. It couldn't be that he was getting a conscience, could it? Maybe it was just that he wanted a clear head when he faced his mother again. If she found out that he had seen Isobel Jacobson again, she was not going to be best pleased.

He was dictating his response to several letters that required his attention when there was the sound of voices in the hall just outside. He recognised his mother's voice and a boy's slightly uneven tones, and, switching off the recorder, he went to open the door.

His nephew, Jaime, was standing outside, apparently in the middle of an argument with his grandmother. 'But Uncle Rafe said he'd let me ride Moonlight before I went back to school!' he was exclaiming, in the curious broken voice he had acquired in recent weeks. At nearly thirteen Jaime was losing his boyish soprano. 'Oh——' He broke off abruptly, when Rafe suddenly appeared, and then continued, less convincingly, 'You did say I could ride Moonlight, didn't you, Uncle Rafe? Gramma says I haven't to bother you, but I've only got another week.'

Rafe rested his forearm against the frame of the door. He had promised the boy he'd spend some time with him these holidays, he reflected ruefully, but somehow he'd never got round to it. The fact was, Moonlight had been Sarah's horse, and in a weak moment he had said that Jaime could exercise the mare. Since then, he'd been putting off doing anything about it.

'I was just trying to explain to Jaime that you're unlikely to want to get on a horse this morning,' the Dowager Countess declared briskly. Her sharp gaze had noted he was still unshaven, and that he wasn't wearing a tie. 'Colin informed me that you were—unwell,' she went on, the euphemism bringing a bitter tightening of her lips. She looked beyond him into the library, and Rafe was sure she had registered the half-filled glass of whisky on his desk. 'Maybe some other time, Jaime. Your uncle is obviously busy.'

'No, I'm not.' Rafe made a sudden decision. 'And I don't know where Colin got the idea that I wasn't—well,' he added, his dark eyes daring his mother to contradict him. 'I can spare an hour to go out with my nephew.' He smiled down at the boy. 'Go and get your coat, Jaime. I'll meet you at the stables.'

Jaime let out a whoop of delight, and then gave his grandmother an apologetic look. 'Sorry, Gramma,' he said, but the words were only perfunctory. They all knew that Jaime couldn't wait to get outside.

But he was sensible enough to know that antagonising his grandmother could still jeopardise the outing, and he bade her a polite farewell, before giving his uncle a conspiratorial grin. But the sound of his heels clattered noisily along the gallery, and Rafe guessed that as soon as he was out of earshot the boy would start running.

'Well...' Lady Invercaldy looked up at her son now with a decidedly disapproving air. 'I should have known better than to try and offer you advice, shouldn't I? But really, Rafe, is this wise? Going out riding! Are you really up to it?'

'I won't fall off, if that's what you mean,' responded Rafe drily, and his mother clicked her tongue.

'Nevertheless, Jaime is not an accomplished rider. He needs someone with him who can offer a strong hand. Someone who can keep his high spirits in check. It's not as if he's ridden Moonlight before. I'm sure Colin doesn't know about this ill-advised junket!'

'Junket!' Rafe's lips twitched. 'Honestly, Mama, there are times when I wonder which century you were born in.'

'And that kind of comment is exactly what I'd expect from someone who needs a shot of whisky to get him out of bed in the mornings,' retorted his mother angrily. 'I may be old-fashioned, Rafe, but at least I know what day it is!'

Rafe's mouth thinned. 'I'm perfectly sober, Mother.'

'Are you?' She brushed past him to gesture at the whisky glass on the desk. 'And that's ginger beer, I suppose. Oh, Rafe, who are you fooling? When are you going to pull yourself together?'

Rafe's nostrils flared, and the mood of optimism that had gripped him so briefly faltered. Who was he kidding? he thought bitterly. Nothing had really changed. Whatever he did, he was never going to escape his conscience...

CHAPTER FIVE

THERE was a quart of milk and a dozen eggs sitting on the doorstep when Isobel got back from the surgery. The milk was in a metal can, with a clip-on handle that held the lid securely in place. To deter raiders like Bothwell, guessed Isobel, carrying both the milk and the eggs into the kitchen. The cat had been curled on the windowsill again, but he sidled past her legs as she opened the cottage door.

Evidently, the Earl had wasted no time in making good his offer, she reflected, as she unpacked the eggs from the carton. But as she gave in to Bothwell's pleas, and poured some milk into his dish, she felt an unwilling warmth invade her neck. Yet he had had no need to make the arrangement for her, she chided herself, and she should be feeling grateful, instead of worrying about the possible consequences of his behaviour. After all, she had no real reason to believe he had treated her any differently than he would have treated any newcomer to the village. It was only Clare's attitude that had soured the situation. That, and her own disturbing reactions to him ...

She moved her shoulders in an impatient gesture, as if brushing away the unpleasant awareness that Rafe Lindsay disturbed her more than was proper for a woman in her position, and went to fill the kettle. It wasn't even a year yet since Edward died. She was lonely, that was all, and this place was still strange to her. She was allowing doubts, and her changed circumstances, to interfere with her emotions.

And, after speaking to the Websters that morning, she should have had no doubts about the impartiality of Rafe Lindsay's actions. It was possible that Clare had primed her parents, of course, but Dr Webster had been at pains to explain that since his wife's death the Earl had acquired a reputation for unpredictability.

'I'm not saying he's ill,' he added hurriedly, when his words aroused a warning look from Mrs Webster. 'But there's no denying that he took Sarah's death very badly. The Dowager Countess—his mother—has spent considerable time and money trying to find a cure.'

'A cure!'

Isobel stared at them blankly, not at all convinced they were even talking about the same man who had treated Cory so tolerantly, and helped her with the Aga earlier in the day. He hadn't seemed ill to her. Just amused, and disturbingly familiar.

'He drinks,' said Mrs Webster shortly, evidently deciding honesty was the lesser of the two evils. 'And poor Colin has been forced to take over more and more of his brother's duties. Since Sarah Lindsay died, Rafe has been something of a—a liability.'

'Oh——' Now it was Dr Webster's turn to look a little askance. 'I don't think we can say that, Laura. As far as I'm aware, Rafe has never neglected the estate. All I'm saying is that Isobel shouldn't take his kindness too personally.'

Which was as pointed a warning as Clare's reaction had been, Isobel thought now, even if the Websters had welcomed her with far more enthusiasm than their daughter. She had left Cory at home, but they had both expressed a wish to meet her, and Mrs Webster had even offered to run Isobel into Strathmoor the following morning to stock up on her larder.

'You'll need to visit the school there, to arrange for Cory's admission,' Mrs Webster had added, as they chatted in the parlour over a friendly cup of coffee. 'The schools started back a few weeks ago, so you'll want to get her settled as soon as possible.' She had smiled. 'And there's a school bus that collects all the children from the surrounding villages every morning, so she won't have any excuse for being late.'

Isobel had smiled, too, though she doubted Cory would find the arrangement so convenient. Starting a new school was just one of the complications her daughter was going to have to deal with, and Isobel had

thought she might let her get used to her new surroundings before forcing any more changes upon her.

But, aside from that, Isobel was quite pleased with
the prospect of working for Dr Webster. The little
surgery, which was situated in an annexe attached to the
Websters' house, was bright and clean, and surprisingly
well equipped. As well as herself and Dr Webster, there
was a practice nurse called Stella Fuller, and they each
had their own rooms opening off the waiting area. Most
minor complaints could be dealt with at the surgery, and
only when serious hospital treatment was needed were
the patients transferred to the infirmary in Strathmoor.
All in all, it was a fairly self-sufficient operation, and
Isobel was relieved to find that everyone seemed to
welcome her.

'I hope you can use a computer!' Nurse Fuller
exclaimed, as she showed Isobel round the office she
was going to use. 'Ever since Miss McLeay left, Dr
Webster and I have been struggling to make sense of her
filing system. Without a lot of success, I have to say,'
she admitted ruefully. 'I hope you won't mind putting
in some overtime. It may be necessary until you get the
records straight.'

'I'll do whatever I can, of course,' replied Isobel,
noting the piles of letters and medical supplies and
samples littering the desk. It was obvious that only the
essential items had been dealt with. It would take her a
couple of days just to open all the packages.

But she was relieved when Dr Webster said that he
didn't expect her to start until the following Monday.
That at least gave her a few days before the weekend to
organise a routine. She had still to unpack her trunks—
when they were delivered—and do something about
clearing out the cottage. Miss McLeay might have liked
to feel herself surrounded by her belongings, but Isobel
preferred a little more space. There was a garage at the
back of the cottage, and she was hoping she might be
able to store some of the smaller items there. She knew
she wouldn't be able to accomplish much in the way of
decoration before the winter, but she intended to do her
best to make the cottage comfortable, and a little
more familiar.

She had seen a little of the village during her walk to the surgery and back again, and it was difficult not to feel optimistic in such surroundings. With the sun shining on the loch, and the mountains that encircled them on three sides pine-clad and majestic, she felt almost privileged to be living in Invercaldy. It might be small, and remote, and very different from what they were used to, but it was full of character, too, and beautiful in its way. It was what she needed, she thought, smiling at the sight of smoke curling from a crooked chimney; it was what they both needed. Far from Mrs Jacobson's jealous influence, she and Cory might stand a chance.

And thinking about Cory forced the realisation that her daughter hadn't come to meet her when she came in. She might not have heard her, of course. She could still be arranging her room. But somehow Isobel didn't trust that explanation. Cory had never been keen on household chores.

The door to the inner hall, off which Cory's room and the bathroom were situated, was open, and, stepping through, Isobel called her daughter's name. But there was no response, and when she entered Cory's room she found out why. She wasn't there. She hadn't even made her bed, Isobel noticed. Though that particular omission meant less than it should in the present circumstances.

Determined not to panic, Isobel went back into the kitchen, and peered out of the window. The cat sprang up on to the window-ledge beside her, as if trying to reassure her by his presence, but she paid him no mind. The garden was deserted, she saw, and beyond the hedge of beech and briar the water meadow was empty, too. There weren't even any of the rather frightening-looking cattle grazing at the water's edge, and only a small boat, far out on the lock, reassured her that she had not stepped into some solitary never-never land.

'Oh, Cory,' she said, half under her breath, and the cat arched its back against her arm, as if in sympathy. But Isobel knew better than to trust its facile charm, and she shooed it out of her way as she walked uncertainly into the living-room.

The clock on the mantel said it was nearly half-past twelve. Which meant she had been out the better part of two hours. With that kind of leeway, Cory could be anywhere. Oh, God, she hadn't run away, had she? Isobel didn't know what she'd do if her daughter had gone missing.

She determinedly calmed herself again. She was over-reacting, as usual. Just because Cory had decided to take a walk by herself was no reason to think the worst. For heaven's sake, she was bound to be curious about Invercaldy. And this wasn't London. It was unlikely she could come to any harm here.

All the same, Cory shouldn't have gone out without permission, a small voice persisted. Isobel had told her they'd go for a walk that afternoon and familiarise themselves with the village. There were things she needed from the village shop, like bread and potatoes. And she'd also promised they'd phone Cory's grandmother today, to let the old lady know they were safely settled in.

She drew another steadying breath, but once again it emerged on a shaky sigh. No matter how she tried to rationalise things, her brain kept turning in the same direction. What would she do if Cory didn't come back? Who was there to help her, if her daughter had disappeared? The Websters? Clare—if she chose to listen? Or Rafe, she appended tensely, despising herself even as she thought of him. But of all of them, he was the only one she thought might care.

Which was ridiculous, she acknowledged impatiently. Hadn't the Websters themselves told her that she shouldn't trust a thing the man said? He drank and he was 'unpredictable'. Hardly someone to rely on in an emergency, even if he was the Earl. And somehow Isobel couldn't see herself phoning Invercaldy Castle to ask for his assistance.

She chewed unhappily at her lower lip. Ought she to go out and look for Cory? The door had been unlocked when she got back, so evidently her daughter had had no qualms about going out and leaving the house un-secured. Probably people didn't worry too much about thieves around here. And, in any case, they had nothing worth stealing.

Going back into the kitchen, she collected the duffel coat she had worn over her skirt and sweater to go to the Websters', and opened the back door again. Bothwell gave her a look of enquiry from the living-room doorway, but apart from waving his tail in a gesture that could have been either distaste or approval he made no move to accompany her.

'Traitor,' muttered Isobel, slamming the door behind her, and then nearly jumped out of her skin at the sight of a boy climbing agilely through the fence at the bottom of the garden. He was a fair, good-looking boy of about Cory's age, but Isobel didn't care for him making free with what she was rapidly coming to regard as *her* property. This was her home now, and she was just about to issue a word of warning when she saw her daughter following the boy through the spiked bushes. Cory didn't make half so good a job of it as her companion. Lack of experience, Isobel hazarded, and she winced as a twig caught the girl's dark cap of hair, dragging a handful out of her scalp.

'Bloody hell!' Cory yelped, but Isobel's instinctive remonstrance was balked by the rueful laughter that followed this outrageous imprecation. It was so long since she had heard her daughter laugh like that, and in any case the boy, who had turned back to help her, was making his own complaint.

'It's not clever to swear,' he said, picking leaves out of her hair, and brushing at her anorak, which Isobel now saw was Cory's best one. 'Any moron can do it. You should have been more careful. It's no one's fault but your own.'

'All right, all right.' To Isobel's amazement, Cory took the criticism without retaliation. 'It nearly scalped me, that's all.'

'And that's an exaggeration,' said the boy, pushing his luck, but his smile was a glowing compensation. And familiar, too, thought Isobel uneasily. He was fair instead of dark, and short instead of tall, but the resemblance to Rafe Lindsay was unmistakable.

His son? she wondered, moistening dry lips, as Cory suddenly realised her mother was standing on the doorstep. For a moment, the shadow of the porch had prevented her from being noticed, but now Cory had seen her. Isobel prepared herself to face her resentment.

But her daughter's first words were not what she had expected. 'Oh—hello, Mum,' she murmured, glancing nervously at the boy beside her. 'I didn't think you'd be back yet.'

'No.' Isobel knew she ought to be taking advantage of the girl's disconcertment to make her own feelings felt, but for the moment she couldn't think of a thing to say. On the one hand, she was relieved that Cory had apparently found a friend, but on the other, she wasn't at all convinced that she welcomed *this* liaison.

'By the way, this is Jaime,' Cory added, and the boy gave Isobel the benefit of his disarming grin.

'How do you do, Mrs Jacobson?' he said, crossing the leaf-strewn lawn to offer her his hand. 'I hope you haven't been worried. We've just been out on the loch.'

Isobel gulped, remembering the tiny boat she had glimpsed earlier. 'On the loch,' she echoed faintly, and Jaime nodded.

'It was quite safe,' he said. 'The water's really calm at the moment. It's cold, I know, but there was no danger of us having to swim.'

'To swim!' Isobel looked beyond them now, and saw the narrow skiff moored in the reeds, and horror surfaced. 'Oh, Cory, you should have waited to ask me before going out in a rowing boat. You obviously weren't wearing a life-jacket. What would you have done if the boat had capsized?'

Cory hunched her shoulders. 'Don't fuss, Mum. I'd have been all right.'

'No, you wouldn't.' Isobel's earlier fears had returned in full measure now, and she wasn't really thinking what she was saying. 'It was totally irresponsible to go out without permission. You know I'd have forbade it. You can't even swim!'

'*Mum!*'

'You can't *swim!*'

The two children spoke in unison, Jaime turning disbelievingly towards his companion, and Cory's face burning with humiliation. And, as she saw her daughter's face, Isobel knew exactly what she'd done. It was obvious Cory had pretended she could swim, in the self-confident way she had, and Isobel should have considered that before opening her big mouth.

And, before she could say anything to retrieve the situation, Cory gave her an unforgiving look, and barged past her into the cottage. The door slammed again, this time almost trapping Bothwell's tail as he emerged, and he came to rub himself against Isobel's legs, as if needing the reassurance.

'You and me both,' muttered Isobel ruefully, bending down to pet the animal, and Jaime gave her an uncertain look.

'I beg your pardon?'

'Oh—nothing.' Isobel straightened, and endeavoured to collect herself. 'I was talking to myself.' She managed an embarrassed smile. 'Does—er—does your father know where you are?'

Jaime shrugged. 'My mother does,' he replied, and Isobel blinked in some bewilderment. 'Well—I told her I was going to see Gramma actually,' he continued. 'I hoped Uncle Rafe would let me ride Moonlight, but I waited at the stables for ages, and he just didn't turn up.'

Isobel's lips parted. 'Ra—that is—the Earl's your uncle?'

'That's right.' Jaime nodded. 'My mother used to go to school with you, didn't she? That's what I told Cory, but I don't think she was impressed.'

'No?' But Isobel could imagine her daughter's reaction to learning he was Clare's son. Not that Jaime was anything like his mother, she reflected. Which was probably why Cory had liked him anyway.

'I'd better be going,' he said now, pushing his hands into the pockets of his parka. 'Tell Cory I don't care if she can swim or not. In fact, I could teach her. Uncle Rafe has a pool. I'm sure he'd let us use it, if I asked him.'

'I—think you ought to ask your mother first,' said Isobel, not wanting to spoil their potential friendship, but doubtful that Clare would feel the same. Besides, she wasn't at all sure that it would be good for Cory getting involved with the Lindsays. It would be far better

if she found friends in the village. Children who were
not likely to make her discontented.

'All right.'

Jaime paused to give Bothwell's ear a friendly scratch,
and then, with a wave, he disappeared round the side of
the cottage. Following him to the corner, Isobel noticed
that he was heading towards the Websters' house, and
with a sense of resignation she went back to the door.

She had expected Cory would be in her bedroom, with
the door closed against all callers, but as it turned out
her daughter was in the living-room. She turned away
from the window as her mother came into the room, and
Isobel guessed she had been watching Jaime, too.

There was a moment when Isobel thought Cory might
still decide she was not speaking to her, and, although
she knew she could hardly be blamed for the lies her
daughter had told, she was tempted to be generous. But
evidently Cory had had second thoughts, too, and,
though she still looked mutinous, she offered an off-
handed overture.

'Has he gone?'

'Jaime?' Two could play at that game.

'Mmm.' Cory hooked her thumbs into the belt of her
jeans and hunched her shoulders. 'What a wimp!'

Isobel's mouth compressed. 'You don't mean that.'

'Maybe I do.' Cory was defensive. 'What did he say
to you after—after I——?'

'Flounced into the cottage?' suggested Isobel mildly,
and Cory pulled a face. 'He just said to tell you he didn't
care if you could swim or not. And—he told me he was
Clare's son. I gather he told you that, too.'

'Big deal!' Cory sniffed. 'That won't win him any
friends.' She paused. 'But Rafe Lindsay is his uncle. Did
you know that? He says the Earl lives in a castle!'

'Really?'

Isobel endeavoured to sound uninterested, but she had
her own reasons for not wanting to get into a discussion
about their benefactor. She still hadn't told Cory that
he had called at the cottage that morning. For some
reason, she had kept that information to herself.

'Yes, really!' Cory exclaimed now, launching into the
description Jaime had given her of the ancestral seat of

the Earls of Invercaldy. 'He says it's very old, and until his uncle became the Earl it was in a pretty grotty state of repair. But he married an heiress, you see,' she grinned, 'just like in all those sloppy love stories Grandma reads, and he's spent a fortune making it really smart.' She grimaced. 'Of course, his wife's dead now. Jaime said she died two years ago, and since then his uncle's not been very sociable. But with relatives like Mrs Lindsay, who can blame him? Although I didn't tell Jaime that. I'm not completely stupid.'

Isobel pressed her palms together. 'I—you didn't tell me how you came to speak to him,' she said, hoping to change the subject. 'I thought I asked you to stay here until I got back.'

'Well, you did.' Cory sighed. 'But I was bored. And— I thought I'd come and meet you. He—that is, Jaime— was hanging about outside the surgery.'

'I see.' That explained a lot. 'Well, the Websters are his grandparents.'

'I know.' Cory nodded. 'But I don't think he was very keen to see them. When I told him who I was, he offered to show me round the village.'

'And you didn't think to let me know what you were doing?' Isobel protested. 'Honestly, Cory!'

'Well—I knew you wouldn't approve if I told you that Jaime had said he knew where there was a boat we could use,' replied Cory ruefully. 'But it was perfectly safe. You heard what Jaime said.'

'Jaime's a child.'

'He's nearly thirteen!'

'As I said, he's a child.' Isobel took a deep breath. 'But we won't say any more about it. So long as you promise not to do it again.'

'All right.' Cory was resigned. Then, just when Isobel was hoping she'd heard the last of the Lindsays for today, Cory added, 'You can see the castle from the loch, you know. That's one of the reasons why he took me out. It's at the other end of the loch, and it looks ever so romantic! Do you think Jaime would take me to see it, if I asked him?'

'I think you should find yourself some other friends, and forget all about Jaime Lindsay,' declared Isobel flatly. 'I know I went to school with his mother, but that was a lot of years ago. We have nothing in common these days, and it's certain that we have nothing in common with the Earl and his family.' She paused, allowing this to sink in, and then added brightly, 'I suggest we have some lunch. Then maybe you can show me around the village. Did you see the stores, by the way? A diet of cheese and eggs is all very well, but I'm dying for a baked potato!'

CHAPTER SIX

THE doves woke her, as they had woken her every morning since they arrived in Invercaldy. Isobel supposed she should have got used to them by now, but she hadn't. Their calls were gentle, but intrusive, and she was still sufficiently restless about the move to find any unusual sound disturbing.

Thankfully, they didn't appear to disturb Cory. But perhaps that was because her bedroom was downstairs and therefore far away from the doves' usual roosting place. Whatever, her daughter had been sleeping really well since they moved, and Isobel guessed she was finding the fresh air, and the unaccustomed amount of exercise they were taking, exhausting.

They had certainly walked more in the last three days than they'd have walked in three weeks in London. There were buses to places like Strathmoor and Fort William, but there was no transport in the village. And, although Invercaldy was fairly small, it was amazing how much time it took to walk to the village stores and back again. Particularly if she was carrying a heavy bag of shopping, reflected Isobel now, feeling the ache of the weight she had carried the previous day probing at her shoulders.

But Mrs Webster seemed to have forgotten all about her promise to take Isobel and Cory to Strathmoor. Isobel had wondered if she'd heard about Jaime's outing with Cory, and this was her way of showing her disapproval. Or perhaps Clare hadn't approved. Whatever it was, they hadn't seen hide nor hair of any of the Lindsays since the day after their arrival.

So Isobel had been forced to improvise. Without a car, she could hardly visit the supermarket in Strathmoor, even if she knew the times of the buses. It was easier to shop at the village stores, even if their prices were considerably steeper.

She wished she hadn't been so precipitate in selling Edward's car now. But there had seemed little use for it in London, and besides, she'd expected to find good use for the money. Here, though, their expenses were considerably smaller, and having a car seemed a real necessity. She wondered if it was possible to buy a good second-hand one with the money she had got from the sale of Edward's saloon. Perhaps it would be a good idea to go into Strathmoor after all. It was obvious there'd be no used-car dealerships around here.

The kitchen was warm when she went downstairs, which was a distinct improvement on the first morning they were here. And, although the radiators didn't crank into action until she turned them on, the heat they engendered made the cottage cosy and comfortable. She had soon learned the knack of keeping the Aga smouldering through the night, and as soon as she opened the damper the flames swept merrily up the chimney.

With heat, and light, and a constant supply of hot water, Isobel had convinced herself she could do anything. She still had moments of indecision, of course, particularly when she realised she hadn't made any arrangements yet for Cory to start school and she was starting work on Monday. After the incident with Jaime Lindsay, she had had a real fear that her daughter might do something foolish. Her mother-in-law already thought she was mad for moving away from London. If anything happened to Cory, however slight, she'd hold Isobel responsible.

Cory was sitting at the kitchen table in her dressing-gown, ploughing her way through her second bowl of rice crispies, when they heard a car pull on to the gravel at the front of the cottage. The farmer who delivered the milk generally used the back door, and Isobel shrugged her ignorance as Cory lifted an enquiring head.

But she was glad she was dressed when the knock sounded at the door. Even if her pink sweatshirt and faded jeans had seen better days. But her hair was still loose, a brown-gold curtain about her shoulders, and with an impatient exclamation she swept it up into a loose knot as she went to answer the door.

It was Rafe Lindsay.

Isobel was still pushing hairpins into the knot as she opened the door, and her heart did a quick somersault before righting itself again. Her hands, too, fell awkwardly to her sides, and the knot wobbled threateningly before remaining where it was.

The annoying thing was, she had spent the last few days trying to put this man out of her mind. And, although she hadn't succeeded entirely, she had managed to convince herself that she was unlikely to see him again. Which suited her just fine, she had decided, after mulling over everything she had heard about him. The last thing she needed was for Clare, or her parents, to think she might have been flattered by his attention. It was obvious it amused him to scandalise his relations, and she wanted no part in his petty little schemes.

'Hi,' he said now, and she thought how infuriating it was to discover he was just as attractive as she had remembered. In dark trousers and a crew-necked black sweater, a dark red suede jacket hanging open to his waist, he looked relaxed and expensive, and she wondered how she'd ever mistaken him for anything but what he was. Yet his hair was still too long, and the knowledge she now possessed gave a reason for the dark lines around his eyes. There was a certain amount of dissipation in his face, she decided, but the net result was no less appealing because of it.

'Oh—hello,' she said now, conscious of Cory's inquisitive ears behind her. 'Um—can I help you?'

Rafe's eyes made a breathtaking appraisal of her appearance, and it took every ounce of will-power she had not to check the unsteady pinning of her hair. Her hand itched to anchor her hair, to hold it manually in place. And then she thought how silly she was to care what he might think of her.

'I thought I might be able to help you,' he remarked, looking at her with a whimsical expression on his face. 'I'm on my way to Strathmoor. I wondered if you might welcome a ride.'

Isobel's breath escaped with an audible rush. 'To Strathmoor?' she fumbled, and Rafe's eyes glinted with a mocking light.

'Unless there's somewhere else you'd like to go,' he conceded, and she felt the betraying heat of embarrassment invade her neck once again. She really was out of touch with talking to men, she thought crossly, but she was perfectly aware of the innuendo that was present in his voice.

And, because she was annoyed with herself and him, her response was less than friendly. 'I don't think so, thank you,' she said, preparing to close the door. 'It's very kind of you to offer, but I don't think it would be quite—proper.'

'Proper?'

His tone was half scathing now, and she hurriedly amended her argument. 'Suitable, then,' she said quickly, inching the door closed. She ignored Cory's gasp of dismay behind her, and offered him a polite smile. 'Thank you for asking, but——'

His booted foot on the threshold brought her tense denial to a halt. 'I don't care what you think about my motives,' he said, as her eyes widened in obvious disbelief. 'Or what moron has given you the idea that we have to conform to some half-assed code of etiquette.' His eyes narrowed, and a decidedly predatory gleam entered their depths. 'I could say that in those circumstances you shouldn't try to annoy me. After all,' he concluded darkly, 'I do own this cottage.'

Isobel stiffened. 'If you think——'

'I don't,' he interrupted her wearily, propping one broad shoulder against the frame of the door. 'Look, shall I go away and come back and we'll start this conversation again? Or do you really dislike me that much that you'd rather take the bus?'

Isobel gave in to the urge to press her hand to the top of her head. The knot appeared to be holding, but she could feel several honey-gold tendrils tickling the nape of her neck. The action separated the hem of her sweatshirt from the waistband of her jeans, and the cool air fanned the narrow width of midriff it exposed. Which caused her to abandon her hair in favour of pulling it down again, but not before his eyes had registered the creamy belt of skin.

'I—you'd better come in,' she conceded, consoling herself with the thought that their prolonged conversation was allowing all the heat to disperse from the living-room. Besides, she had the feeling she was doing herself no favours by keeping him on the doorstep, where anybody passing could observe what was going on.

Of course, she appended, as Rafe stepped inside and she busied herself closing the latch, the vehicle he had come in was just outside, which was an admission in itself. But if he couldn't be seen, no one could be sure of where he was. After all, there were several cottages at this end of the High Street, and he could be in any one of them.

'Hello.'

Cory had finished her breakfast and, with none of her mother's misgivings, was greeting their visitor enthusiastically. It didn't bother her that her winceyette dressing-gown had seen better days, nor that her dark hair was uncombed, and sticking up in short spikes. She was evidently delighted to see Rafe again, and Isobel wished she could be so uninhibited.

'Cory,' he acknowledged, threading his way across the cluttered floor of the living-room with unconscious grace. With his thumbs hooked into the tooled belt at his waist, he appeared relaxed and unconcerned, and Isobel, watching him, had to remind herself forcibly of who he was. 'I hear you've been spending time with my nephew,' he added, as her daughter draped herself theatrically over the arm of a chair. 'Jaime said he'd taken you out on the loch.' His lips twitched. 'You seem to have made quite an impression on that young man.'

'Have I?'

Cory was all coy innocence, and Isobel marvelled at her daughter's duplicity. Yet no one looking at Cory at this moment could doubt that she was flattered by the compliment. The offhand way she had dismissed Jaime's friendship had obviously just been a form of self-protection. Join the club, she thought wryly. She wasn't unaware of her own methods of protection where the Lindsays were concerned.

'Well, let's say your meeting didn't go unnoticed,' remarked Rafe, rather ambiguously, casting a glance over his shoulder at Isobel. 'Tell me, have you seen Clare?'

His meaning was obvious, and Isobel's shoulders sagged. No wonder they hadn't seen Jaime again, if his mother had anything to do with it.

'I—no——' she was beginning ruefully, when Cory gave an indignant snort.

'Yes, we have, Mum!' she exclaimed impatiently, and Isobel knew at once that she had made a mistake. And, while she stood there, incapable of offering any excuses, her daughter went on to describe Clare's visit the night they arrived in Invercaldy in gory detail. 'She was really rude to Mum,' Cory concluded, as Isobel chided herself for not telling her about Rafe's second visit to the cottage. If she had, she might have avoided being made to feel guilty on two counts. As it was, he had only to say the wrong word for Cory to become suspicious too.

'I see,' Rafe said at last, and, feeling those disturbing eyes moving over her, Isobel felt compelled to move away. It was too late now to explain her reason for keeping his visit a secret. Too late now to convince him she'd only been thinking of him.

'She's your sister-in-law, right?' Cory was saying chattily, and, realising her daughter was in danger of becoming too personal, Isobel abandoned any hope of keeping out of the conversation.

'I don't think it's anything to do with us what the— the relationship is between Mrs Lindsay and— and——' she licked her lips '—our visitor.' She flashed Rafe a revealing glance, not quite meeting his eyes before looking away again. 'It's time you went and got some clothes on, Cory. You don't want—people—thinking we spend all morning in our nightclothes, do you?'

Cory grimaced. 'Now!'

'Yes, now,' said Isobel firmly, hoping her daughter was not going to choose this moment to have another battle of wills with her mother. She didn't think she had the strength. Not with Rafe Lindsay watching them, anyway, she amended. She might feel somewhat differently when he was gone.

'Oh, all right.' For some reason Cory decided to be co-operative, and Isobel was just beginning to breathe more easily when she turned to Rafe. 'But you will still be here when I come back, won't you? Are you really going to take us to Strathmoor?'

'No——'

'If your mother wants to go.'

They both spoke simultaneously, and although Isobel's expression warned her daughter of the consequences if she contradicted her Cory was not prepared to give up a chance like that.

'She does really,' she said, refusing to acknowledge Isobel's silent warning. 'Mrs Webster was going to take us—so that Mum could do some shopping at the supermarket—but she hasn't. Do you think it's because Jaime and me got to know one another? I bet she wasn't pleased when she found out about that.'

'Cory!'

There was no mistaking Isobel's anger now, but her daughter was unrepentant. 'Well, I bet she wasn't,' she said, pulling a defiant face. Then, addressing herself to their visitor, 'I'll see you later, right?' She sauntered towards the door. 'I won't be long.'

A pregnant silence followed the closing of the door, and Isobel thought how typical it was that she should be the one to feel embarrassed. Cory's remarks had been tactless and presumptuous, and she was almost glad when Bothwell chose that moment to come and rub himself against her legs. It gave her something to do with her hands, as she bent to tickle his ears, so that when she straightened she felt more capable of handling the situation.

'I'm sorry,' she said, walking through the archway that led into the kitchen, as much to put some distance between herself and Rafe Lindsay as anything. 'Cory had no right to put you on the spot like that.' She glanced behind her. 'Um—can I offer you a cup of coffee?'

'No, thank you.' Rafe confounded her intentions by following her and looking out of the kitchen window. 'Are you settling in?'

'Oh——' Isobel backed away towards the Aga. 'I think so. It's different, of course, but we expected that. And—

Cory seems to like it. She's sleeping well, and eating like a horse! Ah—and thank you for arranging to have the milk delivered. I do appreciate it. It's been so convenient not having to carry it from the shop. I'm very grateful, and the eggs, too. They're so fresh! And delicious. We'll have to be careful, or we'll be in danger of eating too much cholesterol——'

'Why are you so nervous?'

Rafe's quiet voice arrested the accelerating babble of words she was using to keep her thoughts at bay, and she realised how ridiculous she must sound. He wasn't interested in her prattle, particularly when she was thanking him repeatedly for something that had, after all, been a fairly minor favour. All she had succeeded in doing was drawing his attention to herself, the very thing she had been hoping to avoid.

'I'm—not nervous,' she denied, though she could tell he didn't believe her. 'I—just don't think it's a good idea—your being here, I mean.'

'Why?'

He turned to rest his hips against the drainer, folding his arms across his chest, and regarding her with cool, appraising eyes. He looked relaxed, but he wasn't, she thought tensely, and her own nerves tightened at the prospect of dealing with him in this mood.

If only she weren't so aware of him as a man, she thought impatiently. If only when she looked at him she saw the Earl of Invercaldy, instead of someone who feathered her skin and stirred her senses. His voice alone had the power to quicken her pulse, and his muscled frame was wholly masculine. When she looked at him, she found her head filled with all kinds of disturbing images, most of them unprintable, she acknowledged with a sigh.

'I—because you are who you are,' she answered him now, not very convincingly, and his mouth took on a mocking slant. His mouth was disturbing too, she thought, thin yet amazingly sensual. And the lower lip was fuller, with a tiny scar at the corner.

'You don't like me?' he ventured, and her breath escaped on a shivery sigh.

'Don't be silly.'

'Is that silly?' he persisted, and she wished he had accepted her offer of coffee. It would have given her something to do. As it was, she was making a fair attempt at imprinting the shape of the floor unit at her back on her spine and buttocks.

'I don't know anything about you,' she said at last, wondering how she had ever got herself into this situation. It was unreal. Their conversation was unreal. What did he expect her to say?

'There's not a lot to know,' he replied now, lifting his shoulders in a careless gesture. 'I'm not married, and I live in the village. My mother lives with me.'

'At Invercaldy Castle,' said Isobel swiftly. 'You omitted to mention that.'

His eyes narrowed. 'Does that matter?'

'Of course it matters.' Isobel sighed. 'And you're a widower.'

'My, my.' His expression tightened. 'You seem to know more than you think.'

'Well...' Isobel wrapped her arms about her waist '...it's true, isn't it?'

'So?'

'So—why say you're not married?'

'I'm not.'

'But you were.'

'Pedantic, aren't you?' He shrugged again. 'All right, I *was* married. What difference does that make?'

Isobel didn't know. Or, at least, she did, but she couldn't put what she had been told into words.

'I—nothing, I suppose,' she mumbled at last, wondering if she should pretend to make herself a cup of coffee. Whether she'd be able to swallow it was something else. But it would give her an excuse for turning her back on him.

'Which brings us back to your reason for refusing my invitation,' he said softly. 'Your daughter seems to think you'd like to do some shopping in Strathmoor. And it occurred to me you might like to visit the local school. Cory is going to go to the local school, isn't she?'

Isobel took a breath and with some trepidation turned away from him. Resting her hands on the rim of the worktop, she struggled to put her feelings into words, finding it easier to say what she had to say when she wasn't looking at him.

'I—have to work for Clare's father,' she said unevenly, catching her lower lip between her teeth. 'I start on Monday, by the way. And—I don't think it's a good idea for me to—to upset the Websters. Your—your being here, well—they wouldn't exactly approve.'

There was silence for a moment, and she thought at first that he wasn't going to answer her. But then, in a curiously tight voice, he said, 'What else have they told you about me?'

Isobel stiffened. 'I—why—nothing.'

'You're not a very good liar, are you, Mrs Jacobson?' he mocked, and she was dismayed to find he had come to stand behind her. His warm breath moved the fine tendrils of hair at her nape, and caused a faint film of moisture to bead her skin. Though whether that was his fault or the fault of her own agitated hormones she couldn't be sure. 'I can guess what John and Laura have been saying about me.' He paused, and the fear that he was going to touch her caused the blood to run hotly into her temples. 'Let me see—what would be the kindest description they would use? Oh, yes: I'm an eccentric—and I drink too much. Right?'

Isobel moved her head a little too fast, and the knot she had pinned so loosely dipped lop-sidedly above her ear. 'What you do or don't do is nothing to do with me,' she protested, grasping her slipping hair with a frustrated hand. 'But I don't think it's wise to antagonise my future employers, or—or encourage Cory to think you could ever be a friend.'

'Why not?' he asked, his cool fingers brushing her neck as he attempted to help her to push her hair back into place, and Isobel jerked angrily away from him.

'Don't do that!' she exclaimed, and then let out an involuntary cry as her feet tangled with Bothwell, who had been curled around her legs. In her efforts to save herself, she grabbed the Aga, and her cry turned to a groan as a shaft of pain shot across her palm. 'Damn— oh, damn!' she mumbled half tearfully, pressing her injured hand to her mouth, and Rafe uttered a grim oath.

'Let me see,' he said, ignoring her efforts to hide the injury from him, and, half dragging her across to the sink, he turned on the cold tap. The icy water was a shock, but the relief was almost instantaneous. Her palm cooled beneath the chilling spray, and although Rafe continued to grip her wrist she wouldn't have moved, even if he'd let her go.

But he did continue to hold her and, as the pain eased, she became overwhelmingly aware of the intimacy of their position. He was standing half behind her, bent over her in such a way that she couldn't breathe without inhaling his breath. His shoulder imprisoned her arm, and his jacket had parted so that the muscled width of his chest pressed against her back. She could feel the effects the exertion had had on his breathing, feel the solid rhythm of his heart, matching hers beat for beat.

No, not beat for beat, she thought unsteadily. Her heart was palpitating at such a rate that she was sure it was working at twice the speed of his. And because her sweatshirt had ridden up again, the buckle of his belt was digging into her back.

But it was the powerful pressure of his thighs that disturbed her most. That, and the heated scent of his body, which was having such an unprecedented effect upon her senses. Dear God, Edward had never made her feel like this, never drained every ounce of resistance from her, so that all she really wanted to do was lean into him, let his body enfold hers, and give herself over to the sensuous feelings he was evoking...

But she couldn't do that; she shouldn't even *want* to do that, she chided herself fiercely. What kind of a woman was she that she should be having such thoughts so soon after Edward's death? Their marriage might not have been perfect, but he had been good to her. He had cared for her when she was alone and comparatively penniless, and if that had sometimes seemed an unlikely excuse for their union she had been grateful to him at the time.

A coil of hair brushing her neck brought another awareness, and, endeavouring to steady her voice, she said, 'My hair's come down.'

'I know.'

His response was equally controlled, and she did what she had known she mustn't do: she turned her head and looked at him.

It was a mistake. His face was close; too close, she acknowledged, as smoky eyes met startled hazel ones. His eyes really were incredible, she thought, trying to distract herself, but it was the expression in them that made her catch her breath. They were soft, yet sensual, searching hers with a kind of bemused sexuality, warming into an awareness that lit an answering flame inside her.

Her head swam beneath that intensely heated gaze, and she felt her own control slipping. She tried to concentrate on less unnerving details, like the well-marked straightness of his brows or the laughter-lines that fanned his eyes, but all the time she was aware of him watching her, and the dangerous attraction of his nearness. So what if his nose was just faintly crooked, as if it had been broken in his youth, or that there were deeper lines beside his mouth? Even her attempt to guess what had caused the tiny scar she had noticed earlier was all for nothing. She wanted to look at him; she wanted to see what he was thinking.

And, as if sensing the frantic ferment of her emotions, he moved closer, imprisoning her against the sink by the simple method of gripping the unit at either side of her. And, as her breath rushed out in a noisy gush, he turned off the tap and bent his head to the side of her neck.

'Does it still hurt?' he asked softly, and for a moment she didn't know what he was talking about.

Her initial reaction was to say yes, but the pain that was flowering in her stomach and spreading down into her thighs had nothing to do with her scorched fingers. Yet it was pain just the same, and just as discomforting to her peace of mind. It swelled and expanded like a fire out of control, consuming everything in its path.

And when his lips brushed the silky curtain of her hair aside, and his tongue touched the sensitive skin at her nape, her response was purely involuntary. For a moment, time stood still, and she had tilted her head to one side to allow him freer access before she realised what she was doing.

But the heated seduction of his mouth was so different from what she had been used to that her earlier lethargy fled. The pure sexuality of his kiss acted like a brake on her senses, and where once she had been yielding now she struggled to rescue her slipping sanity. The impulse to respond to him, to lean back against him, and let the hand that had now moved to her waist explore the underside of her swollen breast, suddenly repelled her. What was she doing, she asked herself incredulously, letting this man, this virtual stranger, touch her in ways that, at the very least, could be construed as familiar? And with Cory only a dozen yards away, likely to come upon them at any moment.

She froze then, her body stiffening, all her previous doubts congealing into a solid wall of resistance. What did he think she was? she wondered unsteadily. Some kind of easy target? A cheap thrill? Or a woman, on her own, who was desperate for any kind of attention?

Desperate to get laid, she amended bitterly, using the jargon Cory was so fond of to describe what her daughter would think if she ever found out what had been going on. And with a man who, by his own admission, had been called eccentric, and a drunk. Perhaps he was drunk now. She couldn't think of any other reason why the Earl of Invercaldy would find her attractive. Just because she couldn't smell it on his breath didn't mean he hadn't been drinking.

But, if she'd thought he might resist her efforts to get away from him, she was wrong. As soon as he sensed her opposition, his hands fell away, and she was free to put as much space between them as the kitchen would allow.

'I—I think you'd better go,' she said tensely, wrapping her arms across her midriff again, and although she kept her head averted she was conscious of his dismissive gesture.

'If that's what you want.'

His voice was expressionless, and, although Isobel knew she should let it go at that, it infuriated her that he should think he had no need to apologise.

'Did you think it wouldn't be?' she demanded, permitting herself a stabbing glance at his dark face. 'My God! What do you think I am?'

His mouth compressed. 'You're over-reacting!'

'Am I? You come here, unannounced and uninvited, and behave as if the fact that I'm living in your cottage gives you the right to be all over me, and I'm over-reacting! I'm sorry, but if that's what you thought——'

'Don't be so bloody stupid!' His harsh words cut her off, and Isobel caught her breath at the unaccustomed anger in his voice. 'For God's sake, what happened— happened. It was an urge, an impulse, that's all. It wasn't premeditated, and it certainly wasn't intended to promote this kind of a reaction. I thought you wanted me to touch you. Obviously, I was wrong. What do you want? An apology?'

Isobel trembled. 'That would be a start, at least.'

His lips curled, and Isobel's stomach twisted at the realisation of the damage she was doing. And, for all her indignation, she couldn't honestly say that she hadn't wanted him to touch her. She had been as aware of him then as she was now, and the thought that she had probably destroyed any chance of prolonging their association filled her with an aching sense of despair.

'All right,' he said bleakly, straightening his shoulders, and pushing back his hair with aggressive fingers. 'I apologise. I shouldn't have presumed on short acquaintance. Forgive me.'

Isobel swallowed. 'Thank you.'

'My pleasure.'

But his eyes were steely now, and she waited anxiously for him to leave. Something told her she had made an unforgivable error in accusing him of having ulterior motives for his actions, and she was afraid her own nerve would crack if he stayed around much longer.

'I assume this means you won't be accompanying me to Strathmoor?' he declared at last, and Isobel stared at him aghast.

'You can't mean you still want to take me—us!'

'Why not?'

His expression was unreadable, but Isobel had the uneasy feeling that he had successfully reversed their positions.

'Well,' she began, 'well, because after what I said, you can't even—like me.'

His mouth twisted. 'Whatever gave you that idea?' he retorted. And, when she said nothing in response, 'If you change your mind, give me a ring. Invercaldy's in the book. If you leave a message, I'll get it.'

CHAPTER SEVEN

'IT'S your move, Rafe.'

Grace Calder's breathy treble had an aggrieved note, and he realised he had been sitting staring into space, instead of at the chessboard between them. It proved his thoughts were elsewhere than on their game, and Grace was not the type of woman to let that go unchallenged.

'Oh—sorry,' he said now, aware that he hadn't been paying attention to his companion. He scanned the board briefly, and moved his queen into a position where, with his next move, he could corner her bishop. 'I was thinking.'

'Yes, you were,' retorted Grace shortly, taking his queen with a deft move, and giving him a tight smile. 'But not about the game.' She set his queen beside the row of pieces she had already captured. 'Checkmate.'

Rafe stared at the board disbelievingly. It was true. In his haste to prove his attention had not been wandering, he had played right into her hands, and Grace's expression was proof that she knew it, too.

'Well, I'm damned,' he said, leaning back in his chair with what he hoped was a suitably penitent smile on his face. 'You're too good for me, Grace.'

'I just paid attention to the game, that's all,' she replied, doing her best to hide her irritation. 'You're a far better player than I am, Rafe, and you know it. You were winning, until you—lost interest.'

Rafe threaded the fingers of one hand through his hair. He could deny it, but he knew it was true. About losing interest, at least. For the past couple of weeks he had found it difficult to sustain any interest in anything. And, while he assumed his family would put it down to his normal lack of enthusiasm, he knew his present dilemma had nothing to do with his late wife.

On the contrary, it was days since he had even thought about Sarah. And that in itself should have been a cause for concern. For so long he had awakened each morning with the guilty awareness that, no matter what he did, or how he abused himself, he was still alive, while his wife and child were dead.

Yet for more than a week now that awareness had ceased to torment him. Of course, he wasn't drinking as much as he used to. And he wasn't waking with the agonising hangovers that had become such a part of his life. The absence of that particular form of self-flagellation might be the reason he was feeling this sudden surge of restlessness. But somehow he was not convinced.

He was more inclined towards the theory that *someone*—not something—was responsible. And, although it was ridiculous, he knew exactly who that someone was...

'Why don't we go for a walk?'

Once again, Grace's voice disturbed his reverie, her appeasing tone revealing a determined persistence to regain his attention. Grace was nothing if not single-minded, and the fact that his mother had—supposedly—persuaded her to stay on after her uncle, Sir Malcolm Calder, returned to Glasgow was proof that she approved of their liaison.

But then, Lady Invercaldy would approve of anyone who could coax her son to behave 'normally' again, Rafe thought cynically. Providing she was reasonably young, wealthy, of course, and single—qualities Grace possessed in full measure.

He'd wondered why Sir Malcolm had brought his niece with him to Invercaldy. A weekend's hunting, shooting and fishing had not seemed the most appropriate choice for a young woman of Grace's sensitivities, and it was true, she hadn't joined in any of the sporting activities.

Nor had Rafe, but while there were other guests at the castle he had been able to leave their entertaining to Colin. He and Clare came into their own on occasions like this, and Rafe was quite content to let his brother play host in his absence.

But when the weekend was over, it had proved harder
to avoid his mother's remaining guest. Grace was per-
sistent, and he had no doubt that her sights were set on
becoming the next Countess of Invercaldy. He didn't
flatter himself that it was his own irresistible charm she
was attracted to. He had been barely civil to her, and
she must know he wasn't interested. He had no intention
of marrying again, no intention of ever putting himself
through the same kind of torment he had suffered when
Sarah died. And really that was all his mother wanted:
a son of his to carry on the line.

Besides, he hardly knew Grace, he thought irritably,
as a frown dug a furrow between his dark brows. His
lips twisted. There was someone else he hardly knew,
too—another woman; but in her case it didn't seem to
matter...

The knowledge didn't please him. He might not have
forgotten their last encounter, but the memory of it filled
him with distaste. He must have been mad, he thought
grimly, acting like that! She had had every right to resent
his behaviour. Every right to accuse him of taking advantage of the situation, and order him out of the house.

His mouth tightened. Initially, though, she had
responded, he remembered, with an unwilling stirring of
his senses. When she'd turned her head and looked at
him, it hadn't been rejection he'd seen in her eyes. Oh,
no. They had been all light and fire, and when he'd
rubbed his lips against her neck, and tasted that soft
skin with his tongue, she'd been fairly panting with
emotion.

But something had happened, something he had done
or some memory of her husband perhaps, that had
caused her to change her mind—which had been just as
well for both of them. He had been in danger of forgetting who he was with and what he was doing, and
that was something he couldn't—he wouldn't—allow to
happen.

Particularly with a woman like her, he thought disparagingly. One of his own tenants! It was pathetic. She
wasn't some raging beauty, someone whose appearance
might excuse the quite unforgivable urge he had felt to
touch her. And not just touch her, he acknowledged bit-

terly. For the first time since Sarah died he'd wanted to
bury himself in a woman's flesh, wanted to feel her
softness closing around him, wanted her moist heat to
give him the release he had so urgently craved...

God! Why? Why her? She was—ordinary. Presentable
enough, perhaps, but in no way startling. She had nice
eyes—but they weren't markedly different from other
eyes he'd seen. Her lashes weren't even especially long,
and they were bleached a lighter shade at the tips, which
made them less rather than more noticeable. Her nose
was fairly prominent, too. Not long, but straight and
uncompromising, marking the place between cheek-
bones that were less pronounced because her face was
round rather than angular. Her mouth—well, again, her
mouth wasn't particularly noticeable. It was wide and
generous, with a fuller lower lip that might be construed
as sensuous, but, when put together with her other features, simply blended into a face that was pleasant rather
than striking.

She had lovely hair, of course. But it was too long to
wear loose, and she generally had it confined in a chunky
braid. Except when she'd tried to pin it up into that knot,
and it had tumbled down about her shoulders. He'd
wanted to wind it round his hands then, to thread his
fingers through it, and kiss her with her hair soft across
her lips. He'd imagined it spread across a pillow, and
himself poised above her, his taut body already anticipating how it would feel when he——

'Rafe...'

Oh, God——

'Rafe, did you hear what I said?'

For someone who professed to have found her appearance so ordinary, he was remembering an inor-
dinate amount of detail, he thought tensely. Which was
another reason to stay the hell away from her. She was
dangerous—to his life, to his future, to his peace of mind.

'Rafe—are we going out or aren't we?'

Grace's resentful tone finally penetrated his fogged
senses, and with a determined effort he applied himself
to answering her. In fact, her offended expression was
almost a relief, requiring, as it did, no more than a
cursory exertion on his part. He could handle Grace

Calder, so why in God's name couldn't he handle Isobel Jacobson?

'Um—if you like,' he replied now, aware that his response was less than enthusiastic. But Grace had got her own way, and she was delighted.

'Oh, good!' she exclaimed, jumping to her feet. 'I'll go and get my coat. I won't be long.'

'Don't hurry,' said Rafe drily, but that was after she had let herself out of the door and he was alone in the period beauty of his mother's parlour. He was committed now, but he didn't have to like it. And, as it would be dark in an hour or so, hopefully it wouldn't be a prolonged outing.

He got to his feet then, crossing the faded beauty of a carpet that had been made in France during the last century. This room in the castle was essentially French in appearance, with its delicately carved tables and chairs, and an escritoire that was reputed to have belonged to Marie Antoinette herself. That it had been furnished by Rafe's great-grandmother, many years before the present Dowager Countess was born, did not alter the fact that he had always regarded it as his mother's room, and when she had invited him there earlier that afternoon he had not known her intention then had been to leave him and their guest alone together. Balked by his avoidance of meals, taken in the family dining-room, his mother had been forced into connivance, and as he stood at the window now, staring towards the distant mountains, he wondered how long she intended to continue this charade. She must know he wasn't interested, know that no amount of persuasion on her part was going to get him to change his mind. There would be no second Countess of Invercaldy. Jaime was his brother's son; he would inherit the title.

Clare was in the hall when he went downstairs. She had apparently just arrived, and was in the process of handing her gloves and scarf to the waiting housemaid. Because of the shadowy beams that fanned the high, arching roof of the hall, whose stone walls were hung with crossed swords and other ancient weapons, lamps already cast their mellow glow across its worn oak floor. Shredding tapestries shifted in the breeze that marked the closing of the door, and an errant beam of sunlight slanted down from a high window and shone dully on the pearls that encircled Clare's throat.

In a cashmere sweater and plaid skirt, she already looked every inch the chatelaine of Invercaldy, and Rafe felt a certain cynicism at the tight-lipped glance she cast in his direction. She always behaved as if she didn't like him. She didn't approve of him, but anything else was moot. Before she had settled for the younger son of the Earl and Countess of Invercaldy, they both knew she had made an abortive play for the elder. For almost a year, she had used every means she knew—and some she didn't—to make Rafe take notice of her. It was only when people had begun to talk that she had turned to Colin, pretending he had been her objective, when everyone knew he hadn't.

But that was many years ago now, and time had dimmed the circumstances of their marriage. These days, she was known simply as the Earl's sister-in-law—the Honourable Mrs Colin Lindsay—and while he suspected she still harboured some resentment the title seemed to please her.

'Rafe,' she greeted him now, adopting the faintly patronising air of an adult speaking to a child. 'Are you going out?'

As he was wearing a thick suede jerkin over matching trousers and a chunky cream sweater, Rafe thought that was fairly obvious, but he humoured her by saying, 'Briefly. I thought we might take a walk. Is it cold?'

'Extremely,' she replied, warming her hands at the huge fire that was burning in a grate big enough to roast venison. 'Is—is Grace going with you?'

'She is.' Rafe joined her at the fire. 'Want to come with us?'

'What?' Clare gave him a startled look, and then, seeing the mockery in his eyes, her lips thinned. 'Oh—no. No, thank you, Rafe. I'm afraid I'm much too busy.'

'Really?' Rafe arched a dark brow. 'Doing what?'

'I'm here to see your mother about the autumn fair,' Clare replied shortly. 'Someone has to arrange these things, and as the vicar's wife went into hospital on Thursday——'

Rafe's smile was ironic. 'You're all heart, Clare.'

'Well, you can mock, but someone has to keep these customs alive, care about tradition.'

'And you're the ideal candidate, right?' Rafe inserted drily. 'What a pity Colin didn't inherit the title. You'd have made such an impeccable Countess!'

Clare's eyes glittered. 'You enjoy baiting me, don't you, Rafe? Well, take care someone doesn't beat you at your own game. There must be a woman somewhere who'll wipe that smug smile off your face!'

'Not a chance.' Rafe found himself responding with unnecessary violence, the memory of his thoughts earlier enough to bring a scowl to his lean features. 'You spoiled me for other women, Clare,' he said, deliberately taunting her in an effort to hide his own uncertainty. 'Tell me, did you ever tell Colin about that weekend in Aviemore?'

Clare's expression was bleak. 'Nothing happened in Aviemore,' she insisted tensely, but Rafe wouldn't let it be.

'My fault rather than yours, I fear,' he responded maliciously. And then, growing tired of the contest, he changed tack. 'Have you heard from Jaime?'

Clare took a deep breath and visibly restored her composure. 'Since he went back to school, you mean?' she enquired stiffly. 'Yes. We had a letter yesterday.'

Rafe inclined his head. 'He's settled in?'

'Why wouldn't he be?' Clare was clearly finding it difficult to suppress her indignation. 'His friends are there. I think he finds it lonely when he's on holiday. The village children are very—clannish, if you'll excuse the pun.'

Rafe hesitated, but the temptation was too great. 'What about Cory Jacobson?' he asked innocently. 'I understand they spent some time together. You and her mother were friends. Why shouldn't your children be the same?'

Clare clenched her fists. 'I know what you're trying to do, Rafe, but it won't work. I will not rise to your bait this time. You know as well as I do that Cory Jacobson is an entirely unsuitable companion for Jaime. According to her mother, the main reason she was so

keen to move away from London was because of Cory's
wild behaviour. The girl was quite impossible, apparently: into drugs——'

'*Drugs?*'

'Well, glue-sniffing, anyway,' Clare amended huffily.
'And shop-lifting, and absenteeism, and goodness knows
what else. And, as far as I can gather, she's no better
here.'

Rafe's good humour fled. 'Why? What has—Mrs
Jacobson—said to you?'

'To me? Nothing.' Clare tossed her head. 'I've only
seen Isobel a couple of times since she started at the
surgery. But I know she's already had a phone call from
the headmaster at the comprehensive in Strathmoor,
complaining about Cory's attitude. Daddy says he thinks
the girl is completely out of control.'

Rafe's dark brows descended. 'Why?'

'Who knows?' Clare shrugged. 'It not my problem.
I'd just as soon not get involved with them. Daddy says
Cory takes advantage of her mother's absence. But, as
long as Isobel does her job——'

'He won't fire her,' finished Rafe sardonically. 'Do
you have any opinions of your own, Clare, or does
Daddy advise you about everything?'

Clare gasped. 'Don't you criticise my family!'

'Why not?' Rafe was unrepentant. 'I dare say they're
not averse to criticising me, on occasion.'

'Can you blame them?' Clare was a little reckless now.
'You haven't exactly given them anything to admire you
for these past couple of years. If it weren't for
Jaime——'

She broke off then, but Rafe refused to let her get
away with it. 'Go on,' he said. 'If it weren't for Jaime—
what?' His eyes glittered like cold steel. 'Come on, Clare.
Spit it out! What does Jaime have to do with it?'

Clare's hands fluttered. 'I—nothing,' she said, refusing to meet his eyes. 'It was nothing.'

'Why don't I believe you?' Rafe stepped closer, and
she found herself trapped between him and the fireplace
at her back. His eyes narrowed. 'You think if it weren't
for Jaime Invercaldy wouldn't have an heir, isn't that

right? Well, forgive me, Clare, but I'd have thought that
was exactly what you wanted!'

'It is!' she hissed suddenly, driven to such a point that
she no longer cared what he thought of her. 'And you
know what? He'll make a damn sight better job of it
than his uncle!'

Rafe stepped away from her. 'Will he?' he said flatly.
And then, again, half mockingly, 'Will he?' He pulled
a wry face. 'We'll see.'

The sound of Grace's footsteps on the stairs was almost
a relief. Rafe hadn't thought he would ever be pleased
to see the other woman, but he was suddenly desperate
to get out into the fresh air. Clare's bitter words had
soured the atmosphere in the hall, and although it wasn't
the first argument they had had it was one of the worst.
The trouble was, he couldn't hurt Clare without hurting
Colin as well, and he had too much affection for his
brother to do anything to destroy his happiness.

'Ready, darling?' carolled Grace, and for once Rafe
was glad of the casual endearment. It caused Clare to
give the other woman a biting look, and Grace's, 'Lovely
to see you again, Clare,' fell on stony ground.

And, just for good measure, Rafe slipped his arm
about Grace's slim shoulders. 'Of course,' he said, in
answer to her question, 'Clare and I were just discussing
family relationships, weren't we, Clare? I guess we all
have our problems.' His smile was only slightly malevolent. 'By the way, Grace, did you know that Colin's
wife and I——'

'Rafe!'

Clare's protest was shrill, but Rafe only offered her
an innocent glance as he finished '—share an interest in
skiing?' He guided Grace towards the door. 'See you
later, Clare. I hope you won't find you're wasting your
time.'

Clare glared at him. 'Wasting my time?'

'Organising the autumn fair,' he reminded her mildly.
'The vicar's wife may recover. Then your—er—contri-
bution won't be needed.'

Beyond the walled gardens of the castle, acres of grazing
land undulated towards the distant mountains. The

Invercaldy estate had once stretched as far as the eye could see, but these days death and taxes had taken their toll. Nevertheless, Rafe still got pleasure from the thrill of ownership, and he was never happier than when he was here, on his own property. He didn't mind that these days its glens and coverts were used mainly for stalking deer, and where once brigands had lurked in the undergrowth now all you were likely to flush out was a poacher. There was salmon in the rivers, and game in the woods, and an abundance of wildlife of every shape and kind.

He had collected two of the dogs from the kennels on his way out, and now the excited retrievers raced ahead of them. The air was crisp, and scented with the smoke from the gamekeeper's bonfire, and Rafe pushed his hands into his pockets and endeavoured to school his thoughts.

He didn't know why he'd felt it necessary to make that parting shot. It wasn't as if he hadn't known that his brother and his wife anticipated that Jaime would eventually succeed him. And sooner rather than later, if he continued to abuse his liver with alcohol. It was just her attitude, that was all. The vicious way she had rounded on him, when he had challenged her reckless assumption. She was such a snob. Such an out-and-out bigot. He wanted to cut the ground from under her, and she'd known exactly what he meant.

Grace attempted to slip her arm into his, but he made the excuse of bending and picking up a twig to throw for the dogs to avoid the unwanted intimacy. The truth was, it had been Clare's remarks about Isobel and Cory Jacobson that had caught him on the raw. His own shortcomings he could stand. He was used to them. And he was used to being censured for them. But it was the disparaging way she had spoken of Isobel that had really fired his blood. And he was having some trouble dealing with it.

The ground beneath their feet was mushy. As they tramped through the copse of oak and sycamore trees that edged the loch, their feet squished in the mulch of leaves that covered the ground. The winds that had accompanied the rain earlier in the week had left the trees almost skeletal in appearance, and Grace started to complain that her short boots were not really waterproof.

'Couldn't we take the Rover, and go and have a meal in Strathmoor?' she suggested, revealing that that had been her intention all along. 'It's so muddy here. And I'm cold.'

'I don't think the dogs would appreciate the drive,' Rafe retorted drily, and as Grace gave him a wounded look he reflected that it had definitely not been his afternoon for making friends and influencing people. Clare was unlikely to forget what he had said, and Grace would probably take her complaints to his mother.

The barking of the dogs was a welcome diversion, and, seeing that they appeared to have found something dredged up among the reeds at the edge of the loch, he abandoned any thought of placating Grace, and quickened his stride. As he drew nearer, he saw what appeared to be the carcass of some animal clinging to the shore, and, guessing it was either a drowned deer, or an otter, he whistled for the dogs. He didn't want them rescuing some putrefying corpse and bringing it to him for his approval. But they ignored his summons, and, telling Grace to stay where she was, Rafe squelched into the reeds.

It was just as well he was wearing rubber boots, he thought, as the dogs continued to yelp and cavort about their quarry. Not that they wouldn't get the rough edge of his tongue, once he had secured them on a leash. Stupid animals, he swore impatiently. Not only were they covered in mud, but soaked to the skin as well.

And then the creature moved. For a moment, Rafe thought it was the drift of the current, or maybe a trick of his eyes in the fading light. It was almost dark, after all, and the lowering skies had shortened the afternoon considerably. But then he heard a soft moan, and with a sense of horror he realised it was human.

Careless now of splashing his suede trousers, Rafe surged forward, feeling the sucking pull of the reeds brushing against his legs. Every step was hazardous, threatening as it did his own immersion in the loch, and he could only assume that whoever it was had lost their balance and fallen into the water.

The body was curled in on itself, and Rafe had to step into deeper water to be in a position to offer any assistance. He was afraid that whoever it was was only half conscious, and the dangers of hypothermia were foremost in his mind as he bent to lift the body out of the reeds.

It was Cory.

As his arms took the weight and he discovered how little she weighed, her head fell back over his arm. Her face, pale and streaked with mud, was unmistakable, even in the poor light, and her eyes flickered feebly in his direction.

'Rafe?' she said faintly, and he thought how ironic it was that she found his name so easy to use, when her mother didn't.

'Cory,' he acknowledged grimly, ordering off the dogs as he settled her more comfortably against his chest. She was wet through, and he could feel the moisture seeping through his own jerkin. In heaven's name, what had she been doing? And wasn't she supposed to be at school, or at least on her way home, at this time of the afternoon?

'I'm cold,' she said, and as if to endorse this statement she shivered, making him aware of how chilled her skin was. She was in danger of contracting pneumonia, as well as anything else, and with a feeling of helplessness he strode out of the water.

'Who is it? What's going on?'

Grace's questions were only half concerned. Her main consideration was that her afternoon was being ruined by a pair of dogs and a half-drowned individual who should have known better than to fall into the loch.

'Cory,' said Rafe, without really answering her. 'Cory Jacobson.' He knew that name would mean nothing to her. 'She's soaked to the skin.' He paused for a moment, trying to think. 'Dammit, what should I do?'

'Put her down, before she ruins a perfectly good coat,' declared Grace distastefully. 'For heaven's sake, who is Cory Jacobson, Rafe? And what does she have to do with you?'

Rafe's eyes were cold as they speared her resentful face. 'What would you have me do?' he demanded. 'Leave her to die of hypothermia, pneumonia, what? She's just a child, Grace. She's cold, and scared, and a long way from home.'

'That's not my problem.' Grace sniffed. 'Nor yours either, I don't suppose. Who is she? One of the village children? Where are her parents? Don't they care where she is, or what's been happening to her?'

'I doubt if anyone knows,' said Rafe grimly, remembering what Clare had told him that afternoon. He could imagine how Isobel would feel when she found out about this.

And thinking about Isobel reminded him that every minute he spent arguing with Grace Cory was getting colder and colder. Which made his decision that much easier. He would have to take her to the castle. As he had said, she was a long way from home, and returning her to the cottage would entail driving the five miles or so of country roads between. Not to mention the fact that the chances were that Isobel would not be there, and if the cottage was locked Cory would have spent another fifteen minutes in wet clothes with nothing to show for it. For now, it was important to get her out of her wet things and into a hot bath. Now was not the time to doubt the wisdom of such a resolution.

Without another word, he started off towards the castle, with Grace and the dogs at his heels. It was the better part of a mile from where they had found Cory to the gates of Invercaldy, and although Rafe had considered himself reasonably fit his arms were trembling by the time they reached the gatehouse.

It was amazing how heavy the girl had become as the distance he had carried her increased, and the fact that she swam in and out of consciousness made her like a dead thing in his arms. He just hoped that that was not an option. Having lost her husband less than a year ago, Isobel couldn't afford to lose her daughter as well.

CHAPTER EIGHT

ISOBEL sat beside Rafe in the plush front seats of the Range Rover and tried to stop herself from shaking. It was so galling, feeling herself going to pieces like this, and she hoped he hadn't noticed her knees knocking together below the lighted curve of the dashboard.

That was what came of wearing a skirt on occasions like this, she thought foolishly. In jeans or trousers, her distress wouldn't have been half so noticeable. But she always wore a skirt at the surgery. Dr Webster preferred it. And besides, it looked better beneath the white lab coats he liked his staff to wear.

She had been wearing her lab coat when Rafe had walked into the surgery. She'd thought he was another patient, and she'd come out of her office prepared to tell him that Dr Webster was making a house call. She'd been shocked out of her mind when she'd seen who it was. He was the last person she had expected to meet there.

And her first thought had been one of panic: panic that he might have come to see her. She had worked so hard at keeping her head down, at putting him out of her thoughts. Yet when he'd walked into the surgery, her whole system had gone into overdrive.

She hadn't realised until then how much she'd wanted to see him again. Or how vividly his image had remained in her memory. His lean face was painfully familiar, and in a dark shirt and trousers, with an olive-green parka hanging open from his shoulders, he was just as disturbing as she remembered. For a few moments, it was incredibly difficult to control her rioting senses, and, woman-like, she'd wished she had thought to shed her coat before leaving her office. She had no illusions that the stark absence of colour suited her. It robbed her face

of all warmth, and with her hair tucked into a coil at
her nape she looked plain and middle-aged.

Not that she had flattered herself that Rafe might care
how she looked for long. It was more than two weeks
since that morning he had come to the cottage. But he
hadn't acted like a man who was eager to see her again.
On the contrary, he had shown a total lack of interest
in her, and she had been in the process of assuring herself
that she was glad, that, whatever Cory had said, she
didn't want to get involved in any relationship with him,
when he had dropped the bombshell on her.

Cory had had an accident. She wasn't hurt, just
shocked, he thought; but he had taken her to the castle.
She had been found, soaked to the skin and only half
conscious, at the edge of the loch, and as soon as Dr
Webster could be located he wanted him to come and
take a look at her. But for now he had come to fetch
her.

That was when Isobel had gone to pieces. She hadn't
screamed, or cried, or burst into floods of tears, but her
legs had given out on her, and it was only Rafe's swift
reaction that had saved her from collapsing in a heap
on the floor. Instead, with fairly impersonal hands, he
had helped her into the nearest chair, and summoned
Nurse Fuller to come and deal with her.

Isobel guessed he had expected the nurse to give her
something to calm her, but she had refused to take anything. A glass of water, sipped while Rafe quickly apprised Nurse Fuller of the situation, had been all she
would accept, and when he'd finally looked at her again
she'd got unsteadily to her feet.

'I'm ready,' she'd said, fumbling with the buttons of
the lab coat, and Rafe and the nurse had exchanged a
knowing glance.

They had probably been feeling sorry for her, Isobel
thought now, gazing out at the ribbon of winding road
reflected in the headlights of the vehicle. It was common
knowledge that Cory was something of a problem child,
and she knew, from her own experiences, that it wasn't
all that easy to be accepted in Invercaldy. People around
here tended to be suspicious of foreigners, and their name
and their accent had set them apart from the rest.

That was one of the reasons why Cory was having such a hard time fitting into the school at Strathmoor, she assured herself fiercely. It had proved to be a very conservative establishment, and it had been obvious that her daughter would stand out like a sore thumb. Apart from anything else, Cory was not the kind of child to efface herself—as Mr Dougall had informed Isobel only a couple of days ago.

And now this! Isobel shivered again, cold, in spite of her warm duffel and the car's heater going at full blast. What had Cory been doing? As far as Isobel knew, she had boarded the school bus that morning, as usual. But how could she have? If she'd been found earlier that afternoon she couldn't possibly have been to school.

'Are you all right?'

Rafe's voice was low and solicitous, but Isobel didn't delude herself that it was more than a perfunctory enquiry. He must be heartily sick of the Jacobsons, she thought miserably. Since they arrived, they had been nothing but trouble.

Even Clare, whom she had vainly imagined was her friend, had proved to have feet of clay. When she came into the surgery—which wasn't very often—she was more friendly towards Nurse Fuller than she was towards Isobel. She continued to treat her with the faintly condescending air she had conceived the night they arrived, and having Cory's headmaster phoning Isobel at the surgery to complain about her daughter's behaviour had not endeared her to Dr Webster either.

Now she pressed her knees together, trapping her palms between them, and said, 'Why was Cory taken to—to the castle? Wouldn't it have been simpler to bring her home?'

'No.'

Rafe's response was curt, and she thought what an ungrateful creature she was to suggest that anyone had had anything but her daughter's best interests at heart.

'Because—because she was nearer to the castle when she was found?' she suggested, in a more conciliatory tone. 'What—how do you think she got there?'

Rafe cast a brooding glance in her direction, and she cringed. She couldn't exactly see his expression, but she could sense his irritation. She hoped he didn't think she suspected him of having anything to do with Cory's accident.

'She was wet through and in danger of contracting pneumonia or hypothermia or both,' he stated tersely. 'I'm afraid I didn't give a lot of thought to how she got there.'

'Oh.' Isobel swallowed. '*You* found her.'

'Yes, me,' he agreed bleakly. 'Does that make a difference?'

Isobel licked her lips. 'Only to the extent that—that I haven't thanked you,' she stammered unhappily, and with a muffled oath Rafe took one hand off the steering-wheel and gripped her thigh.

'You're not fit to thank anyone,' he declared roughly, his hard fingers digging into the quivering flesh above her knee. 'Dammit, Isobel, I don't want any thanks. It was pure luck that we chose to walk along the shore of the loch. If we hadn't taken the dogs with us, I doubt we'd have even seen her.'

'Thank God you did.' Isobel caught her breath. 'But what was she doing there? She was supposed to be at school.'

'Who knows?' Rafe removed his hand, and a ripple of something incredibly like regret spread from the lingering imprint of his fingers. 'She was in no condition to give us any explanations when we found her. But one of the gamekeepers says he found a skiff in the reeds earlier in the afternoon. He suspected poachers, but there was no one about.'

Isobel gazed at him. 'You think she might have been out on the loch?'

'It's possible.'

Rafe slowed to turn between two stone gateposts and, as he changed gear, Isobel's eyes were drawn again to the narrow-boned elegance of his hands. It was crazy, but she wanted to grasp his hand and hold on to it, as if it was the only constant in a continuously changing world. Oh, God, she thought, she shouldn't have come to Invercaldy. And not just because of Cory. She was in danger, too.

'I suggest you let Cory stay where she is tonight,' Rafe remarked, after a moment, and Isobel was forced to look at him again.

'Stay where she is?' she echoed blankly. 'I—but why?'

'Why not?' he countered, and, just for a moment, she thought he was angry with her again. 'When I left, Mrs Fielding—my housekeeper—had orders to supervise her a hot bath, and put her to bed. I don't think it's a good idea to consider uprooting her again. Not until morning, at least.' His lips twisted. 'We have plenty of room.' He paused. 'You can stay with her, if you wish.'

'Oh, no.'

Isobel was very definite about that, and Rafe cast her a scornful look. 'That's up to you, of course,' he drawled. 'But if you change your mind, let my house-keeper know, will you?'

The set-down was deliberate, but Isobel was too distressed to take offence. 'I—haven't decided whether Cory should stay here yet,' she replied stiffly, her slippery palms an indication of how precarious her control was. 'I'm grateful for the offer, but——'

'We'd have plenty of chaperons, you know,' he cut in sardonically. 'This isn't a ploy of mine to get you into my clutches. My mother's at home, and her guest. Not to mention any number of curious employees!'

Isobel gasped. 'I never thought——'

'Didn't you?'

He changed gear again, and her unwilling gaze was drawn to the powerful muscles outlined by the tight-fitting fabric of his trousers. His thigh flexed as he bore down on the foot-brake, and the memory of how he had cornered her in the kitchen at the cottage, and of how he had felt, close behind her, was suddenly a vivid image in her head.

Had he really done that? she wondered incredulously. Or had she just imagined it? It was difficult to compare this moody, sarcastic stranger with the disturbing man who had scattered her senses and fired her blood.

Yet that was what he was, she reminded herself unsteadily. Disturbing—and disturbed. Unpredictable, as Mrs Webster had warned her. Never to be taken for

granted, and far too complex a character for someone
like her to understand.

'You're quite safe, you know,' he said now, and she
wondered if he had read her mind. He made a
disparaging sound. 'It's—oh, *weeks* since I did any
raping and pillaging!'

Isobel straightened her spine. 'Don't be silly!' she
exclaimed nervously, and he snorted.

'Then don't *you* be silly,' he retorted, as the wall of
a stone edifice appeared in the headlights. 'You're sitting
there terrified I'm going to jump your bones!'

'I am not!' Isobel was indignant, but he wasn't
listening to her.

'We're here,' he said instead, and she swallowed the
panic that rose again inside her as they swept beneath
an arched opening in the wall and drove through what
had once been part of the outer bailey of the castle.

Although Isobel told herself she was in no mood to
admire her surroundings, floodlights illuminating its grey
façade made it impossible for her not to notice the harsh
beauty of the building that lay ahead of her. Time—and
neglect—had reduced the inner bailey wall to a ruin, and
the stark bulk of the keep stood unchallenged against
the early evening sky.

But the keep was unoccupied, she saw at once, and a
second examination found jagged cracks in its stone
walls. Some of the crenellations on its battlements were
worn and crumbling, and birds and climbing creepers
had aggravated the problem.

Yet, for all that, it had a timeless beauty. It was something to do with the fact that it had stood here for
hundreds of years, strong and inviolate, and only very
slowly was it conceding defeat to the hazards of the
twentieth century.

But beside the keep was another building, equally old,
Isobel thought, but in a much healthier state of repair.
It was attached to the keep by a long gallery, but judging
by its many long windows, and the absence of any for-
tifications, it had never been intended to withstand any
attack.

And, remembering what Jaime had told Cory about
Rafe's wife, Isobel's stomach tightened. According to

him, it was her money that had been used to restore the castle, and she had to remember that these people married for other reasons beside love. Rafe might have loved his wife; if his behaviour since her death was anything to go by, he certainly had. But honour, and prestige—and the accumulation of wealth—passed down from generation to generation, that was what really mattered. Love—*sex*—could be bought, but not inherited, and much more cheaply than in marriage...

She was hardly aware that the Range Rover had stopped, until her door was opened and a gnarled hand was offered to help her to alight. It wasn't Rafe's hand, and she cast an anxious look over her shoulder. But he had already left the vehicle, and as she made a rather ungainly passage to the ground she found him standing waiting for her.

The fact that the high seat caused her skirt to ride up somewhere around her thighs caused her no small embarrassment, and she hurriedly brushed it down. But not before Rafe had seen and enjoyed her little flurry, and he smiled as he captured her arm just above her elbow to guide her into the building.

'You see; I was right,' he mocked, as she gave a startled word of thanks to the old man who had helped her out of the car. 'You are a puritan after all.' He resisted her attempt to get free, and his smile deepened. 'That was Cummins, by the way. One of our oldest *retainers*.' He used the word deliberately, she was sure. 'He started here as my father's valet, many moons ago. As a matter of fact, he's been here at Invercaldy longer than I have.'

'My lord!'

The wavering summons arrested them, and Isobel was so shocked by the realisation that this was how most people addressed him that she didn't take advantage of his momentary distraction to release herself.

'Will you be wanting the Range Rover again this evening, my lord?' Cummins enquired, deferentially, and Rafe looked down at Isobel with the question in his eyes.

'We—I *will* be going home,' she said hurriedly, aware of what he was asking. There was no way she was going to stay at the castle. She would see Cory, assure herself that she was fit to travel the few miles to the cottage, and they would go home.

But it wasn't going to be that simple.

As soon as she saw her daughter, Isobel knew she had underestimated the problem. Rafe was right. Cory was not fit to move. She was running the kind of temperature Isobel had previously believed was impossible without losing consciousness entirely, and her skin felt papery thin and brittle.

That Cory was conscious at all was due more to her excitement at her surroundings than to her efforts to fight the high temperature she was running. It was obvious she was sweating, and only the fact that she still knew where she was gave Isobel any reassurance. Even Rafe seemed disturbed by the feverishness of her condition, and he had a low-voiced exchange with the woman who had been tending her while Isobel moved to the bed.

'Isn't this some place?'

Cory's first words were a relief, and Isobel forgot all the words of reproval she had been nurturing on the journey from the village, and clasped her daughter's hand in her own icy cold one.

'Isn't it, though?' she agreed, looking briefly round the lamplit bedroom. She could quite see why Cory would be so impressed. Its size alone was imposing to someone used to the modest dimensions of ordinary houses, though the bed was quite in keeping, being four-square and four-postered, with carved pillars and an embossed canopy.

'I'm all right, you know,' Cory added, as Isobel smoothed damp hair back from her daughter's forehead with a slightly unsteady hand. 'I'm just so hot, that's all. And who's the old woman? Do you know, she tried to bath me? I told her—I'm not a baby. I'm old enough to bath myself.'

Isobel glanced round at the elderly woman Rafe was talking to, and hoped she had not heard Cory's unflattering description of her. Mrs Fielding, as Rafe had said the woman was called, was the only person Isobel had seen, apart from Cummins, since they

arrived at the castle. Rafe had brought her straight upstairs to see her daughter.

'Where's Jaime?' Cory asked suddenly, clutching her
mother's hand, and Isobel frowned.

'Jaime?'

'Yes. I wanted to tell him; I wanted to show him I
could row a boat as good as he could. He said I couldn't
do it. He said *girls* weren't as strong as boys. But he's
wrong, isn't he, Mum? I'm as strong as he is. Or I was,
until——'

She broke off, and Isobel sank down weakly on to the
side of the bed. 'You've *seen* Jaime?' she echoed faintly.

'Oh, not today,' said Cory fretfully. 'Aren't you
listening to what I'm saying? I took the boat out on my
own. I rowed it, just like he did. Only the oars wouldn't
stay in place, and—well, I suppose you know what
happened.'

'No.' Isobel's voice was strained, as the realisation of
what Cory was telling her sank in. The thought that her
daughter had been out on the lake, her daughter who
couldn't swim, on that deep water——

She shuddered, but Cory was too agitated to notice
her mother's expression. 'I had to swim, you know,' she
added, as if that was some kind of achievement. 'Really
swim. You didn't know I could, did you? Well, I can.
I proved it. You ask Rafe. He'll tell you it's true.'

Isobel shook her head. She felt numb with horror.
That Cory was alive at all was a miracle. How could she
berate her for her recklessness, when it had obviously
been a matter of life and death?

'Isobel...'

Rafe's hand on her shoulder—how she knew it was
his hand and not Mrs Fielding's she didn't care to
speculate at that moment—was absurdly comforting, and
she turned tear-glazed eyes up to his dark face.

'Mmm?'

She didn't trust herself to speak without breaking
down completely, and he increased the pressure in such
a way that she rose obediently from the bed and turned
to face him.

'The doctor's on his way,' he said gently, and she concentrated on the place where the opened neckline of his

shirt exposed a V of brown skin. It was safer to look at that hair-roughened skin than into his eyes that were softer then she'd ever seen them; safer to speculate on the particular colour of his shirt than to wonder how it would feel to give in and bury her face against the broad expanse of his chest.

'You've—you've managed to contact him?' she got out jerkily, and Rafe nodded his head.

'Mrs Fielding was just telling me they reached him at Dalbaig. He'll be here very shortly.'

'Thank goodness.'

Isobel wanted to thank him, but she was tired and anxious, and when Cory started to speak again she turned instantly back to her daughter. However, Cory's words were mumbled now, and although she attempted to push the bedcovers away from her she was drifting in and out of consciousness. That she was exhausted was obvious. Isobel just hoped that was all it was.

She lifted her eyes to Rafe's now, and he grasped the hand she fluttered desperately in his direction. 'It's all right,' he said reassuringly, and almost unthinkingly, it seemed, he brought her fingers to his lips. 'I won't let anything happen to her.' His eyes darkened almost savagely. 'To either of you.'

Isobel's lips parted. 'Rafe——'

'What is going on, Rafe?'

The strident enquiry came from the doorway, and Isobel swung round guiltily, realising from the woman's tone and appearance that this was not another of the servants. Dressed for the evening, in an elegant black gown and pearls, a serape of plaid flung over one shoulder, the woman fairly exuded pride and outrage, and Isobel had little difficulty in identifying her as Rafe's mother.

She snatched her hand from Rafe's then, backing up against the bed almost protectively, as if the simple barrier of her body could hide Cory's presence from view. The Dowager Countess's expression alone was enough to cause the marrow in her bones to freeze on the spot, and she wondered what Rafe had told his mother when he'd brought Cory back from his walk.

'Mama,' he greeted her now, and, listening to his voice, Isobel could detect no trace of concern. On the contrary, he was regarding his mother with something akin to a challenge in his eyes, and the Countess fussed with her wrap, before asking tersely,

'How long is this going to take?'

Rafe shrugged, pushing his hands into the pockets of the parka he had not yet thought to discard. 'We'll know better when Webster gets here,' he replied evenly, and Isobel was impressed by his air of detachment.

She was still trembling from the sensuous brush of his lips against her skin. Still horrified that she could have responded to him at a time like this, when she should have been thinking of Cory. Her hands, clasped behind her back, were there as much for her protection as anything else. The guilt she was feeling wasn't just because Lady Invercaldy had interrupted them. It was more to do with her own lack of self-control.

But Rafe was behaving as if nothing untoward had happened. As if his mother catching him kissing a strange woman's fingers were an everyday occurrence in this household. He didn't even seem to care how his mother might regard it. It wasn't as if Isobel had any right to be here.

'By the way, this is Mrs Jacobson, Mama,' he remarked now, turning back to Isobel with a certain tightening of his mouth. 'But I'm sure you know that already.'

'Mrs Jacobson.'

The Dowager Countess's acknowledgement was barely polite, and Isobel couldn't honestly blame her. Her own, 'My lady,' was equally perfunctory, and she hoped it was the proper form of address. But just at this moment she couldn't worry about that.

Rafe's level gaze observed the awkward introduction, and Isobel was half afraid he was going to make some outrageous comment. Presenting her to his mother so offhandedly was not likely to win the Countess's approval, and she wished she could just take her daughter and get out of there at once.

'So—what is going to happen after Webster has given his opinion?' Lady Invercaldy enquired now, and Isobel realised that neither of them was likely to say anything controversial in front of her and Mrs Fielding.

'Your guess is as good as mine,' responded Rafe smoothly. 'I'm not a doctor, Mama. I only act on instinct.'

'Don't you always?'

There was a trace of some other emotion in his mother's voice now, but although her nostrils flared she only brushed past Mrs Fielding and approached the bed. She stood for a few seconds, looking down at the girl lying flushed and helpless on the pillows, and then turned to fasten eagle eyes on Isobel herself.

'You realise this has been a most unfortunate incident, Mrs Jacobson?' she demanded coldly, her gaze moving over Isobel's short pleated skirt and pale blue angora sweater with faint contempt. 'If my son hadn't found her, your daughter might well have died.'

'I know.' Isobel also knew she should have appended the woman's title, too, but she didn't. This whole affair was rapidly becoming too much for her to handle, and the woman's hostility was the last straw. 'I'm sorry.'

'You're sorry!' The words gave the older woman the opening she had been seeking. 'There's not much point in being sorry, is there, Mrs Jacobson? What I think you should be asking yourself is what she was doing there. Shouldn't she have been in school? She does go to school, I trust? Don't you ensure that she takes the bus every morning?'

'That will do, Mama.'

Rafe's voice was mild enough, but his expression seemed to give his mother pause. In any event, she seemed to respond to it, and after casting another glance at the girl in the bed she walked back to the door.

But, as she passed her son, she made one final statement. 'I think Clare should have given some thought to Mrs Jacobson's inexperience of the dangers inherent in living in an isolated community,' she declared pointedly. 'We simply cannot be held responsible for every accident that happens on the estate.'

Isobel caught her breath at the injustice of being accused of something she had never even thought of, but

before she could say anything in her own defence Rafe
took his mother's arm and guided her out of the door.

'It's not your concern, Mama,' he informed her
crisply, his eyes promising retribution if she said anything more. 'Why don't you and Grace have supper? I'll
get something later, after I've spoken with Webster.'

Grace? Who was *Grace*?

Isobel despised herself for even caring at that moment,
and she swung round abruptly to find Mrs Fielding's
eyes upon her. She had scarcely noticed the housekeeper
earlier, but now she was conscious of her guarded appraisal. And why was the woman looking at her like that?
Was it only because she felt sorry for her, because of
what had happened to Cory? Or was there some other
emotion stirring her to a reluctant communion?
Curiosity, perhaps? Or pity? Or was she rueful at the
pathetic attempt Isobel was making to hide her reactions
to Rafe?

'You can go, Mrs Fielding,' Rafe told her now, coming
back into the room. 'But as soon as Webster arrives,
show him up.'

'Yes, sir.'

The housekeeper bowed her head, and after giving
Isobel a polite nod she too left the room. She didn't
close the door entirely, but she did pull it to behind her,
and Isobel was immediately conscious of being isolated
with Rafe in circumstances that could only be described
as familiar. And improper, she thought unhappily. She
was sure his mother would not approve of this situation.

'How is she?'

Apparently uncaring of what his family might think
of his behaviour, Rafe had come to stand beside her,
and Isobel sent a wary look in his direction.

'I—don't know,' she said after a moment. 'Hot, fe-
verish, a little confused, I think.' She concentrated on
Cory and tried to remember that he was being only naturally concerned. He had found her, after all. 'She didn't
care for the fact that your housekeeper apparently
expected to help her take a bath.'

'Ah.' Rafe nodded, and stretched out his hand to rest
the back of his hand against Cory's forehead. 'She's
running quite a temperature. But I think we found her

in time. Don't worry. As I said before, I won't let anything happen to her.'

'How can you be sure?'

The words were torn from her, but if she hoped they
might dispel the strange intimacy that was growing between them she was mistaken. Instead of taking offence,
Rafe only transferred his attention from her daughter to
her, and before she knew what was happening he had
pulled her into his arms.

'Because I say so,' he told her roughly, his hand
cupping her head against his shoulder.

It was meant to be a comforting embrace, she knew
that. He was trying to reassure her, and she was foolish
if she thought it meant anything else. But when his
fingers moved against her scalp they sent shivers of
awareness down her spine, and when she closed her eyes
the sheer relief of his nearness overwhelmed her
inhibitions.

'But—you don't know,' she persisted, trying to hang
on to some semblance of sanity. But her lips were moving
against the curve of his neck, and she could taste the
male texture of his skin.

'Yes, I do,' he contradicted her softly, moving so that
her hip was cradled between his thighs. 'Trust me,' he
added, his hand caressing her nape under the heavy coil
of hair. His mouth brushed the top of her head, and she
thought his breathing was becoming as uneven as her
own. 'The doctor will be here shortly. And if there's
anything she needs, I'll see she gets it.'

'But why should you?' she argued, not because she
doubted him, but just to keep her mind focused on what
was real. She felt surrounded by him—by the heat of his
body and the faint awareness that he was sweating, too.
Yet even that musky scent was disturbing, and she sensed
his arousal even before she felt its betraying hardness
against her hip.

She knew she ought to move, *had* to move, before
something even more mindless happened, but still she
lingered. It was like starting a fire, she thought dizzily,
as his thumb circled the delicate coil of her ear. There
was just a spark at first, but then it flickered into life,

and before you knew what was happening it was rioting out of control.

Yet when the pad of his thumb tipped her chin, turning her face up to his, she didn't resist. Even though she knew what she was inviting, what he wanted from her. For the moment, she was incapable of thinking for herself, and when he bent his head and let his tongue taste the parted softness of her lips her knees almost buckled.

'Why shouldn't I?' he breathed against her mouth, and she had the unwilling feeling that it wasn't her question he was answering but one of his own.

'I—Cory may wake up,' she choked, but the words died on her lips as his tongue invaded her mouth. With a swiftness that had her heart pumping, and the blood thundering hotly through her veins, his kiss lengthened and hardened, turning her from a startled victim to a helpless participant. With her head swimming and her senses seeking some mindless quest of their own making, all she could do was cling to him as he took her with him beyond any chance of control.

And then Cory made a sound, and the world swam back into focus. But Rafe didn't immediately let her go. 'Later,' he said huskily, resting his chin against her forehead. And before she could make any sense of that remark, 'Excuse me now. I think Webster has arrived.'

CHAPTER NINE

It was broad daylight when Isobel opened her eyes. The sun was streaming through a crack in the curtains, and she lay for several minutes wondering why the doves were silent this morning. They hadn't disturbed her as they usually did, and in fact the room seemed strangely quiet and remote.

And then the realisation of where she was came back to her. And with it the uneasy recollection of the events of the day before. Oh, God! Cory had been found, half drowned, in the loch, and if Rafe hadn't found her...

She blinked, swallowed hard, and lifted a heavy wrist to see what time it was. It seemed odd to have to peel back the sleeve of her sweater to do so, and even as she gaped at her watch she could feel the discomfort of her skirt rucked up beneath her body.

The fact that it was nearly eight o'clock was enough to send her stumbling from the bed, but one glimpse of her reflection in a long cheval-mirror brought her abruptly to a halt. She had been dashing, headlong, for the door, her only objective to assure herself that her daughter's condition hadn't deteriorated in her absence. But the sight of tangled hair and crumpled clothes was daunting. She couldn't treat the castle like her own home. However anxious she might be, she had to make some effort to tidy herself first.

Not that it was going to be easy, she acknowledged, looking in vain for either a brush or a comb. And although she had been sure she wouldn't sleep when she lay down on the bed, she obviously had. Which was why she looked such a mess now. If only she'd taken off her sweater and skirt and plaited her hair. But at four o'clock in the morning she hadn't given much thought to anything.

Not even her surroundings, she admitted now, glancing round the room. The comfortable appointments of the guest bedroom, with its tapestry-hung walls and canopied bed, had meant little to her in the early morning hours. It had been a place to rest, that was all. Somewhere to lie down for a couple of hours, while someone else kept an eye on her daughter.

She caught her breath as she remembered who it was who was sitting with Cory. She was sure Stella Fuller had never expected to spend a night at the castle. And clearly Dr Webster hadn't approved of the arrangement.

The doctor's first prognosis had been that perhaps Cory might be better off in the infirmary at Strathmoor. He had been all for calling an ambulance, and shifting the responsibility for the child's recovery on to someone else. And, incidentally, removing her from the castle, too, acknowledged Isobel ruefully. The Websters had obviously not endorsed the present state of affairs.

And who could blame them? she wondered, biting her lip. Had it been her decision, and hers alone, she would probably have agreed with the doctor. After what had happened the previous evening, she was as desperate as anyone else that they should leave the castle. She didn't know what game Rafe was playing, but she knew she was going to get hurt.

But, naturally, Rafe had demurred. After listening intently to what Dr Webster had had to say, he had declared that Cory should stay where she was. She was ill, but with modern medicine and proper nursing there was no reason why she shouldn't make a swift recovery. She was young, and resilient, and he was sure Isobel would prefer it if her daughter were more easily accessible.

Of course, Isobel would, though she could think of other places than the castle. The cottage, for example. As soon as Cory was fit to move, she would take her home.

But, for the present, there was nothing she could do. Even if it was going to cause more problems with the Websters. She wasn't naïve enough to think that she'd heard the last of it. Clare was bound to resent it, and she made her protests felt.

But last night Rafe's words had carried the day. And when Dr Webster had objected that Nurse Fuller might not be prepared to leave her home and family overnight, Rafe had offered to find a private nurse. He had even gone so far as to suggest that if Dr Webster didn't feel he could handle it himself he could arrange for the services of another doctor. But that was adding insult to injury, and the matter hadn't been raised again.

Besides, Dr Webster did have the experience necessary. In his years working in hospitals in both England and Scotland, he had encountered every kind of illness and injury. Isobel didn't doubt that her daughter was in good hands. Whether they were willing hands or caring hands was another matter. And at least Stella Fuller had offered no complaint.

In consequence, Isobel had spent the hours until four a.m. sitting with the nurse by her daughter's bed, watching Cory sleep. It was fitful sleep, and the child's temperature was still giving cause for concern, but Stella was a wonderful companion. She assured her that the antibiotics the doctor had administered before leaving to attend another patient would bring her temperature down. How long it might take was arguable. But everything that could be done was being done. There was nothing to be gained by worrying herself unnecessarily.

And she knew this was true. But that hadn't stopped her worrying just the same. She still didn't know how Cory had come to be out on the lake in the first place. And the prospect of dealing with the consequences was something she didn't want to face.

She also knew she ought to ring Mrs Jacobson. Edward's mother ought to be told that her granddaughter had had an accident. But the idea of admitting her own ignorance of the situation to Mrs Jacobson was discouraging. The older woman would be bound to catch the next train to Scotland, and all the old recriminations would be resurrected again.

She wished she could leave Rafe to deal with her mother-in-law as well. Obviously, he'd have an easier time of it than she would. Mrs Jacobson was as snobbish in her way as Clare. She might even overlook Isobel's shortcomings if Rafe invited her to the castle.

Which was a silly idea, she thought impatiently. She couldn't go on relying on Rafe for every little thing that happened. Maybe his mother hadn't been so unreasonable after all. Perhaps she was giving the impression that she needed his support.

Not that she'd seen much of him since the doctor had departed, she assured herself now, finding her shoes, and crossing the thickly carpeted floor to the window. The room was cool, though not as cool as her room usually was at the cottage, but her feet were cold. After Nurse Fuller's arrival, she'd presumed he'd gone to bed. It wasn't until he'd appeared again in the early hours, still dressed, and with the shadow of a night's growth of beard on his jawline, that she'd realised she'd been wrong.

And he'd been angry, she remembered. Angry that she had spent most of the night sitting on a straight-backed chair that could hardly be called comfortable, and angry that no one had thought to offer her anything to eat. Nurse Fuller had obviously had her evening meal before coming to the castle, but Isobel had come straight from the surgery.

As she drew back the curtains, she wondered what Stella must have thought of their relationship. It was hardly conventional, and to someone used to treating the Lindsays with a certain amount of awe it was obviously curious. She was glad in a way that their conversation had ended in him summoning one of the servants to take her to this guest room. She could imagine what Stella would have thought if he'd taken her himself.

But she hadn't wanted to leave Cory, even so. And that was why her exchange with Rafe had been so confrontational. As a means of spiking his guns, she had refused to drink any of the tea or eat any of the sandwiches that had been delivered to the guest room. Though looking at the untouched tray now, she had to concede she had probably achieved nothing by the gesture.

Impatient with herself, she barely cast a glance at the view of sun-kissed loch and purple mountains before leaving the window to find the bathroom. A second door,

other than the one through which she had entered the
night before, looked promising, and although she opened
it tentatively she found what she was looking for.

And a brush and comb, she saw with some relief. After
sluicing her face and hands, and cleaning her teeth with
her fingers, she hurriedly brushed her hair, before
threading it into a thick braid. There was nothing she
could do about her clothes, but at least she looked tidier.
She just hoped she didn't meet the Dowager Countess.
Somehow she knew that would not be a happy
coincidence.

'Coffee, my lord?'

Rafe opened one eye and wondered why Cummins was
hovering over him like a predatory crow. His head was
aching, and when he tried to move his back protested
with a stabbing pain in his lumbar region. He felt stiff,
and grubby, and not in the best of moods.

He grunted, and Cummins took it as a sign that he
hadn't heard him. 'I asked if you'd like some coffee,
my lord,' he repeated patiently. 'It is only eight-fifteen,
but I was sure you'd wish to know that Miss Jacobson
seems a little better this morning.'

Miss Jacobson. *Isobel*! No, Cory.

Rafe made an effort to straighten his spine, and
discovered he was sprawled in the leather chair behind
his desk. Which accounted for his aching head, and the
absence of any suppleness in his bones, he reflected
broodingly. But at least he didn't have a hangover.
Despite the temptation, he hadn't touched a drop of alcohol last night.

'Thanks,' he said now, wondering why Cummins
didn't just put the tray down on the desk in front of him
and go. The old man should know that he was never at
his best in the mornings. Though in this case the reasons
were more obscure.

'Yes, my lord.' Cummins deposited the tray, and then
stood back, his hands linked and hanging beneath the
slight swell of his stomach. 'Thank you, my lord.'

Rafe managed to drag himself into a slightly more
comfortable position, and after rasping the palm of one
hand across his jawline his mouth took on a sardonic

twist. The fact that Cummins was still there, was being exceptionally subservient in fact, spoke volumes, and before reaching for the coffee-pot Rafe narrowed his eyes in his direction. 'Well?'

Cummins sniffed. 'Is everything to your satisfaction, my lord?' he enquired politely, and Rafe stifled an oath.

'Everything's fine,' he said, casting a careless glance across the tray. 'Don't worry, Cummins. I'm quite fit, and quite sober, I assure you. You can tell her ladyship I shall be joining her for breakfast very shortly. So don't worry.'

'I'm not worrying, my lord,' replied Cummins stiffly, evidently offended at the suggestion. 'And I'm delighted to hear that you're feeling so well, considering the disturbed night you've spent. I—just thought you'd like to know that the Dowager Countess is visiting the patient at the moment. I believe she's delighted with her progress, too, and is at present discussing, with Nurse Fuller, the possible continuation of treatment at Miss Jacobson's own home——'

'What?'

He had all of Rafe's attention now, and Cummins stepped back a little nervously. 'I said——'

'Dammit, I know what you said.' Rafe hauled himself painfully to his feet, and winced as his spine protested at the effort. 'Why didn't you tell me this at once?' He swore again. 'Since when does my mother make house calls on patients she'd rather were not here?'

'That's why I'm here, my lord.' Cummins gave an aggrieved twitch of his stooped shoulders. 'I came to tell you at once.'

'Right. You're right.' Rafe's tone was hardly conciliatory, but he offered the old man a rueful grimace. 'And I'm an ungrateful——' He broke off, aware that Cummins would not approve of the appropriate expletive. 'But now, if you'll excuse me, I'll save this appetising brew until later. Duty calls, as they say. We can't have my mother giving our guests the wrong impression, can we?'

The mockery in his voice belied the formality of his words, but Cummins knew better than to question his decision. The young Earl, as he was still referred to by his staff, did not suffer fools gladly, and only a fool would interfere in something which had given them all hope for his sanity.

Not that Rafe cared particularly what anyone thought as he strode along the gallery and up the carpeted stairs to the next floor. He was too intent on reaching his objective, and discovering for himself what his mother had in mind by approaching Nurse Fuller behind his back. Did she really think she could spirit the Jacobsons out of the castle without his knowledge? Did she actually believe herself safe, because he was usually unapproachable in the mornings?

Rafe expelled an impatient breath. It wasn't really her fault if she did. He doubted if she'd noticed he wasn't drinking the way he used to. She had been too busy manipulating his association with Grace.

He heard the voices before he reached the open door of the room Cory was occupying. Raised voices—which would have been surprising had they been those of his mother and Nurse Fuller. But he had no difficulty at all in recognising Isobel's voice as well, and his nerves tightened with unwelcome emotion at the protective instincts it inspired.

He reached the room, and paused in the doorway, surveying the scene that met his bitter gaze. They were all there: his mother, Nurse Fuller and Isobel, two of them engaged in a noisy harangue that could hardly be helpful to the patient.

Isobel's face was red, he saw at once, his eyes drawn against his will to her unguarded features. Eyes bright, possibly with the glint of tears; soft cheeks flushed, and stretched by close-pressed hands; generous mouth, parted and vulnerable, the full lower lip—which he had caressed with his tongue—bruised by the nervous gnawing of her teeth. Her hair had been braided, but evidently with an unsteady hand. Wisps of sun-streaked brown hair frayed against her temple, and tiny curls of silk danced against her nape.

Rafe's stomach clenched. She was adorable, he thought incredulously. To him, she was absolutely and totally adorable. And yet there was nothing especially striking about her. Brown hair, eyes that were more green than hazel this morning, a figure that was built more for comfort than sophistication; what on earth did he see in her? He didn't know. He didn't even want to think about it. But whatever she was, whatever she had, he found her completely irresistible. Her warmth and womanliness appealed to him in a way no other woman had before. Not even Sarah...

But that was too much. Too much for him to handle, too much for him to accept. He felt sorry for her, that was all, he told himself savagely, unaware that the women in the room might attribute his expression to other causes. He had kissed her—but he doubted he was the first man to do that since her husband died. The fact that he wanted to strip that soft, curvaceous body naked, and find his own release in her moist flesh, was purely carnal. He had been too long without a woman. He was letting his starved libido rule his head.

The words his mother was using meant little to him at that moment. Things like 'taking advantage' and 'unwarranted presumption' rebounded from the blind pull of his senses. For several seconds he stood there, resenting the emotions Isobel aroused in him. And then her passionate, 'That's unfair!' penetrated his skull.

But before he could intervene, Cory did it for him. Evidently she was feeling a little better this morning, for the hectic flush that had stained her cheeks was gone, and although she still looked pale and drained her eyes were quite alert. She was lying against the pillows, listening to her mother defend herself to Lady Invercaldy, and obviously enjoying the notoriety.

And, conversely, he found this awareness didn't please him. Oh, he was pleased that Cory hadn't developed any life-threatening symptoms, for Isobel's sake, if nothing else. But the realisation that his mother might have some grounds for her resentment gave a cutting edge to his feelings of frustration.

'Hi there!'

Cory's greeting, weak though it was, transfixed the other occupants of the room. Although Nurse Fuller hadn't been involved in the altercation, she looked aghast at Rafe, standing so aggressively in the doorway. Even his mother seemed dismayed by this sudden diversion, and Isobel tucked her hands under her arms in a gesture of defence.

'What the hell's going on here?'

Rafe knew his challenge was unwarrantably harsh, but the sight of Isobel's agitated face did merciless things to his insides. He had never considered himself anyone's hero before, but at that moment he felt he would have fought all the hags of hell to restore her tattered pride.

Not that anyone could describe his mother as a hag, he admitted unwillingly, as she drew herself up to her full height and faced his censure with cold defiance. Even at this hour of the morning, her hair was expertly coiffed and her plaid skirt and pearls were immaculate. She was every inch the aristocrat as she countered his opposition, and once she would have cowed him too, with her scornful deprecation.

'I don't think there's any need for that kind of—saloon language here, Rafe,' she declared, apparently deciding there was no point in equivocation. 'If you have a headache, I suggest you take it somewhere else. Mrs Jacobson and I were just discussing her daughter's recovery.'

'Were you?' Rafe was not disturbed by her attempt to belittle him.

'Yes.' Not to be outdone, the Dowager Countess held up her head. 'You look—tired, Rafe.' That was a euphemism for disgusting, he knew. 'Perhaps you should leave this to me. I'm sure Dr Webster will agree, it's all been a storm in a teacup.'

Rafe lodged himself against the door-frame, aware of Isobel's discomfort, but in no mood to give in. This combat with his mother was long overdue, and he was not about to lose his advantage. So, 'What precisely?' he enquired, arching a conspiratorial brow in Cory's direction. 'Enlighten me, Mama. With what will Webster agree?'

His mother's lips tightened. 'I'm sure you understand me perfectly well, Rafe. That's why you're here, isn't it? I imagine someone—Cummins, no doubt—took it upon himself to inform you that I was having this interview with Mrs Jacobson. I expect he also told you that——' she gestured impatiently towards the bed

'—that this—child is not as ill as you first suspected. As you can see, she's much better this morning, and there's absolutely no reason why she shouldn't be transferred to Miss McLeay's cottage to recuperate. A couple of days' rest and she'll be as good as new——'

'No.' Rafe straightened and took a few steps towards the bed. He flicked a tight smile at Cory, and then let his gaze linger on her mother. 'And it's Mrs Jacobson's cottage now. Not Miss McLeay's.' He reluctantly turned his eyes back to the girl. 'So—how are you feeling?'

'What do you mean, no?' His mother's strident question prevented him from hearing anything Cory said. With uncharacteristic violence, she caught his arm and swung him round to face her. 'I've already discussed this matter with Mrs Jacobson, and she agrees with me. It simply isn't—sensible—to keep her here any longer.'

'I said no,' said Rafe evenly, although the edge was audible in his voice. 'Last night, Webster said he'd know better in forty-eight hours. I intend to keep to that time-table, however you might try to persuade him to the contrary.'

Lady Invercaldy expelled a noisy breath. 'Oh—you're drunk!' she exclaimed dismissively, provoked beyond discretion. She cast a malevolent glance in her son's direction, and when that produced no immediate rejoinder she marched to the door. 'I'll speak to you later, Rafe,' she declared, and it was definitely a threat, not a promise. 'When you've had time to—to recover your senses.'

There was a heavy silence after her departure. Rafe guessed Nurse Fuller was wishing she had somewhere to escape to as well, and Isobel looked bitter now as well as distressed. And so she should, he reflected ruefully. He'd never known his mother to behave so indecorously before. It was as if she was desperate to get the Jacobsons out of the castle. But why? What had they done to deserve such treatment?

'She doesn't like us, does she?'

With her usual lack of respect, Cory took much of the tension out of the situation, and with evident relief Nurse Fuller took the opportunity to slip, unnoticed, into the adjoining bathroom. It was only when the door clicked behind her that Rafe realised what she had done, but judging by Isobel's expression it was not a popular move.

Forcing himself to concentrate on Cory, he smiled. 'She's angry with me, not you,' he assured her lightly, striving for a casual tone. 'I must say you look a lot better this morning. When I found you, you resembled nothing so much as a drowned rat.'

Cory grinned, but before she could say anything Isobel intervened. 'I want to move Cory back to the cottage,' she stated stiffly, and Cory's indignant protest merely endorsed Rafe's instinctive denial.

'I don't think that's very wise,' he began, wishing he had taken the time to have a shave when her scornful gaze raked his face. But he doubted it would have made any difference to anything except his self-esteem.

'I don't care what you think,' she retorted, and he thought in passing how far they had come in the past twenty-four hours. She flushed, as if her thoughts echoed his, and then hurried on, 'I want to take Cory home now, today. I didn't ask for her to be brought here, and I surely don't need anyone accusing me of "taking advantage of a brief acquaintance". She——' and he didn't need to be told who Isobel was talking about '—she said I was "presuming" too much. That I shouldn't take anything you said too seriously at the moment, and that Cory's being in the castle might give your tenants the wrong impression.'

'Isobel——'

'I appreciate what you've done for Cory,' she persisted, not allowing him to break in. 'I know...' She paused to take an unsteady breath. 'I know that without you she could have been much worse. All right——' this, as he arched his dark brows interrogatively '—she could have died! But she didn't. She survived. For which I'm grateful. But there's no earthly reason why she shouldn't leave with me.'

'Oh, Mum!' Cory gazed at her mother in total disgust. 'Don't let her get to you! That's what she wants, don't you see? She's just peeved because Rafe likes us better than he does that wimp Grace!'

'*Cory*!' Isobel was horrified now, and her hurried, 'Apologise at once,' was accompanied by an embarrassed gesture of her hands.

But, even though it was Isobel's feelings he was concerned about and not her daughter's, Rafe chose not to endorse her chastisement of Cory. 'It doesn't matter,' he said, wishing he could take hold of her and make her look at him instead of anywhere but. 'I expect she overheard part of what was said between my mother and Grace when we arrived here yesterday afternoon. I'm afraid she might be right. My mother thinks she can order my life to suit her own ends.' His lips twisted. 'She can't.'

'Even so——'

'Even so, nothing.' His patience was slipping, and he didn't enjoy the feelings of aggravation she was engendering by her determination to have her way. He didn't even know why he was so adamant that Cory shouldn't leave here, but he was. The more obvious explanation was one he didn't choose to entertain at that moment, and his tone was sharp as he appended, 'Do you want to take the responsibility for a possible relapse on your own shoulders?'

'You're exaggerating!'

'Am I?' Perhaps he was, but he refused to acknowledge it. 'Who will look after her at the cottage? Or do you intend to take time off work to nurse her yourself?'

He could see her indecision. Even without the troubled cast of her expression, he could sense it in the way she shifted her weight from one foot to the other and locked her hands in a white-knuckled clasp. 'Cory doesn't need a nurse,' she said at last, and he was rewarded by a glimpse of the anguish in the tear-bright eyes she turned up to him. 'It's only a chill!'

'And if it's not?'

She took a laboured breath, and the scented warmth of her body heat assailed his nostrils. It was intoxicating, and for a moment he was incapable of hiding his feelings. His eyes softened, gentled, searched and found the uncertain parting of her lips with an intimacy that was unmistakable. For a few breathless seconds, he felt the bewildered strength of her response, and he knew that the memory of what had passed between them the night before was paramount in both their thoughts. The temptation to assuage his own needs at the expense of hers was almost uncontrollable, and he could feel his body's involuntary reaction to that purely physical awareness.

But then she snatched her gaze away again, and, as if the need to break that brittle bondage was desperate, she gave in. 'All right,' she said, and he could tell she was nearing the end of her tether. 'All right. If—if Dr Webster thinks it's best, Cory can stay here until tomorrow. And now—now I've got to go.'

CHAPTER TEN

RAFE took Isobel home after the doctor's visit, in a compact off-road vehicle. It was smaller than the Range Rover, but built on similar lines, and she was able to distract herself by dwelling on its various accoutrements. It had five forward gears, and an optional four-wheel-drive facility. Just the thing for a wet country road, strewn with the leaves and other debris brought down overnight by the wind.

Not that Rafe seemed in any mood to pursue their earlier discussion. Now that he had got his own way, he seemed quite content to give most of his attention to his driving. That moment in Cory's sickroom, when she had sensed his dangerous attraction, might never have been. He was cool, almost remote, apparently immune from the nervous tension she was suffering. It was all a game to him, she thought, not for the first time, played not with her, but with his mother.

'I doubt if Webster will expect you to work today,' he remarked suddenly, and Isobel was quite proud of the indifferent face she turned in his direction.

'Why not?'

It was a pointless question, and the sardonic compression of his mouth indicated that he was well aware of it. 'I should get some rest if I were you,' he said, as if she hadn't asked it. 'You look tired. And—edgy. Cory's going to be all right, I promise you. You heard what Webster said. He's quite satisfied with her progress.'

'Is he?' Isobel found she couldn't answer him with as little emotion as he was showing. 'Then wouldn't it have been simpler if you'd allowed me to bring her home?'

Rafe allowed the air to leave his lungs on an audible sigh. 'I thought we'd settled that——'

'No. *You* settled it, not me,' retorted Isobel, stung by his dispassionate response. 'I don't appreciate your using Cory and me—um—Cory and I——'

'You were right the first time,' remarked Rafe mildly, and she flushed before continuing.

'—as—as pawns you can move against your mother. I know you can't really want Cory at the castle. Not—not while your girlfriend is there. It's just a means of annoying your family——'

'I don't have a girlfriend.'

Rafe's response was predictably oblique, and for a moment Isobel was speechless. Then her head swung round. 'You do!'

'I don't,' he insisted, depressing the brake, and, although Isobel had spent the journey wishing for their arrival, now she noted their whereabouts with a bitter feeling of frustration.

They had arrived. Rafe had parked outside the cottage, and Isobel gazed at its sightless windows with a feeling akin to despair. There was no reason for it. She was here, where she wanted to be, and if Cory wasn't with her she soon would be. Just because the sun had disappeared, and the sky was now overcast again, it was no reason to feel so gloomy.

But, conversely, when Rafe turned off the ignition and thrust open his door, she wished she had alighted with more alacrity. The last thing she needed was another argument with him, particularly when there was no one around to act as arbiter.

'I—thanks,' she said offhandedly, forestalling him by pushing open her own door and scrambling out before he could offer to help her. 'For the lift,' she added, with a careless tilt of her shoulders. 'Oh—and for everything else. I'm sorry if I seem ungracious.'

'Are you?'

He leant against the car, playing with the keys, and, unable to deal with him at that moment, Isobel went blindly up the path to the door. To her relief, she found her key at the first attempt, and after inserting it in the lock she turned. 'I—what time do you think I should come for Cory tomorrow? Is nine o'clock too early? Ten?'

'We'll talk about it.' Rafe left the car and came up the path towards her. 'Can we go inside?'

'I—I have to get to work!'

It was a weak excuse and they both knew it. 'Later,' he affirmed, leaning past her and pushing open the door. 'Let's go inside. I want to check that everything's OK.'

'I can do that.'

Isobel strove for control, but it wasn't easy when he was so close that she could feel the draught of his breath against her cheek. He knew it, too, she thought unsteadily. Dear God, how could he do this to her? Without any apparent effort on his part, too.

'Do you want me to tell you what *I* can do?' he demanded, looking down at her, and the blood ran thickly in her veins. 'Inside, Isobel. Before I decide to show you.'

She went straight through to the kitchen, using the excuse of checking on the Aga to give her time to compose her expression. To her relief, she discovered it was still smouldering, if only just, and she fed it some wood from the basket before reaching for the kettle.

'Coffee?' she asked coolly, aware that he had closed the front door, crossed the living-room, and was now standing with his shoulder wedged against the archway that divided the two rooms. It was all she could think of to say, the only reason she could think of why he might have chosen to come inside. They had nothing more to say to one another. It had all been said before.

'If you like.'

His acceptance was hardly enthusiastic, and although she was in no real state to conduct the interview she turned and propped her hips against the drainer. 'It's not what I like that counts, is it?' she declared tensely. 'For the moment—for the moment, you're calling all the shots.'

Rafe heaved a sigh. 'What shots?'

'This.' Isobel waved a hand. 'Your being here. Cory's staying at the castle. It's not my choice, is it?'

'No.' Rafe straightened. 'No, you've made that patently obvious.'

'Well, what did you expect?'

'I expected we might have a friendly conversation for once.'

'A friendly——' Isobel broke off. 'You and I can never be friends.'

'Apparently not.' His cheeks hollowed. 'Is that your fault or mine?'

Isobel felt the heat entering her face. 'It's no one's fault,' she said, ashamed in spite of herself. 'We—we just can't.'

'Because of what my mother said?'

'No. I—well, yes. Perhaps——'

'Or because of what happened last night?'

Isobel swallowed. 'Nothing happened last night,' she said, fidgeting with a tea-towel. 'We—you—I was—overwrought.'

His mouth curled. 'Is that the best you can do?'

'Rafe——'

'Ah—you remembered my name.'

'How could I forget?' she muttered unsteadily, and then, before he could use that to his own advantage, she hurried on, 'About Cory——'

'Why did you think I had a girlfriend?'

His question stunned her, and for a moment she could only stare at him. 'I—um—does it matter?'

'It does to me.' He toyed with the buckle of his belt riding low on his hips. And, when she said nothing, 'Talk to me.'

Isobel licked her lips, instantly aware of where her eyes had been dwelling. Those long brown fingers, easing their way inside the belt, were distinctly sensual, drawing her attention to the snug fit of his trousers.

'Cory—Cory mentioned someone called Grace,' she said at last, not prepared to admit that she had been curious since he'd used the name to his mother. 'Who is she?'

'Grace?' he drawled. 'Well, let me see . . .' He transferred his weight from one foot to the other and, in so doing, consciously or unconsciously, she couldn't be sure, narrowed the space between them. 'Her name is Grace Calder, and she's Sir Malcolm Calder's niece. Sir Malcolm is—was—an old friend of my father's.' He raked back his hair with a thoughtful hand, and frowned. 'I don't think I know anything more about her.'

His mockery was evident, and because he was now only a few inches from where Isobel was standing she had to catch her breath before saying, 'If you say so.'

'You don't believe me?' His hand left his hair to tuck a strand of beige silk behind her ear. 'Oh, Isobel, what am I going to do with you?'

Her breath whistled uneasily. 'I didn't say I didn't believe you.'

'No, I did.'

'You know what I mean.' She braced herself against the drainer. 'I'm sure you know exactly what I'm saying.'

He considered her anxious face with sudden intensity. 'Perhaps I do at that.' He paused, and the hand that had lingered by her ear now traced the line of her chin to the swiftly moving rise and fall of her throat. His knuckles brushed the sensitive tip of one breast with seemingly accidental intimacy as his hand fell away. 'The question is, what do you want me to say?'

'Nothing,' she choked, dry-mouthed. 'I don't want— I don't think you should say anything else.'

'No?' His eyes followed the betraying curve of her breast to its peak. 'Are you sure?'

'Oh, *God*!'

With a groan of despair, Isobel tucked her chin against her chest. She couldn't cope with him at this moment. The fact that he was here at all, that he could so effortlessly overset her plans, was frightening, and she knew, without a shadow of a doubt, that he was aware of her vulnerability.

'What's wrong?'

He was too close, and she had no place to go. With his hands spread at either side of her, he made any kind of retreat impossible, and although his question was innocent enough she didn't trust him.

'You are,' she said tensely, refusing to respond to his sympathy. 'I—think you ought to go.'

'You don't mean that,' he said, and the trouble was, she knew he was right.

But, 'I do!' she insisted, unsteadily, concentrating on the toe of his boot, which was just visible below the muscled curve of his leg. 'Just—just tell me when I can collect Cory. I—I'll arrange for a taxi. Clare—Clare mentioned someone called Mr—Mr MacGregor——'

'To hell with Clare,' said Rafe, softly, but succinctly, his hand finding the stubborn dip of her chin and wresting it upwards. 'Are you afraid of me, Isobel? Is that what it is?' His thumb brushed across her lower lip with sensuous abrasion. 'What are you afraid of? Me? Or yourself?'

He was going to kiss her again. She knew it. There was that look in his eyes, that consuming, sensual warmth that sent a bolt of excitement rocketing through her veins. A wave of heat pooled in her stomach, and spread down into her thighs. She wanted to move away from him, but he had moved against her, and her treacherous body was already yielding to the exciting thrust of his. He had parted his legs to balance himself, and she could feel the tightness of his arousal taut against his zip.

'Don't—don't be afraid of me,' he whispered, as his tongue dampened her lips. And then, as if his own desires had overwhelmed his patience, he crushed her mouth beneath the fever of his.

His lips were hot, and hungry. His tongue in her mouth was urgent and possessive. Wet, and velvety smooth, it stroked and sucked and tantalised, plundering her senses and teasing her into submission. Her blood was on fire, reason spinning wildly out of control. She was dazed, and dizzy, and compliant, sensually intoxicated, and mindlessly content.

With a helpless moan, she wound her arms around his neck. Her fingers slid into his hair, where she now realised they had wanted to go, as long as she had known him. His hair was thick and smooth, too, and incredibly vital to the touch. It clung to her fingers as her nails raked his scalp, and she used it to pull him closer, opening her mouth wide to the sensuous invasion of his.

For long impassioned moments she forgot all the promises she had made to herself, and let her senses have free rein. No one—especially not Edward—had ever made her feel as Rafe made her feel, and it was magic. He—Edward—had always told her she wasn't an emotional woman. He'd said she was sweet, but passive—but it wasn't true. Rafe aroused her in ways she had only dreamed about, and for that brief spell of madness she let her conscience drift.

Afterwards, she was horrified by her own shamelessness. She had even wondered if Edward had suspected what she was really like, and deliberately kept it from her. But no! Edward's needs had matched his character: undemanding, and moderate. He was not the type to lose control, to make love to her in the kitchen!

But when Rafe's teeth found her ear, biting the tender lobe before moving on to find her neck, she didn't try to stop him. When he loosened her braid, and caused her hair to tumble wildly about her shoulders, she let him have his way. There was something intensely sensual in tasting her hair on his lips, and his muffled groan of approval sent shivers down her spine.

She was too bemused to do anything but respond to him, and when his hand slid intimately beneath her sweater she expelled a little moan of her own. She wanted him to touch her. She wanted him to caress her breasts and abrade her aching nipples with his palm. She wanted him. Oh, *God*! She actually *wanted* him. Which was more, so much more, then she'd ever wanted before.

But, ultimately, it was the awareness of her own vulnerability that brought her—unwillingly at first—to her senses. The awareness that if she didn't stop him he might not stop at all. She had the feeling he was using her, to assuage some desperate need of his own, and while it was flattering to think he wanted her she was very much afraid it wasn't true.

And—dear God!—they were in full view of the kitchen window. If anyone came to the door, they couldn't fail to see them. Did she really want to destroy her reputation, acting as substitute for the woman Rafe really loved? The gossips would have a field-day. Not just an outsider, but shameless as well.

But she wasn't, she thought fiercely, scrubbing a hand across her face. Yet, with her sweater pulled all askew, and her bra unfastened, and her skirt riding up around her thighs, who would believe her? Using her fists, she pushed him away from her. One of them had to be sensible. One of them had to prove that the woman Edward had loved was not this wild-eyed wanton.

Rafe's eyes were glazed with emotion, and he made a muttered protest when she shook him into awareness. What would he have done, she wondered, if she hadn't stopped him? Would he have made love to her there, propped so inelegantly against the drainer? Her skin feathered, as much in revulsion at her own reactions as his. Or would he have taken her upstairs, to the bedroom under the eaves—that virginal bedroom, which she was sure Miss McLeay had never violated? The idea of Rafe sharing her bed, the bed she had come to regard as her own, was both tantalising and disturbing. When Edward died, she had been sure she'd never want to share a bed with anyone ever again. Even thinking about doing so with Rafe was a betrayal of all she'd believed.

Side-stepping him now, she thrust back her hair, pushed her sweater down, and went to turn off the boiling kettle. Bothwell was sitting on the window-ledge outside, and she wondered rather foolishly what he must be thinking of her behaviour. His furry face looked pinched and indignant, and she wondered if he had been there all night. At least he couldn't talk about what he'd seen, she mused wryly, opening the door to let him in. He was totally dependable. Probably the only thing that was.

'Do you drive?'

While she had been purposely avoiding looking in Rafe's direction, he had moved to rest his hips against the sink unit. Unlike her, there were no overt signals to betray what he had been doing, and if his eyelids looked heavier than usual and there was a faint incoherence to his speech she doubted anyone else would have noticed.

'Do I drive?' she echoed now, keeping her shoulder firmly between them. 'I—why do you want to know?'

'I take it that means yes,' he declared flatly, pushing his hands into the pockets of his jacket. He straightened, and because she was alert to every move he made she saw the somewhat ironic expression that crossed his lean face. 'You can use the Shogun, then,' he added, stepping towards the archway. He dropped a set of keys on to one of Miss McLeay's many occasional tables. 'I suggest you come back about half-past six.'

'Come back?' Isobel knew she sounded stupid, but she couldn't help it. What was he talking about?

'To the castle,' he explained levelly, and his eyes were as cool now as they had been hot earlier. 'You can join Cory while she has her supper. I know she'll be glad to see you, and it will give Nurse Fuller a break.'

Isobel stared at him. 'Tonight?'

'Well, I don't mean in the morning, do I?' he enquired, rather tersely. 'Then, after Webster's given his verdict, you can bring her home.'

'Tonight?'

'Is that all you can say?' Rafe cajoled tightly. 'No.' He expelled a weary breath. 'Tomorrow morning. Haven't I just said so? You'll join us for supper, of course, and spend the night——'

Isobel gulped. 'That's impossible!'

'Why is it impossible?'

'Because it is.' Isobel couldn't believe he was even suggesting such a thing. 'I—your mother——'

'My mother has nothing to do with it.' His tone was definitely cool now. Cool—and unyielding. 'You're my guest. My mother will respect my wishes.'

'And if she won't?'

'She will.' He was uncompromising, and she shivered at the detachment in his tone. 'You can't stay here,' he added, shrugging. 'Ergo, it's the obvious solution.'

Of course, it wasn't. It was no solution at all, and afterwards she recognised that if she hadn't been so eager for him to leave she'd have told him so. But she had been eager, not to mention anxious, and afraid. Not just of the power he had exhibited over her, but of her own weaknesses as well. Even then, conducting that rather odd conversation, she had been intensely conscious of the danger.

The fact that she hadn't made a very satisfactory job of restoring her clothes to rights hadn't helped. Her breasts had felt sore and the fine wool of her sweater had proved a constant irritation. Had he known that? she wondered. Had he sensed how nervous she was?

She'd felt as if a layer of skin had been removed, and
the tender flesh beneath was being punished.

By the time he'd let himself out of the cottage, she
was shaking so badly she didn't even absorb the fact
that he had left his keys behind him. It was only then
that she realised what he'd meant by his questions, and
the identity of the Shogun was quickly understood.

Of course, she snatched up the keys and went after
him, but she was too late. And when she saw him
climbing into the passenger seat of the Range Rover, she
realised he'd planned to leave the vehicle all along.

She had a bad moment when she realised the Range
Rover had a driver. Just for a minute, she wondered if
the man had possibly come to the door without them
hearing him. But then, despite her fears, she discarded
the notion. Rafe was the Earl of Invercaldy. No one,
least of all a chauffeur, would attempt to intervene. Besides, he had been parked some way along the street.
Patiently waiting, she'd mused bitterly. For however long
his employer might choose to take.

Which meant she had the use of the car all day. Not
that she intended to use it. Not initially, anyway. It wasn't
until she arrived at the surgery—albeit on foot—and Dr
Webster insisted she take the day off that the advantages
became apparent.

Not that Mrs Webster endorsed her husband's decision. Roped in to fill the gap that Stella Fuller's absence had created, she was less than sympathetic in her
opinion. 'You can't have Cory running about the estate
causing all manner of upset. Maybe Clare's offering you
this job was an error of judgement. A child like your
daughter is evidently more used to city streets. The
dangers there are just as real, I'm sure, but less likely
to offend other people.'

What other people? Isobel wanted to ask, but she
knew. The Dowager Countess wasn't the only one who
objected to her association with Rafe. If only she could
explain that it wasn't her doing that had created this
unlikely liaison between herself and the Earl.

But, at that moment, she had more pressing matters
to attend to. She needed to ring Mrs Jacobson first of
all. And then, she thought, she'd take a trip into

Strathmoor. For once she was independent and she decided to stock up on all Cory's favourite foods at the supermarket while she had the chance.

Mrs Jacobson predictably received the news of Cory's accident with even less understanding. Even the fact that her granddaughter was presently being cared for at Invercaldy Castle did little to assuage her dismay. She had little hesitation in blaming Isobel for what had happened. And, despite all assurances, she succeeded in convincing herself that Cory was at death's door.

'I'm coming up tomorrow,' she declared, and Isobel forcibly closed her mind against the possible consequences of such a visit. The past three weeks had taught her that there were worse things than Mrs Jacobson's over-protectiveness. Quite honestly, she wished she had someone to protect her against the insidious effects of Rafe's attentions.

However, she did succeed in putting off the older woman's visit for another day. Until Dr Webster had given Cory the OK, she couldn't be sure her daughter would be coming home tomorrow. Until she did, she ventured, it wouldn't be fair to expect the Earl and his family to accommodate a stream of visitors to the castle.

Of course, Mrs Jacobson had objected that the child's grandmother hardly constituted a 'stream of visitors' but she'd seen the logic of the argument. 'Just make sure they take good care of her,' she'd stated finally. 'Cory's not just any child. She's *my* granddaughter.'

Isobel doubted that would mean much to Rafe's mother, or the Websters either, for that matter, but the prospect of the evening ahead was enough to deter any deliberation on that score. Whatever Rafe said, she could not believe any of the Lindsays would welcome her presence at their supper table. It was another of Rafe's provocations, and she was being forced to bear the brunt.

But, despite her declared unwillingness to return to the castle, Isobel found herself back there at half-past six precisely. She parked the Shogun near the entrance, not knowing where else to put it, and then breathed a sigh of relief when Mrs Fielding came out to meet her.

'Your daughter's waiting for you, Mrs Jacobson,' she said politely, and Isobel guessed she had had orders to make sure her arrival didn't disrupt the smooth running of the household. 'Just leave the car where it is. Lucas, or one of the other men, will put it away later.'

And, as before, Isobel saw no one on the journey up to her daughter's room. It was dark, and lamps with beaten bronzed shades cast long shadows on high, arching walls. The walls were hung with gloomy portraits of long-dead ancestors, and Isobel could feel their eyes watching her as she followed Mrs Fielding along the gallery. Even the fact that some of the pictures of men in Highland costume reminded her of Rafe was no comfort. Their stiff features were cold and un-friendly, and possessed none of his warmth of character.

Cory was waiting for her, as the housekeeper had said, and over an appetising bowl of beef casserole—which Isobel noticed her daughter swallowed with evident en-thusiasm—she confessed she'd be glad to go home after all. It had evidently been a long day, and Cory soon got bored when she had nothing to do. She'd seen Rafe, she said, which caused her mother no small *frisson* of alarm, but apart from his visit she'd mostly been left alone.

'They don't have televisions in the bedrooms here,' she added, after one of the maids had taken her tray away. 'Can you imagine that? All their money, and no television!'

Isobel had to smile. 'Not everyone wants to spend all their free time glued to the box,' she declared. 'There are other things.'

'Oh, yeah. Right.' Cory grimaced. 'Like magazines, I suppose. Mrs Fielding lent me some magazines, but they were boring too. All about horses and dogs and fishing! I thought they'd buy *Vogue* and *Tatler*. Stuff like that.'

'They probably do,' said Isobel drily, guessing that Rafe's mother was unlikely to contribute any of her magazines to keeping Cory occupied. 'Anyway, you'll be coming home tomorrow. And the day after that your grandmother's coming for a visit.'

'She is?' Cory was delighted, and Isobel had to admit that as far as her daughter was concerned her grand-mother's arrival meant sweets and presents, and an ally to call on if her mother got heavy. 'Is she staying long?'

'I'm—not sure.' Isobel wished she knew the answer to that herself. 'We'll see.' She paused. 'Now, do you want to tell me why you weren't at school yesterday?'

'Because I wasn't.' Cory shrugged, and then said, shrewdly, 'You're dressed up tonight. Are you going somewhere?'

Isobel sighed. She'd wondered how long it would take before Cory noticed she was wearing something special. The slim-fitting black velvet was plain and simple, but its long sleeves were flattering and its short skirt displayed her legs.

'I'm—that is—I've been invited to have supper with—with the Earl and his family,' she admitted swiftly. 'Now, why weren't you in school, instead of playing dangerous games on the loch?'

'You're having supper *here*!' Cory's astonishment was not feigned, and although Isobel knew she was once again avoiding the issue she could hardly blame her daughter for echoing her own feelings.

'Yes,' she said now, checking to see that her hair was still secure in its knot. She had braided it this evening, and wound the braids into a coronet on top of her head. It was more sophisticated than the way she usually wore it, and she hoped it would give her confidence. 'Um— the Earl invited me. Didn't he tell you?'

'No.' Cory made a sound of astonishment. 'So that's why creepy Grace was snooping about this afternoon.'

'Grace?' Isobel cleared her throat. 'I mean, Miss Calder?'

'Yes. Do you know her?'

'I know—of her,' admitted Isobel warily. She didn't want to be too obvious, but she had to ask, 'What did she want?'

'This and that.' Cory was definitely more her old self, Isobel thought drily. There was a decided gleam of speculation in her eyes now. 'She asked about you, actually. Now I know why.'

Isobel moistened her lips with a nervous tongue. 'What—what about me?'

'Where we lived; whether you were married; how old you were.' Cory shrugged. 'I told her Rafe was a friend of ours. Well, he is, isn't he? Why else would he invite you to supper?'

Why, indeed?

Isobel wished she had a satisfactory answer for her. 'I—think he just felt sorry for me,' she said at last, wondering if perhaps that wasn't the truth after all . . .

CHAPTER ELEVEN

Rafe stood at the open window, letting the cold evening air clear his aching head. It wasn't that he had been drinking—or, at least, no more than anyone else. A Scotch before supper, two glasses of wine with his meal and a brandy afterwards were definitely not enough to cause him any discomfort these days. Once, they might have done; but in recent years he had been known to empty a bottle of Scotch all by himself, and the social tippling he had done this evening did not come anywhere near that record.

In fact, he hadn't felt like drinking at all. Keeping his mother and Grace civil had proved a full-time occupation, and although Isobel had stood her corner there was no doubt that she had not enjoyed it.

And that was the real reason he had a headache. No matter what excuses he made, how often he told himself that his infatuation with the Jacobson woman was just that, an infatuation, his senses told a different story.

The trouble was, he wanted her. Even now, standing here, with a chill wind blowing in his face, he wanted her. Even thinking about her warm lush body, and that fine silky hair, which he knew fell almost to her waist, caused a painful tightening in his groin. He had touched that hair; he had threaded it through his fingers, and wet it with his lips, and he could imagine how it would look on a pillow. And not just any pillow, he acknowledged tensely, as his body stirred of its own volition. *His* pillow; *his* bed; he wanted her there, naked beneath him.

The constriction his unwelcome arousal created brought an unwilling hand to ease his trousers. He had flung off his jacket earlier, and now he loosened his belt, and the button at his waist, and released the zip partway. The relief was only temporary, and his lips curled at the admission. But at least there was no one else around to witness his frustration.

What in hell was wrong with him? He'd never felt like this, not even when he and Sarah had first got married. He had always known their relationship was more cerebral than physical anyway, and despite having lived a fairly hedonistic existence before their marriage he had convinced himself that what he and Sarah shared was enough.

Besides, the very idea of Sarah permitting the kind of liberties Isobel had permitted at the cottage that morning was ludicrous. It would have been an insult to her sensitivities. She had been a lady, in every sense of the word. If he had treated her as he had treated Isobel she would have been hurt, and humiliated. Any kind of overt sexuality had embarrassed her, and he had soon learned not to advertise his needs.

But he had loved her, he told himself fiercely. Dammit, he loved her still. He was letting the darker side of his character dictate his mood. Letting a physical attraction seduce his finer feelings.

With a muffled oath, he slammed the window shut on the darkness outside, and paced broodingly about the apartment. He was like a callow youth, he thought disgustedly. All he could think about was getting Isobel Jacobson into bed. If he was so desperate for a woman, why didn't he just go into Glasgow and find one?

But he knew he'd find no satisfaction in some casual sexual encounter. He was desperate for a woman, yes, but not just any woman. God, if that were the case, Grace was fairly panting at the bit. Ever since her uncle had departed, she had tried everything she knew to get him interested. Of course, she was playing for higher stakes, but she had had no guarantees.

Still, after this evening, even she must have got the message, he mused grimly. His mother had, he was sure. That was why she had been so anxious to get Cory Jacobson out of the castle; why she had been so incensed when he'd told her he had invited Isobel to join them for supper.

'I really think you must have taken leave of your senses, Rafe!' she had exclaimed, the faint quaver in her voice revealing the intensity of her emotions. 'Isn't it enough that we have Webster and his nurse coming and going at all hours? Why must I entertain her mother? Might I remind you, Rafe, this is my home?'

'It's my home, too,' he had replied neutrally, aware that his mother's anger had lost much of its bite. 'Why shouldn't I invite a female guest if I want to? It makes a change from you doing it for me.'

'If it were a suitable female guest, I would agree with you,' Lady Invercaldy had retorted. 'Oh, I'm well aware of what you're really doing, Rafe. This is your way of getting back at me for inviting Grace to stay on, isn't it? Very well. If you insist on it, I'll ask her to leave forthwith.'

'Not on my behalf,' Rafe had demurred evenly.

If only it were that simple, he thought now. He wished someone could tell him what there was about Isobel Jacobson that was causing him to act so out of character. It wasn't as if they had anything in common. Yet he couldn't seem to get her out of his mind.

'Well, I think you're irresponsible,' his mother had declared finally. 'And, whatever you say, I know I'm not far off the mark. I don't believe you're seriously interested in Mrs Jacobson. You're just using her as a means to frustrate me.'

Rafe sighed now, the breath leaving his lungs on a weary gasp. She was probably right, he conceded bitterly. She had to be right. He picked up his late wife's picture from where it always stood, on the table beside his bed, and stared grimly at her gentle image. His interest in Isobel wasn't serious, he assured her silently. It was just an aberration. A minor inconvenience. She was the only woman he had ever loved.

And yet...

The knock on his door arrested further thought. A swift glance at his watch informed him it was after eleven. It was unusual indeed for anyone to disturb him after he'd retired.

The possible explanation had his heart quickening rapidly. Cory, he thought grimly. It had to be Cory. Her condition must have deteriorated after all. He had told

Mrs Fielding to let him know if there was any cause for concern.

Setting down the picture again, he crossed the room swiftly, throwing open the door without hesitation. The brief hope that it might be Isobel came and went as his booted heels covered the carpet. But he squashed it down determinedly. Apart from anything else, she didn't know where his apartments were...

It was Grace.

Rafe clutched the door weakly, aware of a crippling sense of disappointment. Whatever logic had dictated, the fact that it was another woman, and not Isobel, who had invaded his sanctuary left him feeling raw and vulnerable. Destructive, too, he acknowledged savagely. Was this another of his mother's ideas? If it was, perhaps he ought to exploit it.

But he knew he wouldn't. He couldn't. No matter how tempting the thought of thwarting his mother might be, he had no desire to sleep with Grace—with or without conditions. Besides, as his anger subsided he knew his mother would never have condoned such behaviour. Grace had come here, clothed only in a black satin robe, for her own purposes. But as soon as she started to speak he wondered if his mother hadn't indirectly had something to do with it after all.

'Oh, Rafe!' Grace exclaimed, her gaze alighting on him with evident avidity, before darting over his shoulder into the room beyond. 'I hoped you'd still be up.' She looked at him again, and he was well aware that his state of semi-undress hadn't gone unnoticed. 'I'm leaving in the morning, and I wanted to say goodbye.'

'Goodbye?' Rafe knew he sounded blank, but he couldn't help it. It was the last thing he had expected, and it was difficult to hide his confusion.

'Yes, goodbye,' repeated Grace softly, one hand tracing a provocative line from her throat to the deep V of the robe. Her fingers lingered there, in the hollow between her small breasts, as she held his startled gaze with her own. 'I know you sometimes go out early, and I was afraid I might miss you.'

Rafe managed to hide his disbelief at this statement by offering a half-truth of his own. 'This is rather sudden, isn't it?' he protested politely. 'I thought you were in no hurry to return to Glasgow.'

'Well...' Grace's fingers spread tantalisingly towards her nipples '...I thought you might be glad to see me go. Elizabeth says you're having some sort of an affair with Mrs Jacobson, and I wouldn't want to get in your way. I must say, I didn't believe her at first. I mean, since Sarah died you've been virtually unapproachable. But maybe an affair is what you need right now. And after this evening——'

Rafe's jaw clenched. 'When did my mother tell you I was having an affair with Mrs Jacobson?'

'Does it matter?' Grace looked beyond him again, before meeting his dark gaze with appealing eyes. 'Why don't you invite me in, and we can discuss it? It is rather draughty in this corridor, and, as you can see, my robe is rather thin.'

Rafe stared at her angrily, and then, out of the corner of his eye, he glimpsed another movement. Someone else was there, at the end of the corridor; someone who quickly concealed himself, as soon as he realised he—or perhaps it was a she—had been noticed.

'What the——?'

With a curse, Rafe brushed Grace aside, and stalked grimly along the corridor. The suspicion was growing that it was his mother, after all, come to observe the outcome of the poison she had spread earlier, and it incensed him. How dared she discuss his behaviour with Grace? How dared she accuse him of being irresponsible, and then imply his interest in Isobel was both transient and sordid?

The fact that he had been making a similar deduction earlier didn't even occur to him at that moment. The assessment he had made of his attraction to Isobel was as far from his thoughts as the woman he had left standing at his door. He was angry, and resentful, and the opportunity to vent his frustration in any form was welcome.

But when he reached the bend in the corridor there was no sign of his mother. The dark-clad figure hurrying rapidly in the opposite direction was Isobel herself, and it took no feat of deduction on his part to realise it was

she, and not the Dowager Countess, who had seen Grace
at his door.

His reaction was swift and unequivocal. Despite all
his efforts to convince himself that Isobel meant nothing
to him, that her effect on his senses was physical and
nothing else, the sight of her obvious panic cut him to
the core. He could guess what she was thinking, having
glimpsed Grace's half-naked figure, and before he could
stop himself he had called her name.

She stopped, but he could tell by the rounding of her
shoulders as she turned to face him that she hated having
to do it. There was humiliation as well as reluctance in
her expression, and although she was obviously making
a concerted effort to appear composed her eyes were
bright and unfocused.

'Were you looking for me?'

Rafe's question was hardly sensitive, and he knew,
even before she spoke, that he wouldn't get a satisfactory answer.

'I—I must have taken the wrong turning,' she offered
through taut lips, unwillingly retracing her steps, and
Rafe admired the determination that was giving her the
courage to deny him. 'I've just been checking on Cory.'
She licked her lips. 'She's asleep.'

'Is she?' Rafe took a breath to steady himself. 'I
thought you'd be too.'

'Yes.' Isobel's lips took on a faintly bitter curve. 'I'm
sure you did.'

Rafe glanced behind him. Then, content that Grace
was too far away to overhear their conversation, he said
something completely crazy. 'Why don't you come and
see where I sleep?'

Isobel's response was wholly predictable. 'I don't think
so.'

'Why not?'

'Why not?' He guessed she was giving herself time to
think. 'Um—don't you think one—visitor—is enough?'

'I didn't invite Grace here,' he retorted swiftly. And
when Isobel's brows arched in obvious disbelief he felt
the familiar pang of irritation that he should need to
defend himself to her. 'I didn't,' he insisted harshly,
telling himself he didn't need any of this, but going for

it all the same. 'God, do you think she'd have been standing at the door if I'd wanted her company? She turned up a couple of minutes before you—missed your way.' The irony in his voice was unmistakable. 'It's the truth.'

Isobel's eyes darted towards the other woman, as if assessing the veracity of what he had said. 'Well,' she ventured, 'I suppose that's feasible——'

'Thanks!' His mockery was intense.

'But——' her eyes flickered over his loosened belt, and he wondered how two women's eyes could cause such contrasting reactions '—you must admit, there is room for doubt.'

'I was getting ready for bed,' said Rafe, exasperated as much by his own capacity for lying as by her for doubting him. Then, tightly, 'We have to talk. Please.'

Isobel looked anxious. 'Not now.'

'Why not now?'

'Miss Calder——'

'To hell with Miss Calder,' retorted Rafe harshly, his hand moving of its own accord to fasten around her wrist. 'Isobel——'

'Well, excuse me!' Grace's sarcastic tone couldn't quite hide her fury as she paused beside them. Without either of them being aware of it, she had joined them at the other end of the corridor, and Rafe knew at once that he should have waited for her departure before showing his feelings quite so clearly. 'I'll see you later, darling,' she added, allowing the black silk to slip and expose one white shoulder. 'I can see you've got your hands full at present. Don't do anything silly, will you?'

Her gaze slid mockingly over her rival's flushed face before she sauntered off along the corridor, and Rafe knew before Isobel opened her mouth what she was she going to say.

'I've got to go——'

'Why?'

Isobel raised her eyes heavenward. 'You know why,' she spat, as Grace cast one final smirk in their direction, before disappearing into her own room. 'This—this isn't sensible.'

'What happened this morning wasn't particularly sensible either,' he declared grimly, stung into a defence that could hardly help his case. And then, urgently, 'Isobel—I *need* you. I mean it. I do. Don't—don't turn away from me now. At least come and have a nightcap with me.'

She shouldn't have given in to him. She knew it. But, as far as he was concerned, that was all she ever seemed to do. And why? Because she believed him when he said he needed her? Because she felt sorry for his having lost his wife, and sympathetic for the strain that had been put upon him? *No*!

If she were honest, she'd admit that her association with Rafe Lindsay had as much to do with her needs as his. No matter how she tried to defend herself, nothing could alter the fact that tonight's events owed more to her weaknesses than to his.

She hadn't intended to explore the castle. She hadn't intended to do anything but go back to her own room and try to sleep. Not that she had felt much like sleeping after the uncomfortable couple of hours she had spent in his mother's and Grace Calder's company. But that was over now, and unlikely to be repeated. All she had planned to do was check on her daughter and then retire to bed. She'd had no thought whatsoever of venturing further.

Or had she? In all honesty, she had wondered where Rafe's bedroom was. The room she had been allotted was so attractive and so comfortable, she'd told herself, it was only natural that she'd be curious about the Earl's own apartments. But when she'd left Cory's bedroom, it hadn't been a conscious decision to turn in the opposite direction. In fact, she had covered several yards of thick Turkish carpeting before she had realised what she was doing. And then—well, the temptation to go on had overwhelmed her inhibitions, and it was only when she'd turned the corner and seen Grace at Rafe's door that she'd realised where her apparently innocent transgression had led her.

'I'm afraid I can only offer you the local brew,' Rafe said behind her now, and she turned in some confusion to find him handing her a cut-glass tumbler.

'Oh, I—don't drink whisky,' she protested, but he pressed the glass into her hand anyway.

'Make an exception,' he said wryly, raising his own glass to his lips and looking at her over the rim. Then, 'I'm sorry about this evening. It didn't work out the way I'd expected.'

'No, I don't suppose it did.' Isobel sniffed the whisky half suspiciously and took a tentative sip. Then she pulled a face. 'Well, it worked out exactly as I expected.'

Rafe scowled. 'If Grace hadn't been there——'

'Your mother would have reacted just the same,' Isobel assured him drily. 'Just as she'd react if she knew I was here.' She allowed her gaze to wander round the surprisingly spartan apartment. 'This is your bedroom, isn't it? Even if we are still fully dressed.'

Rafe expelled his breath on a heavy sigh. 'Let's start again, then, shall we? I'm sorry about this evening. I am. I didn't want to embarrass you. I just wanted to spend some time with you.'

Isobel gave him an old-fashioned look. 'In company with two people who, for different reasons—or perhaps the same one,' she amended, 'hate my guts?'

'It wasn't meant to be that way.' Rafe regarded her with some impatience. 'This morning——'

'This morning is best forgotten,' Isobel interrupted him shortly, taking an inadvertently large mouthful of the Scotch and almost gagging. Moving away, she set the glass down before she made any more mistakes of that kind, and mentally stiffened her shoulders before turning back to him.

'You don't mean that,' he told her now, setting down his own drink, and the threat implicit in that simple action had her nerves tingling anxiously.

'I do mean it,' she averred hurriedly, before he could get any other ideas. 'Contrary to your belief, I'm not one of those women who, just because their husbands are dead, are desperate for a man's attention. I—the physical aspects of our marriage were never—never that important to me——'

'I can believe that.'

His laconic acceptance of her denial had her momentarily blinking her eyes, but then, suspicious of any statement he might make, she hastened on, 'And—and having an affair with you doesn't—doesn't interest me.'

Rafe's eyes narrowed, and she was struck by the way it concentrated their darkening intensity. 'Have I asked you to have an affair with me?' he enquired, and she was chilled by the awesome challenge in his voice. 'As I recollect it, I invited you in here for a drink; nothing more. An innocent enough suggestion, wouldn't you agree?'

Isobel's lips worked in silent agitation. Then, because she had very little to lose anyway, she exclaimed, 'That's not true, and you know it! You didn't ask me in here just to have a drink. I know it and you know it, so why don't you stop playing games?'

Rafe's dark brows ascended. 'So why did you accept my invitation?' he asked softly, and Isobel, who realised she hadn't thought it through before opening her big mouth, was nonplussed.

'I—well, because I did believe you—at first,' she lied unhappily. And then, knowing he didn't believe that either, she added wearily, 'Look, why don't I just leave—now—before either of us says something we don't mean?'

'Or does something?' suggested Rafe quietly, and she expelled her breath on a rueful nod. 'Even if, as you say, that's what we both want?'

Isobel caught her breath. 'That's not what I said.'

'No?'

'No, I just explained——' She broke off. 'I thought you understood.'

'Understood what?'

She flushed. 'Well——' She licked her lips. 'When I said the—the physical aspects of my marriage to Edward weren't—weren't that important, you said you could believe it.'

'So?'

Isobel shook her head. 'You're just being deliberately obtuse.'

'No, I'm not.' Rafe tucked his thumbs into the waistband of his trousers, drawing her eyes—

deliberately, she was sure—to their precarious fastening. 'I can believe your relationship with your late husband was not a particularly physical one.'

'Why?' Isobel swallowed. 'Oh, I suppose I'm not—experienced enough?'

'Something like that.'

His response infuriated her, and she wondered why. She should have expected it. She was inexperienced, after all. No one could have called her relationship with Edward a passionate one. They had been friends first and lovers second. A situation that had suited her very well—until now.

'I'll have you know Edward and I had a very happy marriage,' she declared bitterly.

'Did you?'

'Yes.' Isobel clenched his fists. 'And just because your wife——'

'Leave Sarah out of this!'

His scowl had returned with a vengeance, but Isobel was tired of being threatened. 'No. Why should I?' she retorted resentfully. 'She died too, and I'm sorry, but I'd rather be accused of being frigid than eccentric! Which is just a polite way of saying you can't handle it!'

'Shut up!'

'Oh?' Isobel arched her brows in defiance. 'It's all right for you to make fun of me, but not for me to——'

'I said shut up!' he snarled, and before she had time to enjoy her little victory his hand shot out and grabbed her wrist, jerking her towards him. 'Shut up,' he repeated raggedly, his free hand trembling as his thumb came to smear her lips, and then, with a muffled groan, he replaced his thumb with his mouth.

Isobel's hands balled against his midriff, but she didn't attempt to push him away. Not that she'd have succeeded, even if she'd tried, she reflected ruefully. Her strength was small when compared to his, and whatever nerve her reckless words had pricked had driven Rafe beyond the point of conciliation.

Besides, with his angry mouth plundering hers, and his hands tumbling her hair from its braid, she had little

will to fight his aggression. In all honesty, she knew this
was what she had been wanting ever since they had sat
across from one another at the supper table that evening,
when every questing look he had sent in her direction
had caused a curious melting sensation in the pit of her
stomach. She had tried not to look at him, particularly
as his mother and Grace Calder had been watching their
every move. But the hunger she'd had had been wholly
physical, and she hadn't always been able to restrain her
wandering eyes.

And now that hunger was being assuaged by the most
urgent means possible. Or, at least, a part of it was, she
mused dizzily, aware that however closely Rafe's arms
might imprison her it would never be enough. No matter
that one arm was wrapped around her waist, moulding
her warm body to his. No matter that the fingers that
had abraded her lips were now locked in her hair. It
wasn't enough; they were not close enough. She wanted
to be closer still, without the annoying barrier of their
clothes between them.

Her palms spread against his midriff, feeling the taut
muscles flex beneath her fingers. Beneath the fine silk
of his shirt, his skin was lightly spread with hair, and
he sucked in his breath when her finger probed between
the buttons and found his puckering flesh. It caused him
to remove his mouth from hers and stifle a taut oath
against the scented curve of her cheek. But when the
button popped, allowing her free access to his stomach,
his mouth sought hers again, with a desperation that
owed nothing to anger and everything to his own inflamed senses. His tongue plunged deeply into her
mouth, possessing and possessive, and her tentative imi-
tation was met with a muffled groan of approval.

His hands moved now, sensuously caressing the curve
of her spine, before sliding down her back to her bottom
and lifting her fully against him. The action brought her
into intimate contact with the throbbing heat of his
arousal, and instinctively she allowed her fingers to slip
down his belly to where his belt hung open.

'God!' he gulped, against her lips, as the sensations
her innocent fingers were evoking caused him to thrust
more urgently against her. He ground his body against

hers, and his mouth spun its magic ever more sensually, and she slid her arms around his waist and let him part her legs and ease his thigh between.

'God-dammit, Isobel, you must know what you're doing to me!' he muttered, when she rubbed herself against his leg, and, looking up at him, she saw that his eyes were not cold now, but dark and smouldering with emotions he was as incapable of hiding as she was. 'You do know, don't you?' he added, looking down at her with a mixture of bitterness and frustration. 'And, unless you want me to do the same thing to you, you'd better get out, now!'

'Is that what you want?' she asked huskily, but she already knew the answer. She didn't care what she was inviting any more. Nothing she had shared with Edward had prepared her for the aching needs she was experiencing in Rafe's arms, and the idea of leaving him and making the lonely journey back to her own room wasn't even worthy of consideration.

'You know what I want,' Rafe said now, the unsteadiness in his voice betraying his own shredding control, and although she knew exactly what he meant she had to push him to the limit.

'For me to be—Sarah?' she ventured, needing that final reassurance, and he swore before pushing his face close to hers.

'No!' he growled harshly. 'Sarah never—she was never like this!' And, with another oath, he swung her up into his arms and carried her to the bed...

CHAPTER TWELVE

RAFE awakened with an unusual feeling of well-being. For several minutes he just lay there, enjoying the unaccustomed sensations of a clear head and a healthy body, without allowing the reasons for his present state of mind to impinge on his consciousness. He was a little sore, perhaps, and there was an unfamiliar ache around his lumbar region, but that didn't trouble him. It was enough to know that he hadn't thought of his late wife as soon as he opened his eyes, and the sun streaming through the uncurtained window was a pleasure and not a bane.

But, inevitably, the reasons for that uncurtained window began to bother him. His valet always drew the curtains, and if they weren't drawn now it was because he must have opened them. But when? And why? And why hadn't he closed them again? Despite the sense of lethargy, he forced his brain to make the connection.

And it did. Much too quickly for his peace of mind. He had been standing at the window the previous evening, before Grace had come knocking at his door. Before Isobel had interrupted them, and he'd brought her back in here...

His body jack-knifed then, rearing back against the pillows as he swung round in the bed. With his heart hammering painfully in his chest, and the blood rushing swiftly to his face, he stared disbelievingly at the empty space beside him. Isobel, he thought blankly. He had brought Isobel to his bed. He blinked, as consternation gave way to irritation. So where the hell was she? God, what had he done?

There was no possible hope that he might relax again now, and with a savage imprecation he threw himself out of bed. He winced as the stiffness in his spine forced him to move a little less energetically, and the realisation that he was completely naked had him reaching for his robe. But not before he glimpsed the streaks of blood that scarred his shoulders, and he twisted before a long pier-glass to access the possible damage. The marks were consistent with his remembrance of Isobel's nails digging into his flesh as she wound herself about him, and for a moment a foolish feeling of smugness brought an involuntary smile to his lean lips. But it was short-lasting, even if the memory of what had happened the night before could not so easily be displaced.

He closed his eyes for a moment, willing the unwelcome thoughts away, but his brain was functioning clearly now, and it refused to be diverted. Pictures of himself and Isobel entwined together were imprinted indelibly on the back of his eyelids. He couldn't escape their imagery, and he couldn't deny their passion.

Dear God!

He opened his eyes to the awareness that his hands were sweating and not entirely steady as he tied the cord of his bathrobe. And it angered him. Was he to escape one prison, only to be ensnared by another? And how could he have done such a thing, with Sarah looking on?

He snatched his late wife's picture from the cabinet, but this time there was no reassurance to be gained from her reflection. With a feeling of desperation, he thrust the photograph into a drawer, unable to face her, unable to face himself.

Yet the remembrance of what had happened the night before refused to be dislodged. In spite of his guilt at his betrayal of Sarah's memory, there was also the suspicion that he had betrayed Isobel too. It was all very well consoling himself with the thought that she had been as much to blame for what had happened as he was, but was that really true? He had known as soon as he touched her—not just last night, but weeks ago—that she was a virtual innocent when it came to sexual relationships. She had been married, sure, and no doubt she considered herself as experienced as any other married woman, but it wasn't true. Whatever she had had with that husband of hers, it hadn't been a passionate affair. He had loved her, perhaps, and no doubt she believed she had loved him. Perhaps she had, in her way, he admitted, though rather less willingly. Nevertheless, the physical side of their marriage had never achieved the fulfilment they had found in each other's arms last night. Indeed, Rafe knew, albeit equally unwillingly, that he had never found that satisfaction with anyone else either.

But it had only been a *physical* satisfaction, he reminded himself, striding irritably into his bathroom. And maybe he had exaggerated its importance because it was so long since he had made love with any woman. Since Sarah died, that aspect of his nature seemed to have died, too, and no one had succeeded in getting under his guard. He had considered himself numb, inviolable, until that afternoon he had seen a curvaceous but fairly ordinary woman waiting at Glasgow Station . . .

His jaw clenched. It wasn't true, he told himself. He had felt sorry for her, that was all. And the urge to irritate his mother had overridden his reason. The fact that he enjoyed talking to her—baiting her even, he conceded tautly—had nothing to do with love, and everything to do with sex.

He leant towards the mirror, examining his overnight growth of beard with more determination than it warranted. It felt rough against his palm, and he deliberately scraped his hand upwards in an attempt to rid himself of the unwanted recollection of how smooth Isobel's skin had been. Smooth, and silky soft, he remembered, his masochistic attempt to divert himself failing abysmally. She had been all warmth, and heat, and sultry passion, blossoming beneath his touch like a flower to the sun.

And he remembered every small detail of what had happened after he had carried her to the bed. He remembered depositing her on the satin coverlet, and her involuntary shiver when he unzipped her dress, and her back touched the cold satin for the first time. He remembered she had slipped her hands about his neck then, delaying his efforts to draw the sleeves of the tight-fitting dress down over her arms, and although he had been impatient at the interruption the tantalising taste of her tongue in his mouth had more than made up for the distraction. She had taken his tongue between her lips and sucked on the tip, he remembered unevenly, revealing a totally uninhibited side to her nature.

Of course, eventually, he had succeeded in drawing the dress down to her waist, and, although she had also worn a bra, her full breasts, taut and swollen, had almost overspilled the lacy cups. He remembered he couldn't wait to release the clip, and weigh those generous globes in his eager hands. Then he had taken each of them into his mouth in turn, suckling like a babe at their rosy peaks.

God, he had wanted her then. Even unbuckled, his trousers had been unbearably tight. But, when he had drawn back to unfasten the zip, Isobel had brushed his hands aside. With her tongue lodged provocatively between her teeth, she had removed the constriction herself, opening his trousers with exquisite precision and baring his aching sex to her waiting hands.

And that had been exquisite, too, he conceded tensely, as his breathing quickened. Feeling her soft hands touching him, caressing him, moulding his throbbing length between her palms. And, when she had bent her head and tasted the tiny pearl of moisture that had beaded on its sensitive tip, he had gone wild.

Damn, he groaned, he was becoming aroused just thinking about her, about what they had done. She had been so sweet, so eager, so responsive! She'd wanted so badly to please him. How could he have guessed what her unsophisticated lovemaking would do to him?

But, by that time, he had been beyond the point of worrying about some as yet unthought-of future. For the first time in his life, he hadn't been thinking, he was only feeling, and he was blind to any thought of the possible consequences of his actions. He wanted Isobel. He wanted to be a part of her. He wanted to bury himself in her warm flesh, and assuage the hunger she had initiated.

He remembered removing her dress and tights with little attention to detail. He remembered tearing off his own clothes with even less discrimination. The need to have her in his arms, to lie beside her on his bed, hip to hip, and skin to skin, had been all he could think about. It had seemed—only at that moment, he assured

himself—that his whole life had been but a prologue to
this point. And he had wanted to expand it, to prolong
it, to luxuriate in its undoubted perfection.

And it had been perfection feeling her full breasts
crushed beneath his chest, her soft stomach a cushion
for the hair-roughened cavity of his belly, and her hips
cradling his sex. He recalled how she had opened her
legs to make him more comfortable, and then made little
whimpering sounds of pleasure when he had rubbed his
hairy thigh against her.

Of course, his luxuriation hadn't lasted long. He had
wanted her too badly, and every innocent move she had
made had only inflamed his already burning senses. Even
so, when he had lifted himself on to his elbows and
looked down at her, the need to draw out the moment
even more, to make it as perfect for her as it was for
him, had overwhelmed him.

With infinite tenderness he had used his lips to trace
a path from the tip of her breasts, down across her flat
stomach, and lower to where a cluster of moist curls
marked the junction of her legs. Then, equally tenderly,
he had slid his fingers into the curls, parting their
softness, and exposing the sleek nub of her femininity.

Her constricted breathing, and the convulsive way she
had clutched his shoulders, had revealed her innocence
in this aspect of lovemaking, and he remembered it had
crossed his mind that in that respect she had resembled
his dead wife. But only fleetingly, he acknowledged
tautly, aware that Isobel's response to his probing fingers
and tongue had been exactly what he wanted. Her gasps
of delight and pleasure, the way she had arched her back,
and thrust against his hand, had driven him to the limit
of his own endurance, but when he had eventually eased
himself into her the slickness of his passage had made
it all worthwhile.

Nevertheless, he hadn't been unaware of the faint trace
of consternation that had crossed her face when she'd
felt him filling her and expanding her taut muscles. He'd
been quite sure she didn't think she could take all of
him, and proving to her that she could had been only a
small part of the enjoyment her reaction had given him.
He hadn't wanted to think of her late husband at that

moment, but he couldn't help the purely smug feeling of satisfaction he got from knowing that Edward must never have inspired such a response, and feeling her tightly clasped around him had almost sent him over the brink.

But concentration, and a degree of determination, had kept him sane, and with careful consideration he had let her get used to him before making any unnecessary movements. Besides, the few minutes he waited had given him the time he needed to get his own emotions under control again, so that when he had begun to move he was not like some callow schoolboy, incapable of restraint.

All the same, that first loving had not been as leisurely as he had planned. After his prolonged attentions, Isobel's emotions had been far from controlled. With wild abandon, she'd swept away his defences, taking him with her to the point of no return.

They had made love hungrily, hotly, passionately, using each other heedlessly, and reaching a mutual peak of fulfilment in an amazingly short time. So short, in fact, that Rafe had known himself to be still partially aroused, and a second eager loving had followed on the first.

The incredible thing was that although Isobel had responded so deliciously to his demands he had intuitively known she had never experienced anything like it before. His earlier suspicions about her lack of experience were as nothing compared to the way she had received her first climax. The sounds she had made, and the convulsive way she had sought to disguise her reactions, had proved beyond a doubt that she was a total novice when it came to enjoying her body. No wonder she hadn't wanted to talk about her relationship with Edward. The man must have been totally insensitive not to have realised how responsive she was.

While he had been all too sensitive, he acknowledged grimly, remembering how furious he had been when she had accused *him* of having a less than satisfactory marriage. He had been so angry then, so resentful that she could suggest such a thing. He hadn't wanted to think

about Sarah. He hadn't wanted to hear her name on
Isobel's lips. Their marriage had always been sacrosanct.

Yet now he wondered if she hadn't scraped a nerve
after all. Why else had he responded as he had? But no,
he assured himself fiercely. He and Sarah had been perfectly happy together. They had been content, which was
something few couples could boast.

But, and it was a big but, he admitted ruefully, was
contentment   in   marriage   altogether   desirable?
Particularly in a man and woman of their age. Wasn't
contentment for the elderly, for those beyond the fire
and fever of youth? Might he have got bored with Sarah,
if their goal of having a baby hadn't been there to divert
him? And if she, and their child, had lived, would he
always have been as patient as he had been then?

He scowled, snatching up the shaving foam and
lathering his face with the creamy substance. He was
being stupid. He was letting his imagination run away
with him. Just because he and Isobel had spent a purely
lustful night together, he was looking for reasons to
justify his actions. She hadn't had to stay with him. He
certainly hadn't forced her. And just because she had
proved to be more innocent than he had imagined, he
had no reason to feel guilty for seducing her.

No, not seducing her, he told himself savagely,
grabbing his razor and scraping less than skilfully at his
beard. He couldn't have seduced a woman who had been
married for more than ten years! If she regretted what
had happened, if that was why she had disappeared,
slipping away like a thief in the night, then that was her
problem. He hated to admit it, but perhaps his mother
was right. Perhaps it was time he found himself another
wife. He was getting far too introspective. There was a
time when he would have thought nothing of sleeping
with a woman he barely knew. It wasn't as if she was in
love with him or anything. From the first, it was he who
had done all the running.

All the same, as he staunched the several cuts his
careless use of the razor had left on his cheek, he found
himself wondering why Isobel had left him. He told
himself it didn't matter, that he didn't care, but the fact
remained, he was piqued by it. It made him feel small:

as if she was ashamed of what had happened. God, he
had known she was trouble, from the first day he saw
her at the station. But he had thought she'd make trouble
for his mother, not for him. Never for him.

By the time he had showered and dressed it was half-
past eight, and he decided to join his mother for
breakfast, rather than have Cummins fetch him a tray
to the library. The prospect of sitting across the table
from Isobel, with the knowledge of the night they had
spent together fresh in his mind, was both a provocation
and a challenge. Not least because he wanted to prove
to himself that he was exaggerating the importance of
what he had done.

But when he entered the morning-room, where the
family usually took the meal, he found only his sister-
in-law at the table. Clare was drinking coffee, and
flicking through the pages of the morning newspaper,
and his usual animosity towards her was tempered by
his concern for Isobel's whereabouts. Surely she knew
he would expect her to join the family for breakfast. Or
was she sharing the meal with her daughter? He realised
he hadn't given Cory a thought since he'd woken up and
found her mother gone.

'Good morning,' he said shortly, noting that his
mother's place was as yet undisturbed, and that Grace
had either eaten earlier or was having breakfast in bed.
'You're an early riser.'

Clare gave him a tight smile and folded the newspaper
with meticulous precision. 'I came with Daddy,' she
remarked at last, and Rafe's brows descended sharply.

'Daddy?' he echoed, his expression mirroring his confusion. Then, 'Webster's here?' His frown deepened.
'Cory—is something wrong?'

'Of course not.' Clare allowed a little irritation to enter
her voice. 'In my opinion there was never anything wrong
with that child that a little more discipline wouldn't cure.'

Rafe's mouth compressed. 'Yes. Well, I don't believe
I asked for your opinion, Clare,' he responded coolly.
'So do I take it your father is making his final examination of her?' That would explain why Isobel wasn't
at the table, he thought with some relief.

'Oh, he's done that,' replied Clare airily, pouring herself another cup of coffee. She held up the pot. 'Do you want some? It's still hot.'

'No.' Rafe made no attempt to be polite now. Then, with enforced civility, 'Where's Isobel?'

Clare lifted her cup. 'Gone,' she said, with evident satisfaction at the word. 'She left about half an hour ago. Daddy had an early call at Dalbaig, so he called here on his way.'

Rafe stared at her. 'Isobel's gone!' he said disbelievingly, and Clare nodded.

'And her daughter. Daddy pronounced her fit, so there was no point in her staying. They left just after eight o'clock, as I said. I expect Isobel wanted to get home and change before she's due at the surgery.'

Rafe was appalled at the staggering sense of disappointment he experienced at this news. He felt lost; betrayed; abandoned; torn by the twin torments of resentment and betrayal. Dear God, surely she must know he would want to see her this morning. Surely she must know how he would feel at finding her gone. If nothing else, they needed to talk. Or was this her way of showing him how little last night had meant to her?

'You seem—surprised,' Clare observed now, and Rafe wondered if he looked as shattered as he felt.

'How?' he asked obliquely. 'How did they leave? Did you see them go?'

Clare regarded him with malevolent amusement. 'They took the Shogun,' she replied. 'I believe you had loaned it to Isobel, hadn't you?' she added innocently. 'As a matter of fact, Lucas went with her. To help her with Cory, and to bring the vehicle back.'

Rafe swore then, silently but violently, and, judging by Clare's expression, she knew exactly how he was feeling. She was actually enjoying his confusion, and after the way he had baited her in the past he supposed he couldn't entirely blame her.

'I see,' he said then, recovering enough of his equilibrium to make a reasonably controlled departure from the morning room.

'Oh—don't you want any breakfast?' Clare called after him, and although the urge to take his anger out on her was almost irresistible Rafe forfeited the challenge.

CHAPTER THIRTEEN

ISOBEL was washing up the breakfast dishes when someone knocked at the front door.

Aware that the blood was pounding in her ears and her heart was beating unnaturally fast, she stood for several seconds in a state of indecision, knowing she had to answer the door yet desperate to avoid doing so.

Cory was still in bed. She had given her her breakfast half an hour ago, with the adjunct that she could get up if she wanted to. The cottage was warm and cosy, and she guessed her daughter would prefer to spend the day watching television on the sofa rather than spending the day in bed. It was what she had done yesterday, after their precipitate flight from the castle. And until Isobel found the time to go into Strathmoor and speak to her headmaster she had no intention of sending the girl back to school. Besides, her grandmother was coming today. Mrs Jacobson would no doubt have her own ideas about what Isobel should do.

But not at this hour of the morning, Isobel thought uneasily, glancing at her watch. It was barely eight-thirty, and in her experience there was only one person likely to arrive at this time. It had to be Rafe, and, although she had spent the whole of the previous day waiting anxiously for his appearance, as always he chose to disconcert her.

She took a deep breath, and dried her soapy hands on a tea-towel. Well, she had known their confrontation had to come sooner or later. She ought to be grateful Cory was still in bed. It would be difficult enough to face him as it was, without her daughter's curious eyes appraising their every move.

All the same, her knees were decidedly unsteady as she crossed the floor. Dear God, what was she going to do? What was she going to say to him? What did you

154

say to a man who had taken your safe, unadventurous world and turned it upside-down? It wasn't as if he had made any secret of the fact that his attraction to her was a purely physical one. Good lord, it wasn't as if she hadn't been warned. She had known from the beginning how he had reacted to his late wife's death.

Heavens, what had happened had come about because she had dared to challenge his relationship with Sarah. So why had she allowed herself to be so reckless? He wasn't a monster. She knew that. If she had truly tried to escape him, he would have let her go.

The trouble was, she had been totally inexperienced in such matters. Inexperienced in more ways than one, she admitted, remembering her ignorance of her own body's needs. But the years she had spent with Edward had not prepared her for any kind of sexual relationship. She had thought theirs had been a good marriage, and it had. But that was mainly because she had been so innocent of what to expect.

Growing up without a mother, even the confidences she had shared in school had not made any real impression on her consciousness, and in many ways Edward had merely taken her father's place. On the infrequent occasions when he had sought physical satisfaction, he had taken it swiftly and unemotionally, and in her ignorance Isobel had assumed it was her lack, rather than his, that had left her so unmoved.

Besides, in those early years, when she might have questioned that belief, she had had Cory to contend with. She had been totally unprepared for the demands of a baby, and with Mrs Jacobson's assistance she had soon been convinced of her own inadequacies.

That was why what had happened two nights ago had been so shattering, why she had jumped at the chance of leaving the castle yesterday morning, before Rafe was even up. She hadn't needed Clare's barbed suggestion that she had taken advantage of their hospitality long enough. She had wanted to get away. She had wanted to forget.

She'd told herself she needed time: time to think, and time to compose herself, before she saw Rafe again. What to him had been a simple assuagement of the senses had

meant so much more to her, and that was something she
had to deal with. She needed some space, to be on her
own for a while, so that when she did see him again she
could deal with him on her own terms. A few hours, she
had thought, while Clare made arrangements for one of
the castle chauffeurs to accompany her and bring the
car back. That was all she needed. A few paltry hours.
But now here she was, twenty-four hours later, and still
incapable of producing a coherent explanation as to why
she had run out on him.

Of course, she hadn't expected him to accept it. In all
honesty, she was surprised he had given her as long as
he had. He was not a patient man, she knew that. And
he would demand an explanation. If only she could adopt
the same indifferent approach that he could don so easily.

'Aren't you going to answer the door, Mum?'

Cory's voice brought Isobel to a shocked awareness
of the situation. While she had been reliving the momentous events of the night she had spent in Rafe's bed,
her daughter had got out of hers, and was standing
behind her. She wasn't dressed; she was still wearing her
dressing-gown. But her eyes were bright and avid, and
Isobel wondered if their visitor had knocked more than
once while she had been daydreaming.

'Oh—I——' Isobel moistened her lips in some confusion, and the girl's face took on an expression of
concern.

'What's the matter?' she asked curiously, drawing her
brows together. 'Hey—have you been crying?'

'No!' Isobel was indignant, but when she smudged a
defensive hand across her cheek she found it was damp.
'I had something in my eye, that's all,' she lied, appalled
at her own capacity for deceit. 'Um—why don't you go
back to bed, sweetheart? Whoever it is, they won't want
to see you in—in your dressing-gown.'

'Why not?' Cory shrugged, showing no intention of
moving. 'It's probably Dr Webster. He said he'd call and
see me in a couple of days. Don't you remember?'

'Oh—oh, yes!' Isobel's relief was palpable, and the
weight of apprehension lifted from her shoulders instantly. 'Of course. I'd forgotten that.' She hurried to

the door. 'You're probably right. Heavens, I hope he doesn't think I've deliberately kept him waiting.'

'Why should he?' Cory watched her mother with speculative eyes. 'You're not scared of him, are you?'

Isobel had hardly time to give her daughter a troubled backward glance before she had thrown the bolt and unlocked the door. What Cory might have meant by such an obscure remark had to be put aside for the moment, but as she opened the door all her earlier apprehensions returned to haunt her.

'I'm sorry——' she began, ready to offer Dr Webster an unconditional apology for wasting his time, but she was speaking to thin air. As soon as she turned the handle, a querulous hand thrust the door aside, and a stout, elderly woman, with strong, faintly masculine features and dark hair, liberally tinged with grey, stepped boldly over the threshold. She threw her arms wide at the sight of Cory, and, muttering some uncomplimentary comment about useless females who weren't fit to be mothers, she gathered the girl close to her generous breasts.

'Grandma!' exclaimed Cory delightedly, and it was left to Isobel to collect her mother-in-law's suitcase from the step outside and close the door. As usual, Ruth had ignored the social niceties. Isobel had asked her to wait until today, and she had. But she must have travelled up to Fort William the day before, so that she could get here as soon as it was decently possible. It was a wonder she hadn't arrived in time for breakfast, thought Isobel drily. She supposed she should be thankful for small mercies.

'Ah, it's so good to see you again, my darling,' Mrs Jacobson was crooning now, completely ignoring her daughter-in-law. 'I've been so worried about you, Cory. Didn't I say your mother would regret bringing you to this outlandish place?'

'It's not that bad,' protested Cory, meeting her mother's eyes over her grandmother's shoulder half defensively. 'And it wasn't Mum's fault that I fell in the loch!'

'You fell in the loch!' Mrs Jacobson hugged her even tighter. 'First I lose my only son, and now I hear my granddaughter has nearly died of hypothermia! No wonder I'm only a shadow of the woman I used to be!'

Cory wriggled free. 'Don't exaggerate, Grandma!' she exclaimed, laughing. 'The day you stop enjoying your food, I'll start to worry.'

'Cory!'

Isobel felt bound to interject, and as if it reminded her that she hadn't yet greeted her daughter-in-law Ruth turned. 'It doesn't matter,' she said, spreading her hands in an expressive gesture. 'She's right. I'm not losing weight, I'm gaining it. When I'm worried, I eat, and I've eaten a lot since you had this crazy idea of moving my granddaughter away from her home and her family.'

Isobel sighed. 'This is Cory's home now,' she replied evenly, trying not to feel hurt by her mother-in-law's attitude. 'And we're both her family. Not just you.'

Ruth snorted. 'You can say that, when you almost lost her?'

Isobel trembled. 'I didn't almost lose her. Cory—Cory had an accident, that's all. It wasn't my fault.'

The older woman sniffed. 'So what happened? How did she come to fall in the—the water?' She refused to say 'loch'. 'Where were you when it happened?'

'At work.'

'At work?' Mrs Jacobson turned to Cory again, and wrapped a protective arm about her shoulders. 'You can tell me this and still maintain it's not your fault?'

'Yes.' Isobel gave her daughter a helpless look. 'I—I thought she was at school.'

'At school——'

'It's true, Grandma.' Cory pulled away from her grandmother again, but her expression was faintly sulky now. 'Mum thought I'd gone to school, but I hadn't.' Her shoulders hunched. 'I hate that school! It sucks!'

'*Cory!*'

Isobel's protest was automatic, but useless in the face of Mrs Jacobson's look of triumph. As always, Edward's mother was eager to sow seeds of dissension between them, and Cory's obvious unhappiness at Strathmoor was just the spur she needed.

'You should have let her stay with me,' Ruth declared now, urging Cory down on to the sofa and plumping

herself down beside her. 'She'd have been happy at Lady
Eleanor's Academy. It's what I wanted. It's what Edward
would have wanted. And——' she squeezed her granddaughter's shoulders '—it's what you wanted, isn't it,
darling?'

Only the sudden knock at the door prevented the argument from deteriorating into a row. The diversion it
provided gave Isobel time to gather her defences.
Exchanging words with Edward's mother always put her
at a disadvantage, mainly because, unlike Ruth, she
didn't like hurting anyone's feelings.

'Excuse me,' she said, and, leaving them to console
each other, she marched to the door.

It was Rafe. For a moment, the sight of him robbed
her of speech. She had been so sure it would be Dr
Webster this time, and the awareness that her earlier fears
had been realised left her numb and mute. Of all the
people it might have been, he was the one she had least
hoped to see, and she could imagine Ruth's reaction
when Cory told her who it was.

'Hi.'

Rafe's greeting was disturbingly familiar, and Isobel
had to suppress physically the urge to throw herself into
his arms. Despite her apprehension, it was a powerful
impulse. And one which she despised herself for feeling.
But in her present state of conflict he looked so achingly
dependable.

But he wasn't, she reminded herself fiercely. Whatever
reason had brought him here, it wasn't because he wanted
to offer her any support. Curiosity, perhaps, and a spu-
rious need to assuage his conscience, that was all she
could expect from him. Maybe he wanted to thank her—
for being there when he needed a woman. It was certain
now that what they had shared hadn't meant as much
to him as it had to her. Otherwise he'd have come to
find her yesterday, to assure her that what had happened
hadn't been just a one-night stand.

'Hello,' she managed at last, aware that Cory and Mrs
Jacobson were listening to every word. 'Did you want
something?'

Rafe's eyes flickered, and for a moment there was a
trace of impatience in their brooding depths. Then, with

a faint twist of his lips, he inclined his head. 'I wanted to see you.'

'Did you?' Isobel wet her dry lips and glanced half apprehensively over her shoulder. 'I can't imagine why.'

'Can't you?' There was definitely an edge to Rafe's voice now, and she hoped he wouldn't say anything that other ears could misconstrue. 'Can I come in?'

'It's Rafe,' Isobel heard Cory telling her grandmother behind her. 'That's the Earl, you know,' she added, with a certain amount of pride in her tone. 'Ask him in, Mum!' she called. 'I want him to meet Grandma.'

'I——' Isobel knew there was little she could say in the face of her daughter's invitation. Besides, this was his cottage, she reminded herself bitterly. Could she legitimately keep him out? 'Um—come in,' she conceded, stepping aside. 'Edward's mother's here.'

'Ah.'

Rafe's expression cleared, and, as she closed the door, Isobel wondered if he thought that was why she had hesitated. God, could he be that insensitive? she wondered incredulously. Did he really think they could dismiss what had happened and go on as before?

By the time she had secured the latch, Cory had performed the necessary introductions, and Isobel wished she could just collect her coat and handbag and leave them to it. She had to leave for work soon, anyway. Rafe must have known that. Was that why he had come?

'I understand it's you I have to thank for saving my granddaughter's life,' Mrs Jacobson declared, after the introductions were over, and Rafe gave a small smile.

'Quite inadvertently, I can assure you,' he remarked, his eyes registering the fact that Isobel was standing rather indecisively by the door. He arched a quizzical brow. 'Did you arrive last night?'

'No, this morning,' replied Ruth, her attention flickering between their unexpected visitor and her daughter-in-law. 'As soon as I heard Cory had had the accident, I caught the next train to Glasgow.'

'Rafe carried me all the way back to the castle,' Cory inserted, not to be outdone. 'Then he leant Mum a car, so that she could come and visit me.'

'Did he?' There was a certain amount of speculation in Mrs Jacobson's response, and inwardly Isobel groaned. 'But aren't you being a little disrespectful, darling? I'm sure the Earl didn't give you permission to call him—er—Rafe.'

She gave Rafe a sympathetic smile as she said this, but once again Cory chose to be controversial. 'It's what Mum calls him,' she declared, looking defiantly at her mother. 'And he doesn't mind, do you, Rafe?'

'Not particularly,' he replied, before Isobel could get her tongue around an appropriate response. 'So—how are you, Cory? Still running rings around your mother, I see. Obviously that dip in the loch hasn't done you any harm.'

Cory dimpled, delighted to be the centre of attention, but Mrs Jacobson wasn't amused at his levity. 'I'll have you know that "dip in the loch", as you call it, could have killed her!' she exclaimed tersely. 'If you hadn't found her, as you did, Isobel would have been none the wiser. She didn't even check that the child had arrived at school.'

Isobel's face flamed, but, as before, Rafe pre-empted her bid to defend herself. 'Oh, I don't believe the headmaster of Strathmoor Comprehensive would appreciate having the parents of his some five hundred pupils calling in to check that their offspring had actually made it to the classroom,' he remarked mildly, and Mrs Jacobson flushed now.

'I'm not suggesting that, and you know it,' she retorted, as Cory did the unforgivable and giggled. 'But my granddaughter's a stranger here. And, as she says, she doesn't like the school. The least Isobel could have done was assure herself that Cory caught the school bus.'

'Cory's not a child,' said Rafe evenly, and, realising she couldn't let him go on defending her, Isobel stepped forward.

'Well, whoever was to blame, Cory's all right now,' she said tensely, aware of Rafe's eyes upon her. 'And that's what really matters, isn't it?'

'Is it?' Mrs Jacobson took a deep breath. 'I wonder what excuse you'd find if this happened again.'

Isobel gasped. 'It won't happen again.'

'No, it won't.' Her mother-in-law got ponderously to her feet, as if finding the effort of looking up at her two protagonists was giving them an advantage. 'I'm going to take Cory back to London with me, where she belongs. She can start at Lady Eleanor's after half-term. If you insist on staying in this—backwater—that's your affair. Cory is not going to be made to suffer for it.'

'Now look here——' Isobel began hotly.

'I think that's a very good idea.'

Rafe's cool acknowledgement of the older woman's suggestion momentarily silenced her. That he should take it upon himself to offer any opinion was aggravating enough; that he should agree with her mother-in-law's outrageous suggestion was galling.

'I beg your pardon?' she echoed, as Mrs Jacobson adopted a look of smug approval, and Rafe pushed his hands into the pockets of the olive-green leather jacket he was wearing and regarded her enquiringly.

'I said, I think you should let her go.'

'Yes, I heard what you said.'

'Oh?' Rafe looked appallingly complacent. 'I'm sorry. I thought you——'

'What I want to know is why you think you have the right to offer an opinion,' retorted Isobel furiously. 'Cory is my daughter. Mine! I'll decide where she lives, and with whom!'

'I just thought——'

'I don't want to know what you think!'

Isobel glared at him, aware as she did so that she was in great danger of giving in to her emotions and slapping his deceptively innocent face. She felt like taking hold of him and shaking him and beating at him with her fists. How dared he do this to her? How dared he suggest that Cory would be better off without her?

But then she realised that their altercation had not gone unobserved. And how familiarly she had spoken to someone who ought to have been treated with a certain amount of deference and respect. Dear God, she could imagine what Ruth's reaction would have been if she had slapped him. She was already aware that the situation was not all it should be. It wouldn't take much to convince her that she had every right to be suspicious.

'If anyone cares how I feel, I think it's a jolly good idea,' Cory remarked, from the sofa. She drew up her knees and wrapped her arms around them. 'I wouldn't mind going back to London, Mum. You don't need me here. And Grandma's all on her own.'

I'm on my own, too, Isobel protested silently, but she was half afraid that such a declaration would induce her daughter to make some other damning comment. All it needed was for Mrs Jacobson to believe that she and Rafe were having an affair and she'd never let it rest. What was it they called women like her? An unfit mother? Yes, that was it. She knew Edward's mother wouldn't hesitate to call on the law if she thought she could gain custody of her granddaughter.

'We—we'll talk about it,' Isobel said now, the look she gave Rafe crippling in its intensity. 'But not now. I—I have to go to work.' She looked at her watch, though in all honesty she couldn't see it. 'I'm going to be late.'

'I'll take you,' said Rafe at once, and although the thought of getting into a car with him after what he had done made her flesh creep she could hardly say so.

'If you like,' she said offhandedly, brushing past him and going into the little kitchen annexe, gazing about her blindly, not even sure what she was looking for.

'I'll make Grandma some breakfast,' Cory offered, following her, but Isobel couldn't face her daughter either.

'You know where everything is,' was all she could muster, and, snatching up her coat and handbag, she returned to the living-room. Then, taking a breath, 'I'll see you later—um—Ruth. Cory will look after you.'

Outside, the air was crisp and sharp, tangy with the scent of autumn fires. It was only a five-minute walk to the surgery, and now that they were out of the cottage, and out of the earshot of Mrs Jacobson, Isobel had no need to hide her feelings.

'I'll walk,' she said, turning up the collar of her coat in preparation for doing so, but Rafe caught her arm.

'No, you won't,' he said, all trace of complacency absent from his voice now. 'I want to talk to you, and I've no intention of putting it off until later.'

Isobel's stare was hostile. 'Don't you think you've said enough?'

'Not nearly,' replied Rafe grimly, urging her towards the waiting Range Rover, and because there was still a chance that they were being observed from the cottage window Isobel let him open the door and put her inside. But she pressed her knees together, and when he walked round the vehicle and got in beside her she made sure to leave as much space between them as was possible.

If he noticed, Rafe made no comment. He merely put the car into gear and depressed the accelerator. The Range Rover swung smoothly away from the kerb, after giving way to a tractor, whose driver raised a cheerful hand in greeting, and then sped swiftly along the High Street, straight past Dr Webster's surgery.

Isobel immediately objected. 'Stop this car at once!' she exclaimed, fumbling for the handle of the door. But the door was locked, which was probably just as well, she admitted tensely. She could hardly jump out of a car that was travelling at thirty miles an hour.

'Calm down,' said Rafe impatiently. 'I'm not abducting you. I just think what we have to say is better said in private. Or do you want to air our differences in full view of Webster's patients?'

'Don't you mean you don't?' countered Isobel scornfully, though she was perilously near to tears. Not only had he destroyed any peace she'd found, but now he was threatening her relationship with her daughter.

'All right.' With a brief display of temper, Rafe stood on the brakes, and the Range Rover squealed to a halt. They were not outside the doctor's surgery, but they were still in the village, and a woman who had been whitening her step looked up in some confusion. 'We'll talk here,' he said, turning off the engine, and resting his forearms on the wheel. 'I suggest we deal with Cory first. You're mad because I said I agreed she should go and stay with her grandmother.'

'Damn right!' Isobel's voice was tremulous, but full of righteous indignation. 'How dare you interfere between Cory and me? You don't know anything about us.'

'I know that Cory hasn't settled down here. I know that she's not happy in school, and that she's more often absent than not.'

'How do you know that?'

Rafe shrugged. 'Does it matter?'

'I think so, yes. Have you been spying on us?'

'Oh, Isobel!' Rafe ran his long fingers through his hair, and despite all that had gone before she couldn't help remembering how his hair had felt when she touched it. 'If you must know, I'm one of the governors of the school in Strathmoor. It was no especial feat to find out about one of its pupils.'

'And I suppose Mr Dougall is a friend of yours!'

'The headmaster? No, not particularly. As a matter of fact, I think he's a bit of a prig, but that doesn't mean I sympathise with Cory's behaviour.'

'Of course not.'

'Isobel.' Rafe sighed. 'Stop behaving as if I'm your enemy. I'm not.'

'With friends like you, I don't need them.'

'And stop trying to score points. I only want to help you, and I don't believe forcing Cory to stay at Strathmoor against her will is going to solve the problem. Let her go. Let her live with her grandmother for a while. From what I've seen of that old lady, I don't think she'll stay there long.'

'I don't care what you think.' Isobel stared at him, with tears sparkling in her eyes. 'I wish I'd never met you. Just stay out of my life from now on.'

Rafe groaned. 'You don't mean that.' He turned in his seat and put his arm along the back of hers. His fingers brushed the tight coil of hair she had secured at her nape, and she shivered involuntarily. 'You must know that's why I'm here? Don't let Cory come between us. You can't believe that after what happened the other night I wouldn't want to see you again?'

Isobel jerked away from his caressing hand, and the face she turned towards him was taut with loathing. 'I'd have thought that's exactly what you'd have wanted,' she declared, showing her contempt. 'You got what you wanted, now leave me alone. I never want to speak to you again!'

CHAPTER FOURTEEN

ISOBEL finished at lunchtime on Wednesdays. As she often worked Saturday morning, Dr Webster generally allowed her half a day in lieu. She could have been paid overtime, but she preferred the free time. It enabled her to go into Strathmoor, if she wanted to, or potter about at home if she didn't.

At first, the time spent at home had been unbearably lonely. Even though she told herself that had Cory been at school in Strathmoor she would still have spent this time on her own, the isolation got to her. Nothing could make her forget that Cory wasn't just at the local comprehensive. She was hundreds of miles away, in London, and unless Isobel changed her mind and went back too it could be weeks, months even, before she saw her.

It was an appalling prospect, and one she knew Mrs Jacobson expected would eventually work to her advantage. Sooner or later, she was sure, Isobel would give up her crazy schemes and return to London. To the house in St John's Wood, and the enforced protection of her mother-in-law.

And of course she would. Despite what she wanted, despite her own needs, she loved Cory too much to let her go. It was just a matter of time before she handed in her resignation.

That she had let Cory go with her grandmother at all was still a source of some amazement to her. At no time had she ever endorsed such a decision. But it had been what Cory wanted; what her mother-in-law wanted. And after Rafe's unforgivable intervention the odds had weighed heavily against her.

Besides, the prospect of sending Cory back to school in Strathmoor had never been an inviting option. The discovery that her daughter had spent more time out of the classroom than in it had filled her with despair. There was no way she could take Cory to school, no way she could ensure that she stayed there if she did. And, goodness knew, there were many worse things that could happen to a teenager than falling in the loch. How would she live with herself if Cory were abducted, or raped, or worse?

In those circumstances, Lady Eleanor's Academy had held a certain attraction. At least, until she could save enough money to offer a satisfactory alternative. That was why she had given in to her mother-in-law's demands, why she had let her take Cory back to London. She had to accept that, for the present, Edward's mother could do more for her daughter than she could.

Not that she had admitted that to anyone but herself. And particularly not to Rafe Lindsay, she acknowledged, as she left the surgery on Wednesday lunchtime, a month after the traumatic events that had preceded her daughter's departure. Whatever excuses she might make to herself, she couldn't forget that he had agreed with Mrs Jacobson. Even knowing how much her daughter meant to her, he had still encouraged her mother-in-law to take her away.

Of course, he hadn't thought she meant it when she'd said she never wanted to speak to him again. In the days after Cory and her grandmother had returned to London, he had been a frequent visitor to the cottage, turning up at all hours of the day and night, determined to get her to change her mind. He had tried all means open to him, from patient persuasion to downright anger, but all to no avail. Isobel had refused to listen to him, and only now, as the pain of Cory's leaving began to ease, did she detect a deeper significance for her sense of loss.

But that was ridiculous, she told herself fiercely, not allowing the memory of that other betrayal to resurrect feelings she would just as soon forget. What had happened between her and Rafe was best forgotten. She had the feeling that probing that particular weakness might expose a wound that would never heal.

And it wasn't as if he had continued to pursue her. He had soon grown tired of her recalcitrance, and it was weeks now since she had even laid eyes on him. She thought perhaps he might be away, but there was no way she could question the Websters without drawing attention to herself. Besides, it was nothing to do with her, she had told herself firmly. It wasn't as if they owed each other anything. And, despite a momentary fear to the contrary, there was to be no unwelcome outcome of the night they had spent together. Even though she had long stopped taking the Pill, she wasn't pregnant. She didn't have anything to worry about.

But, and it was a big but, she did. Worry, that was. More and more, with each succeeding day. Not about Rafe, she assured herself, in her less discriminating moments. He didn't need anyone to worry about him. But about the way she had treated him; and how easy it had been to blame him for something that really wasn't his fault.

That was why she had this empty feeling inside her every time she thought about him, she decided bleakly. Why she awakened every morning with a feeling of oppression, as if there was something ominous hanging over her head. It wasn't just because she was missing Cory. She missed Rafe as well. By blaming him for her own failure, she had lost his friendship also.

A few spots of rain spattered at her face as she reached the cottage. It was cold, and she guessed the rain might turn to sleet by nightfall. She had already learned that it got much colder here in the Scottish Highlands than it did in London. The locals were already forecasting a hard winter.

Bothwell wasn't in his usual place on the kitchen windowsill when she reached the back door. Which surprised her. The cat was always waiting for her, waiting for the bowl of milk she always gave him. She hoped he was all right. She didn't know what she'd do if he went missing too.

She pulled out her keys, but before she could insert the appropriate key in the lock the door opened. To her astonishment, it was Cory who was standing just inside, gazing nervously at her, Bothwell, his tail arched, rubbing against her legs.

'Hello, Mum.' Cory's voice was strangely husky, as if she had a head cold—or perhaps because she'd been crying. 'I bet you didn't expect to see me.'

That was the understatement of the year, thought
Isobel, blinking, struggling to get her brain back into
gear. 'No. No, I didn't,' she conceded, incapable of
making any coherent judgement at the moment. She
stepped inside almost automatically, and closed the door
by leaning against it. 'Is—is your grandmother with you?
Why didn't you let me know you were coming?'

'I couldn't.' Cory's answer was no less confusing, and
she pushed her hands into the pockets of her jeans, and
regarded her mother anxiously. 'It's lovely to see you
again, Mum. It really is. Have you missed me?'

It was typical of Cory to ask a question like that,
thought Isobel bleakly, brushing past her daughter and
frowning at the empty living-room. 'Where's your
grandmother?' she asked, instead of answering her. 'Did
you stay somewhere overnight? Couldn't you have
phoned me?'

'No.' Cory chewed her lower lip. Then, 'Grandma's
not with me.'

'What?' At last, Isobel felt some measure of com-
prehension, though with it came an awful sense of dread.
'What's happened? Is she ill?' she demanded swiftly, as
a possible reason for Cory's appearance became apparent. 'Oh, God, nothing's happened to her, has it?'
she groaned. 'I know I've grumbled about her sometimes, but I wouldn't want to wish her any harm.'

'No. No, Mum. Nothing's happened to her.' Cory's
denial was sufficiently urgent for her mother to know
she was telling the truth. 'I—Grandma doesn't even know
I'm here.'

Isobel groped for the back of a chair to support herself.
'You can't mean that!' she exclaimed in horror.

'I do.' Cory sniffed, and Isobel guessed that if she had
been crying it was because she had been afraid of what
her mother's reaction might be. 'I—I flew up to Glasgow
this morning—on the shuttle. Then...' she hesitated
'...then I phoned Rafe from Fort William, and he came
and picked me up.'

Isobel stared at her. She had phoned *Rafe*! Her legs
gave way, and she sank down weakly on to the arm of
the chair. All these weeks when she'd not seen him, and

Cory casually phoned him and asked him to pick her up!

But first things first. 'How—how could you pay for a ticket on the shuttle?' she asked faintly. She shook her head. 'Where does your grandmother think you are?'

'In school.' Cory sniffed again, and came to fling herself into the armchair opposite. 'Oh, God, it's been awful, Mum. Much worse than staying at Strathmoor. Grandma takes me to school every morning, and picks me up every afternoon. She never lets me go out; not alone anyway. And the girls at Lady Eleanor's are really dull!'

Isobel tried not to be diverted by the anger her daughter's words engendered. Why had she never seen before how selfish Cory was? Why hadn't she ever acknowledged that Cory thought only of herself?

'The plane,' she reminded her evenly. 'How could you afford a plane ticket?'

Cory's chin jutted. 'I used Grandma's credit card——'

'You what?' Isobel was appalled.

'She said I could!' exclaimed Cory defensively. 'She said if I wanted to order any tapes or CDs I could use her card.'

'Tapes and CDs are not plane tickets,' retorted her mother shortly, mentally reviewing the balance in her own cheque account. 'How much was this ticket, and I mean exactly?'

Cory told her unwillingly, hurrying into more excuses for what she'd done. 'I thought you'd be glad to see me,' she said. 'I thought you'd be pleased I wanted to come back. I've missed you, Mum. I have. I've missed you.' She glanced round. 'And this dumpy cottage. I guess this is my home——'

'Cory——'

'No, let me finish. I mean it, Mum. Grandma was always on my back.' She grimaced. 'Do you know, she even made me clean out the bath every time I used it? And if I left a sock on the floor in my room, she nearly had a fit.'

'You're exaggerating.'

'I'm not.' Cory was indignant. 'I think old people are like that. You know—fussy about stupid things. I suppose it's because they are old. I couldn't wait to get away from there. She can keep her money. I'd rather live with you.'

Isobel got to her feet and turned away, as much for her own sake as Cory's. The trouble was, deep down she could feel herself sympathising. She knew, better than anyone, how infuriating Edward's mother could be if she didn't get her own way.

Of course, what Cory had done was unforgivable, and the first thing Isobel had to do was phone her mother-in-law and tell her where her granddaughter was. Thank heaven she hadn't had time to miss her yet. As far as Mrs Jacobson was concerned, Cory was still in school.

And perhaps that was what she should do, Isobel reflected. Give her daughter a good talking-to, and send her back on the next train. It was what Cory deserved, whatever way you looked at it. If only to prove that her mother wasn't the pushover she apparently thought her.

But there was something else, something she wasn't proud of, but which she was honest enough to admit, to herself at least. After the way Edward's mother had treated her, there was a certain rough justice to be found in her defeat. And, whatever Cory's faults, she had proved she couldn't be bought.

Which was why Isobel knew she wouldn't be putting her on the train to King's Cross. Blood was thicker than water, and she loved Cory more than any other human being. *Except Rafe*, a small voice taunted, her daughter's reappearance forcing her to admit that her feelings for him would not go away. He'd said Cory would come back, she remembered unhappily. Oh, God, she sighed, if only she'd believed him!

'How—how did you get to Fort William?' she asked now, needing the triviality of practicalities to overcome the sense of desolation she was feeling. It was perhaps easier to think of Rafe in terms of how he had treated her daughter. She didn't want to think of how *she* had treated him.

'I took a bus,' said Cory quickly, evidently glimpsing the crack in her mother's armour. 'I did have some cash.

Pocket money, you know,' she added, flushing, eager to
dismiss that aspect of the situation.

'Even so...' Isobel glanced at her watch.

'Oh—you mean, how did I get here so fast?' Cory
interpreted easily. 'I spent the night at a schoolfriend's
house. You wouldn't know her. Her name's Virginia
Harmon. She's a bit of a pain really, but she lives near
Heathrow. It was ideal really. I told Ginny what I was
going to do, and she covered for me. I caught the early
morning flight to Glasgow, and you know what
happened after that.'

'I thought you said your grandmother wouldn't let
you out of her sight.'

'Ginny's different.' Cory sighed. 'Mrs Harmon went
to school with Grandma. She'd never expect there'd be
any problem with me staying at their house.'

Isobel shook her head. 'So, not only have you
deceived your grandmother but you've deceived the
Harmons as well.'

'I told you, Ginny's covering for me.' Cory scuffed
her toe against the carpet.

'Hmm.' Isobel would deal with that later. 'So—what
time did you reach Fort William?'

Cory shrugged. 'I don't know. About eleven o'clock,
I suppose.'

'And why did you phone—Rafe? Why didn't you just
get a taxi to bring you to Invercaldy?'

Cory leaned forward, resting her forearms along her
thighs, and staring broodingly at the floor between her
feet. 'Because—because I knew you'd be mad.'

Isobel swallowed. 'I beg your pardon?'

'I said, I knew you'd be mad. Not because I'd come
back, but at the way I'd done it.'

'I see.'

'Do you?' Cory looked up at her through her lashes.
'I had to do it like this, Mum. If I'd told Grandma how
I felt, she'd have found some way to persuade me I was
wrong. And she'd never have given me the fare. Not
enough to cover the whole fare back here. She wants me
to stay with her, Mum. Not just now but always.'

Isobel's throat constricted. 'I—still don't see why you
had to—involve Rafe.'

'Because I wanted to talk to him.' Cory groaned. 'I thought he might talk to you, if you must know. I knew he was interested in you before I went away, and I guess I hoped he might——'

'What do you mean?' Isobel broke in before Cory could go any further. She took a moment, and then went on stiffly, 'What do you mean, you knew he was interested in me?'

'Well, he was, wasn't he?' Cory looked up at her wearily. 'Oh, Mum! I'm not a child, you know. I saw how he looked at you when he came to the cottage. And that night I had the accident—I wasn't unconscious, you know. I saw him kiss you. You can't pretend I was just imagining it. Rafe admitted that's what he did.'

Isobel's jaw dropped. 'Rafe did what?'

'He admitted it,' muttered Cory, transferring her attention to the floor again. 'But he still wouldn't come and talk to you,' she muttered. 'He said you wouldn't listen to anything he said.'

Isobel put a horrified hand to her head. 'Cory, are you telling me you blackmailed Rafe into helping you by threatening to tell someone of our supposed relationship?'

'No!' Cory was horrified now.

'But you did ask him—personal questions.'

'Only because it came into the conversation,' retorted Cory hotly. 'Honestly, Mum, what do you take me for? Just because you've chosen to forget what Rafe did for me, it doesn't mean I have to do the same.'

'I haven't forgotten!' Isobel could hear her voice rising in her frustration, and she made a concerted effort to control it. 'Some tea,' she said, half to herself, as she removed her overcoat. 'I need a cup of tea.' She glanced back at her daughter. 'Then you can tell me exactly what you said to—to the Earl. And I mean exactly, Cory. Not what you think I'd like to hear.'

'Well, I got the number of the castle from the operator,' explained Cory, some time later, as she and her mother sat opposite each other at the kitchen table. She cradled the mug of tea her mother had given her between her hands, and warmed her fingers on the cup. 'Not that I got to speak to Rafe straight away. It wasn't until his brother eventually came on the line that I convinced them who I was.'

'And?' Isobel prompted tautly.

'Oh—him, Rafe's brother, that is, he would have probably put me off. But Rafe said he and—I think he said his brother's name was Colin—were working together in the library, and I suppose he got suspicious about who was on the line.'

'So you spoke to Rafe.' Isobel tried not to sound too eager. 'What did he——' She stifled the words 'sound like', and added '—say?'

'He said he'd come and get me,' said Cory carelessly. 'What else did you expect him to say?'

'He could have refused.'

Cory shrugged. 'Rafe's not like that.'

'*Out of the mouth of babes...*'

'All right.' Isobel conceded the point. 'He picked you up at Fort William.'

'Outside the railway station,' agreed Cory, nodding. 'He came in this big Mercedes!' Her eyes sparkled. 'I expected him to come in the Range Rover, but he didn't——'

'I'm not interested in what car he came in,' cut in Isobel, trying to keep her patience. 'What happened then? Did he bring you straight back here?'

'Well, we had a Coke and a burger in a café before we left,' said Cory, frowning. 'He looked tired, and I think he was glad of the break. That was when he told me I couldn't expect him to have any influence with you. He said you weren't even speaking to him.'

'Cory!'

'Well, isn't it true?'

'No.' But Isobel could feel her cheeks turning red even so.

'Well, he said it was,' said Cory, looking at her shrewdly. 'He said you blamed him for me going away with Grandma. He said he'd tried to talk to you, but you wouldn't listen.'

Isobel lifted her own mug of tea and concentrated on taking a sip. The last thing she had expected was that Rafe would tell Cory that they hadn't seen one another.

But then, she hadn't expected Cory to try and enlist his help in talking to her mother. What must he be thinking of her? What must he be thinking of both of them?

'Is that true?' Cory persisted now, not at all deceived by her mother's prevarication. ''Cos if it is I think you should apologise. I wrote to Grandma weeks ago, asking if I couldn't come and live with her.' She eyed her mother warily. 'I know I was out of line, Mum, and I'm sorry. I just thought that if Grandma suggested it you might change your mind about staying.'

CHAPTER FIFTEEN

'RAFE, I hesitate to approach you in your present mood, but do you mind telling me why you drove to Fort William this morning?'

Rafe lifted his head from his balled fist and looked up at his mother wearily. Lady Invercaldy had come to find him in the library, and although he knew he ought to get to his feet out of deference he remained where he was, slumped at his desk.

'Didn't Colin tell you?' he enquired, quite sure his brother had lost no time in informing their mother of Cory's call. 'I went to collect Mrs Jacobson's daughter.'

'And bring her back to Invercaldy?' His mother's lips tightened. 'I'm surprised you chose to come back to the castle afterwards. Didn't—Mrs Jacobson—want to show you how grateful she was?'

Rafe's expression darkened, and, as if aware she had gone too far this time, she hurried on, 'Well, you have attempted to see her, haven't you? Colin says you've been to the cottage several times. I'm surprised you haven't started drinking again. Isn't that the way you usually deal with your problems?'

Rafe's hand came down heavily on the desk, and his mother took a nervous step backwards as he came aggressively to his feet. 'You never miss a trick, do you, Mama?' he asked disgustedly. 'I could almost believe you're sorry I'm not still blaming myself for what happened to Sarah.'

'Don't be ridiculous!'

'Is it ridiculous?' Rafe arched his dark brows. 'I haven't touched a drink in weeks, and you know it. Yet still you can't resist putting in the boot.'

His mother tilted her head. 'I wish you wouldn't use those coarse expressions, Rafe. And I don't think you can blame me if I regard your present state of sobriety with some suspicion. It's not as if you've been behaving normally, is it? Apart from this one trip to Fort William, you never leave the castle.'

Rafe scowled. 'I do what I have to.'

'Oh, yes. So long as it doesn't entail visiting any of the tenants.'

'I do employ an agent to handle those things for me,' retorted Rafe, without expression. 'And you've got Colin to run your errands, if Stuart can't handle it. What I do is my affair. Now, if you don't mind, I'm busy.'

'It's that woman, isn't it?' exclaimed Lady Invercaldy tremulously. 'That—Mrs Jacobson. Oh—Isobel, if you will. She's the reason you've become a virtual hermit. Why are you afraid of seeing her? What does she mean to you?'

Rafe looked down at his desk. 'You wouldn't believe me.'

'Try me.'

'All right.' He faced his mother squarely. 'I think I'm in love with her.'

She gasped. 'You're not serious!'

'I told you you wouldn't believe me.'

'But——' His mother sought to find justification for her words. 'You love Sarah!'

'Sarah's dead.'

'All right. You *loved* Sarah, then.'

'I believed I did.' Rafe shrugged. 'But I wasn't *in love* with her.'

His mother gasped again. 'Of course you were.'

'No.' Rafe sighed. 'I know you may find this hard to believe, Mama, but the reason I went to pieces when Sarah died wasn't just because I cared about her. It was because I blamed myself for what happened to her. I felt guilty. If Sarah hadn't been having my baby, she might still be alive.'

'But that's ludicrous!'

Rafe's lips twisted. 'I'm glad we agree on something.'

'No. I mean—it's not true. I saw you, Rafe. I saw how you reacted at her funeral. You were devastated! Don't trivialise your feelings now simply to justify this— this lust you have for the Jacobson woman!'

'I'm not.' Rafe regarded her steadily. 'I am in love with Isobel, Mama. I may not want to be. I may not even like to be. But I am.'

'So what do you intend to do?'

Rafe lifted his shoulders. 'I may never—do—anything.'

'It's not serious, then?' Lady Invercaldy clutched at the straw he had given her. 'Oh, Rafe, I know you're attracted to her. I could see that the night you brought her to supper. But that's not love. Believe me, I know. If you'd slept with her, you'd see this infatuation for what it is.'

'I have.'

'You have what?' His mother's confidence faltered.

'Slept with her,' replied Rafe flatly. 'I'm sorry to disappoint you, Mama, but sleeping with her has only aggravated the problem.'

Lady Invercaldy pressed a hand to her throat. 'Oh, Rafe, you can't mean you're thinking of marrying her!'

'Well, you did tell me to pull myself together, Mama,' he reminded her drily, and she made a distracted gesture.

'I suppose—she—finds the affair highly amusing!' she exclaimed bitterly. 'I'm sure she can't wait to make fools of us all.'

'I wouldn't count on it,' Rafe retorted, his brief spurt of humour extinguished. 'Contrary to your expectations, Mama, Isobel won't even speak to me. I've tried to tell her how I feel, but she doesn't want to know.'

His mother frowned. 'Is that why—is that why you've become as reclusive as a monk?'

Rafe sank down into his chair again. 'If it is, you've got nothing to worry about. Now, do you mind? I've got work to do.'

Lady Invercaldy wrung her hands. 'Oh, Rafe, why do you do this to me? All right, maybe I haven't been as understanding as I should have been in the past, but all I really want is your happiness.'

'Is it?' Rafe looked up at her wryly, and she could see the honest scepticism in his eyes. 'Don't worry, Mama, I don't blame you for anything. And nor do I intend to start drowning my sorrows in alcohol again. As Isobel says, it doesn't prove anything. Except perhaps what a spineless bastard I am.'

It was three miles from the village to Invercaldy Castle using the public right of way. It was further if you used the road, but as Isobel didn't have a car that wasn't really an option. She supposed she could have hired Mr MacGregor's taxi, but she preferred not to advertise her actions. She and Cory had caused enough talk in the village as it was. As residents they made very good outsiders.

The walls of the castle keep loomed ahead, stark against a grey November sky. There had been flurries of snow earlier, and she had warned Cory what would happen if she stepped over the threshold in her absence. But after receiving a dressing-down from her grand-mother, Cory was quite content to snuggle on the sofa. She was very relieved to have the conversation over with. And evidently glad it hadn't been conducted in person.

As it was, Mrs Jacobson had bellowed her disap-pointment into the telephone. Far from being relieved to hear that Cory was safe and well, she had complained about the girl's untidiness, and asked how soon Isobel intended to repay the cost of her air fare. And, although she firmly intended to deduct the cost from Cory's pocket money, Isobel promised she'd put a cheque in the post that very day.

She would get over it, Isobel was sure. Ruth was not likely to abandon her granddaughter that easily. And— who knew?—Isobel thought, she might yet return to London. Even if putting the better part of five hundred miles between herself and Rafe would probably tear her to pieces.

Lucas was working on the garage forecourt. He was washing a car similar to the one Rafe had used to collect Cory from Fort William that morning. It was probably the same car, reflected Isobel, half relieved to see a friendly face. Lucas would probably know where Rafe was. She just wanted to offer her thanks—and her apologies—and leave.

'Hello,' she said, stopping beside him awkwardly, aware that in her grey duffel and faded jeans she was not a prepossessing figure. 'Is—is the Earl at home?'

Lucas's mouth turned down. He was a man in his early forties, Isobel thought, with the square stocky build of a fighter. But he was also a gentle man, and a kind one, and, unlike Mrs Fielding, he had no air of condescension.

'Where else?' he replied now, dropping the wash-leather he had been using into a bucket, and drying his hands on the seat of his trousers. 'Would you be wanting to see him?'

'If possible,' agreed Isobel, nodding, stamping her booted feet against the cold. 'Um—you couldn't tell him I'm here, could you? I'd rather not—disturb the household.'

Lucas's grin assured her that he knew exactly what she meant, but his answer wasn't quite what she expected. 'Tell him yourself,' he said, nodding towards the stables. 'He's in there with Mr Colin. He's thinking of giving one of the mares to young Jaime.'

'Oh.' Isobel's mouth felt dry. 'Oh, well, perhaps——'

But at that moment three people emerged from the stables. One had to be Rafe's brother. She recognised him by his resemblance to his son. Jaime, too, was un-mistakable, clearly delighted by what had occurred. But it was Rafe who held her eyes, Rafe who tore her heart, Rafe who looked older, and tired, as Cory had said. Rafe whom she loved—and always would, unfortunately.

He saw her at once, and although she had half expected some animosity from him he excused himself from the others and strode swiftly across the yard to-wards her. 'Isobel,' he said, and although his tone was controlled his eyes were dark and wary. 'Cory—you've seen Cory? There's nothing wrong, is there?'

Isobel found it difficult to say anything. It seemed so long since she had seen him, and her strongest urge was to grasp his gloved hands and beg him to forgive her. In dark cords and a black overcoat that hung open from his shoulders he was so unbearably familiar. And the intimacy she had always felt with him was still there, just like before.

'N-nothing's wrong,' she assured him at last, avoiding those dark disturbing eyes and concentrating on a point to the right of his shoulder. It meant she was looking almost directly at Jaime, but that couldn't be helped. Rafe's brother knew she was here now so there was no way she could keep it from his mother. 'I just wanted to—to thank you for—for bringing her back.'

Rafe's eyes narrowed, and he looked at Lucas almost impatiently. 'We can't talk here,' he said. 'Come into the house. Colin and Jaime were just leaving.'

'Um—no.' Isobel put out her hand half defensively. Lady Invercaldy's knowing she was here was one thing; meeting her was another. 'I—couldn't we talk out here? I don't have a lot to say.'

Rafe hesitated, glancing round at his brother and nephew, who were, reluctantly in Jaime's case, making their way towards the castle. 'We'll go into the stables,' he said, and although she was uncomfortably aware of Lucas's appraisal he put his gloved hand beneath her elbow. 'Come on. It's warm inside. Lucas, see that we're not disturbed.'

'Sir,' the chauffeur replied, with a polite salute, and Isobel was forced to accompany Rafe back across the yard, with Lucas's eyes boring into her back every step of the way. What must he be thinking? she fretted anxiously, glad that at least the others had disappeared. Yet what did it matter anyway? She doubted she'd be here much longer.

The stables were, as Rafe had said, warm, and more friendly. Several horses snuffled over the doors of their stalls at their approach, and a silver-grey muzzle nudged familiarly at Rafe's sleeve.

Isobel smiled, momentarily distracted by the animal's blatant attempt to gain his attention, and he drew an apple out of his pocket and let it take it from his palm.

'This is Moonlight,' he said, noticing her interest, and Isobel came forward to stroke the horse's nose. 'She used to belong to Sarah, but I'm giving her to Jaime. She doesn't get enough exercise and he's eager to replace his pony.'

'Oh.' The mention of his late wife's name was like a douche of cold water. For a few moments she had forgotten her, even forgotten what had brought her here. It had been enough to be with Rafe, to breathe his air and feel the heat of his body next to hers. But Sarah's name changed all that, and she automatically stepped away.

'You wanted to talk to me about Cory?'

To her dismay, Rafe had followed her, and, realising she was backing herself into corner, both metaphorically and physically, Isobel was forced to stand her ground.

'I—came to apologise,' she said, digging her hands into the pockets of her duffel and bravely meeting his gaze. 'You were right and I was wrong. Cory has come back, just as you said she would. But, of course, you know that. I'm sorry she made a nuisance of herself by ringing you this morning.' She paused. 'And if she asked any embarrassing questions.'

Rafe shrugged, his eyes guarded. 'I didn't mind.'

'I did.' Isobel held up her head. 'She should have rung me.'

Rafe peeled off his gloves and stuffed them into his pockets. 'Perhaps she was afraid you might put her on the next train back to London,' he offered quietly. 'She could hardly have complained. You certainly had the provocation.'

'I wouldn't have done that.'

'No.' Rafe conceded the point. 'Well, then—she thought I'd be her ally. She didn't know we hadn't been seeing one another. She didn't know I stood less of a chance of defending her to you than she did herself.'

Isobel drew a breath. 'Yes. She told me.'

'Did she?' A certain resignation entered his eyes at her words. 'Well, I guess that covers it, doesn't it? You've got your daughter back, and you've made your peace. I hope she'll settle down now.' He hesitated. 'I could have a word with her headmaster, if you think it would do any good.'

'No.'

Isobel's refusal was too swift to be considered, and Rafe frowned. 'As you wish.'

'No—I mean——' Isobel's tongue came to circle her lips in sudden panic '—it's very kind of you to offer, but—but I don't think Cory will be going back to Strathmoor.'

'No?' Rafe took an involuntary step towards her, and then, as if realising he had no right to expect an explanation, he halted. He sucked in his breath. 'So what is she going to do?'

Isobel couldn't sustain his penetrating gaze any longer. Dropping her eyes, she concentrated on the toe of her boot, scuffing bits of straw that were scattered on the stone floor at her feet. 'It's what I'm going to do that matters,' she said at last. 'I'm thinking of going back to London myself.'

There was silence after this statement. So much silence, in fact, that it was almost audible. And through it all Isobel could feel the hammering of her heart. It was pounding so loudly in her ears that she was sure Rafe must be able to hear it too.

When Rafe moved, she jumped almost instinctively. But all he did was rest his back against the wall, beside a mound of hay used to feed the animals. Her covert gaze took in his bent head and rounded shoulders, and the aching look of weariness in his stance.

'Rafe?' she said softly, half afraid there was something wrong with him, something he wasn't telling her, and he rolled his head against the brickwork and looked at her.

'Don't go,' he said harshly. 'Please—don't go. I can live with us being estranged, so long as I know I can see you if I have to. But if you go back to London, I can't answer for my actions.'

Isobel quivered. 'Is that a threat?'

'Hell, no.' His lips twitched in the semblance of a rueful smile. 'How can I threaten you? I don't have anything you want.'

Except yourself . . .

Isobel pressed her hands together. 'Then—what did you mean?'

'Oh, I don't know.' He gave a short mirthless laugh. 'I guess I could always do what Clare wants, and relinquish my right to the title in favour of Colin. She'd love to be the Countess of Invercaldy, and that way Jaime would automatically become his father's heir. The boy will inherit the title one day anyway. And I'm sure my mother believes Colin deserves the position far more than I do.'

'But why would you do that?'

'Perhaps I need to be free too. Who knows?' His mouth curled. 'I may follow you. I've never liked London, but that was before——'

'But you can't do that.' Isobel was horrified. 'I don't care what you say or what your mother wants, Invercaldy is your birthright. You can't give it up. And—and in any case why should Jaime be your heir? You should have a son of your own.'

'But I won't, will I?' said Rafe flatly. 'If you go away, that possibility will be finally put to death.' He rolled his head back, and stared grimly at the eaves above his head. 'Do you know, I hoped you might be pregnant? After all these years of crucifying myself for making Sarah pregnant, I actually prayed that you might be having a baby.'

Isobel swallowed. 'Why?'

He looked at her out of the corners of his eyes. 'Why do you think?' he asked, a little bitterly now. 'Are you being deliberately obtuse, or do you just want to see me crawl?' His lips twisted. 'All right, I'll crawl if I have to: I wanted you to need me. I wanted you to come to me and tell me that you couldn't bring a baby into the world on your own. I wanted you to *want* me,' he groaned, an ugly anguished sound. 'At least half as much as I want you!'

Isobel couldn't believe it. 'I'm—I'm not pregnant,' she stammered, and he gave her a tormented look.

'I know.'

'But—I could be,' she ventured unsteadily. 'I don't mind if you want to try again.'

Rafe's head jerked towards her. 'What?'

Isobel swallowed. 'I said——'

Rafe came up off the wall. 'Damn you, I heard what you said,' he grated harshly. His eyes searched her face. 'What did you mean by it? You said you were going away.'

'I—I didn't know I had an option,' confessed Isobel, putting out her hands towards him. 'I thought you still

loved Sarah. Oh, Rafe, don't look at me like that. I—
I love you. I only want to please you. And—and if you
want a baby, I'm perfectly willing to try.'

Rafe uttered an unguarded sound, as much a howl of
frustration as a moan of approval. 'God, Isobel,' he
groaned, his hands digging into her shoulders as he
jerked her towards him. 'Don't you realise if I have you,
I don't need anything else? You're all I've ever wanted.
You're the only woman who's ever owned me—body and
soul!'

'It's just as well you said you wanted me to have a baby,
isn't it?' Isobel remarked smugly, as her husband
propelled himself out of bed in answer to their son's
lusty wail from the nursery. 'What a pity you can't feed
him too.' She sat up and began unbuttoning her nightdress. 'Did you ever see a baby so greedy?'

Rafe watched his son suckling at his wife's breast with
a certain amount of envy. Since having their son six weeks
ago, Isobel's breasts had grown lush and inviting. Just
as the rest of her had, too, he conceded, sliding back
beneath the covers, and allowing himself the pleasure of
caressing other inviting contours of her body. They had
lived together for almost a year now, and he still couldn't
quite believe it. She was his wife, the mother of his son,
and the woman he loved more deeply every day.

'How much longer will he require a feed at this hour?'
Rafe asked idly, allowing his tongue to taste the warm
hollow of her shoulder. 'When you said you wanted to
feed him yourself, I didn't know I'd be jealous.'

Isobel gave a soft laugh. 'You can't be jealous!'

'I am.' But there was less conviction in Rafe's voice
now. 'No, but I want you all to myself,' he added huskily.
'Thank goodness Cory's gone back to school. At least
we'll have a few weeks to ourselves before Christmas.'

Isobel smiled, and moved the baby from one breast
to the other. The one the baby had left was soft and
milky, and Rafe's tongue moved to rescue a pearl of
moisture from its tip. The sensation of his tongue
brushing that most sensitive of areas caused a corre-
sponding surge of feeling between her legs. Oh, God,

she thought weakly, she wanted him too. She wanted
him inside her, hot and hard and hungry.

With his usual perception where she was concerned,
Rafe recognised the moment when her limbs began to
melt, and his lips curled in a lazy smile. He feigned a
yawn, covered his mouth with his hand, and rolled over
on to his back. 'Oh, God, I'm tired!' he said
deliberately, pretending to close his eyes. 'You'll put
young David back in his cot, won't you?'

Isobel's toes dug into his ribs. 'No, you will,' she told
him tolerantly, propping the drowsy baby on her
shoulder, and bringing up his wind. 'There, he's half
asleep already. Isn't he gorgeous? Come on, Rafe, don't
wait until he wakes up again.'

Rafe gathered up his son and padded obediently back
into the nursery. It was four o'clock in the morning, and
still pitch-dark outside the sleeping castle. At least
David's nanny could handle his early morning ab-
lutions, though Rafe with relief. He could now have
Isobel all to himself for four or five glorious hours.

She was waiting for him when he got back into bed,
her nightdress discarded, and her warm limbs eager and
willing to coil themselves about him. As he sank down
into her warm arms, he thought how lucky he truly was.
Not only did he have the only woman he had ever really
loved, but a precious son to make their lives complete.

And Cory, too, he acknowledged, threading his hands
through the silky curtain of Isobel's hair. With Jaime's
help, his stepdaughter had settled down well at the school
Jaime himself attended, and much to their relief and
astonishment she was proving to be quite an academic.
Whether that had anything to do with the fact that she
wanted to impress Jaime they couldn't be sure, but the
fact remained that she was taking her studies seriously,
and even Mrs Jacobson had been impressed with her
assertion that she intended to go to university.

'I love you,' murmured Isobel against his ear, her
tongue seeking and finding the sensitive pulse beneath,
and he groaned contentedly.

'I should think so,' he reproved, finding her mouth
with easy familiarity. 'Hmm, did I tell you you taste delicious? You must do. My son's no fool.'

'Nor's his father,' agreed Isobel, winding her arms about his neck, as he moved to lie between her thighs. She caught her breath as he nudged her with his engorged manhood. 'Go on. Don't stop now.'

'I have no intention of stopping,' Rafe assured her thickly, letting her guide him into the slick sheath that pulsed so deliciously around him. Her muscles caught him, and held him, drawing him closer, and he groaned as the magic of their union was fulfilled.

Some time later, when he really was drowsy, curled around his wife, her rounded bottom comfortably cushioned against his belly, Isobel spoke again. 'Do you think your mother will join us for Christmas this year?' she asked softly, and Rafe uttered a protesting sigh.

'Does it matter?' he mumbled into her hair. 'We'll talk about it tomorrow.'

'You said she would.'

'*She* said she would,' Rafe corrected her patiently. 'My love, nothing will keep her away. Not now she's got a new grandson to show off to everyone.'

'Hmm.' Isobel sounded doubtful. The previous year, just after their wedding, Lady Invercaldy had taken herself off on a prolonged trip to see her sister in New Zealand, and not until the news reached her that her daughter-in-law was expecting a baby in three months had she come home. Since then, she and Isobel had achieved a kind of amnesty, and although Isobel doubted they would ever be friends they were at least in tune over their admiration of David.

'She'll be here,' Rafe assured her again, realising this was important to Isobel, and she snuggled more contentedly against him. 'And don't forget Mrs Jacobson will be here too. I'm looking forward to those two getting to know one another. I have the feeling they'll be a match for one another.'

'Oh, yes.' Isobel giggled and wriggled in his arms. 'I'd forgotten about Ruth. I never thought I'd say it, but I'm glad she doesn't let anyone intimidate her. Do you remember at our wedding? I thought your mother was going to die when Ruth asked for smoked salmon instead of pâté.'

'I remember.'

'Do you think Clare will ever forgive me for stealing her thunder? I know she thinks I was expecting David before we got married. I'm sure she thought it was quite disgraceful, having a baby a bare nine months after the ceremony.'

Rafe made an exasperated sound. 'I don't particularly care what Clare thinks either,' he assured her. 'All I will say is that if you continue to wriggle about like this you may find yourself pregnant again, sooner rather than later.'

Isobel laughed. 'Did I say I'd mind?' she asked innocently, and Rafe's indulgent chuckle sounded like heaven in her ears.

IT'S FREE! IT'S FUN! ENTER THE

☆ "Hooray for ☆
☆ Hollywood" ☆

SWEEPSTAKES!

We're giving away prizes to celebrate the screening of four new romance movies on CBS TV this fall! Look for the movies on four Sunday afternoons in October. And be sure to return your Official Entry Coupons to try for a fabulous **vacation in Hollywood!**

⭐ If you're the Grand Prize winner we'll fly you and your companion to Los Angeles for a 7-day/6-night vacation you'll never forget!

⭐ You'll stay at the luxurious Regent Beverly Wilshire Hotel,* a prime location for celebrity spotting!

⭐ You'll have time to visit Universal Studios,* stroll the Hollywood Walk of Fame, check out celebrities' footprints at Mann's Chinese Theater, ride a trolley to see the homes of the stars, and more!

⭐ The prize includes a rental car for 7 days and $1,000.00 pocket money!

Someone's going to win this fabulous prize, and it might just be you! Remember, the more times you enter, the better your chances of winning!

ALSO⁺ Five hundred entrants will each receive SUNGLASSES OF THE STARS! Don't miss out. ENTER TODAY!

"HOORAY FOR HOLLYWOOD" SWEEPSTAKES

HERE'S HOW THE SWEEPSTAKES WORKS

OFFICIAL RULES — NO PURCHASE NECESSARY

To enter, complete an Official Entry Form or hand print on a 3" x 5" card the words "HOORAY FOR HOLLYWOOD", your name and address and mail your entry in the pre-addressed envelope (if provided) or to: "Hooray for Hollywood" Sweepstakes, P.O. Box 9076, Buffalo, NY 14269-9076 or "Hooray for Hollywood" Sweepstakes, P.O. Box 637, Fort Erie, Ontario L2A 5X3. Entries must be sent via First Class Mail and be received no later than 12/31/94. No liability is assumed for lost, late or misdirected mail.

Winners will be selected in random drawings to be conducted no later than January 31, 1995 from all eligible entries received.

Grand Prize: A 7-day/6-night trip for 2 to Los Angeles, CA including round trip air transportation from commercial airport nearest winner's residence, accommodations at the Regent Beverly Wilshire Hotel, free rental car, and $1,000 spending money. (Approximate prize value which will vary dependent upon winner's residence: $5,400.00 U.S.); 500 Second Prizes: A pair of "Hollywood Star" sunglasses (prize value: $9.95 U.S. each). Winner selection is under the supervision of D.L. Blair, Inc., an independent judging organization, whose decisions are final. Grand Prize travelers must sign and return a release of liability prior to traveling. Trip must be taken by 2/1/96 and is subject to airline schedules and accommodations availability.

Sweepstakes offer is open to residents of the U.S. (except Puerto Rico) and Canada who are 18 years of age or older, except employees and immediate family members of Harlequin Enterprises, Ltd., its affiliates, subsidiaries, and all agencies, entities or persons connected with the use, marketing or conduct of this sweepstakes. All federal, state, provincial, municipal and local laws apply. Offer void wherever prohibited by law. Taxes and/or duties are the sole responsibility of the winners. Any litigation within the province of Quebec respecting the conduct and awarding of prizes may be submitted to the Regie des loteries et courses du Quebec. All prizes will be awarded; winners will be notified by mail. No substitution of prizes are permitted. Odds of winning are dependent upon the number of eligible entries received.

Potential grand prize winner must sign and return an Affidavit of Eligibility within 30 days of notification. In the event of non-compliance within this time period, prize may be awarded to an alternate winner. Prize notification returned as undeliverable may result in the awarding of prize to an alternate winner. By acceptance of their prize, winners consent to use of their names, photographs, or likenesses for purpose of advertising, trade and promotion on behalf of Harlequin Enterprises, Ltd., without further compensation unless prohibited by law. A Canadian winner must correctly answer an arithmetical skill-testing question in order to be awarded the prize.

For a list of winners (available after 2/28/95), send a separate stamped, self-addressed envelope to: Hooray for Hollywood Sweepstakes 3252 Winners, P.O. Box 4200, Blair, NE 68009.

CBSRLS

OFFICIAL ENTRY COUPON

"Hooray for Hollywood"
SWEEPSTAKES!

Yes, I'd love to win the Grand Prize — a vacation in Hollywood —
or one of 500 pairs of "sunglasses of the stars"! Please enter me
in the sweepstakes!

This entry must be received by December 31, 1994.
Winners will be notified by January 31, 1995.

Name _____

Address _____ Apt. _____

City _____

State/Prov. _____ Zip/Postal Code _____

Daytime phone number _____
(area code)

Account # _____

Return entries with invoice in envelope provided. Each book
in this shipment has two entry coupons — and the more
coupons you enter, the better your chances of winning!

DIRCBS

OFFICIAL ENTRY COUPON

"Hooray for Hollywood"
SWEEPSTAKES!

Yes, I'd love to win the Grand Prize — a vacation in Hollywood —
or one of 500 pairs of "sunglasses of the stars"! Please enter me
in the sweepstakes!

This entry must be received by December 31, 1994.
Winners will be notified by January 31, 1995.

Name _____

Address _____ Apt. _____

City _____

State/Prov. _____ Zip/Postal Code _____

Daytime phone number _____
(area code)

Account # _____

Return entries with invoice in envelope provided. Each book
in this shipment has two entry coupons — and the more
coupons you enter, the better your chances of winning!

DIRCBS